**"Judith Rossner's accomplished novel . . . goes to the heart of matters . . .**

we're given an enormously likable and substantial person who goes through a lot of struggle, though never without self-awareness and irony, to change, grow, and be worthy of our admiring interest and, often, delight."

—*Ms. Magazine*

*Any Minute I Can Split* is a warm, exuberant, outrageous novel whose heroine, in a moment of despair, plunks her elephantine pregnant torso on her husband's motorcycle and takes off! She's leaving her life as victim-in-residence for her rich, sadistic husband and heading toward Cape Cod.

En route, a cold-hearted nineteen-year-old, David, adopts her as his comforter and together they journey to a commune in Vermont. Her first act, on arrival, is to give birth to twins. . . .

D1329037

**Books by Judith Rossner**

Any Minute I Can Split
Attachments
Emmeline
Looking for Mr. Goodbar
Nine Months in the Life of an Old Maid

Published by POCKET BOOKS/WASHINGTON SQUARE PRESS

Most Washington Square Press Books are available at special quantity discounts for bulk purchases for sales promotions, premiums or fund raising. Special books or book excerpts can also be created to fit specific needs.

For details write the office of the Vice President of Special Markets, Pocket Books, 1230 Avenue of the Americas, New York, New York 10020.

# JUDITH ROSSNER

## Any Minute I Can Split

WASHINGTON SQUARE PRESS
PUBLISHED BY POCKET BOOKS NEW YORK

A Washington Square Press Publication of
POCKET BOOKS, a division of Simon & Schuster, Inc.
1230 Avenue of the Americas, New York, N.Y. 10020

ISBN: 0-671-50975-6

First Pocket Books printing October, 1981

10  9  8  7  6  5  4  3  2

WASHINGTON SQUARE PRESS, WSP and colophon are
registered trademarks of Simon & Schuster, Inc.

Printed in the U.S.A.

*For Eva Harrison*

# Any Minute
# I Can Split

SHE had enough irony to nourish an entire block of underprivileged children; on herself it had a less than helpful effect since she generally used it to saw at her own head instead of at the bars surrounding her life.

Her mother, a violent soul in a gentle body, had committed suicide in April, having spent the previous ten years withdrawing from life to a point where she could fail to notice that this was the incorrect season for despair. It was, as they say in another not entirely unrelated context, a long hot summer, the fact being that summers not spent at the seashore are invariably both, and they didn't go to the seashore that year because the house at the seashore had always been haunted anyway, not an object in it unworthy of three flashbacks, and of all the events that can give ghosts dominance in one's life, the death of one's mother is probably the most effective. So they stayed home in the three-year-old raised ranch that didn't remind

9

anyone of anything except maybe the future. This put her husband, who had proposed to her during their first visit to the house at the seashore, into a semi-permanent fury in spite of the fact that it was he who had chosen that very raised ranch in that very suburb on the theory that in such dull surroundings one or the other of his arts must flourish. A philosophy since somewhat tarnished in her eyes by the fact that on the day they'd moved, film making had joined the long list of things like painting and shaving that he didn't do any more.

All that summer and into the early fall she couldn't sleep unless the bedroom door was open in addition to the windows, which of course made it impossible to use the air conditioning. This was all right with her since the one night that summer they'd turned it on she had become convinced that the room had detached itself from the rest of the house, including both bathrooms, and was flying through space with an insufficient oxygen supply.

She was pregnant, due to have her baby—or babies, as the doctor ascertained in July—on October thirty-first. In August the cat, having been romping in a patch of poison ivy, went to sleep against her back as she lay on her side in bed. For several days she scratched what she took to be a particularly loathsome mosquito bite and a week later most of the visible parts of her body and one or two invisible ones as well were covered with the maddening rash. She could not be given a shot of cortisone because she was pregnant. She could not take oral medication because, her mother having orally medicated herself out of existence, she had a tendency to become hysterical at the suggestion that she take so much as an aspirin into her mouth. On the rare occasion when she fell asleep for a few minutes, she invariably dreamed that her mother was scratching her back and then she would wake up crying.

She weighed, at this juncture, two hundred and fifty

pounds, having gained an even seventy-five pounds in the first seven months of her pregnancy. Since she was just an inch under six feet tall she cut a fairly impressive figure but it was hard for her to find clothes. She made herself two dresses out of tablecloths while she could get just close enough to the sewing machine to see the stitches but this still left her with a wardrobe problem in hot weather, a problem she finally solved by spending all her time at home and naked. Something about her shape made her appear to be sitting down even when she was walking.

At the end of September her husband went on a camping trip with some old school ties. A sudden end to Indian summer brought them back to the house, where Margaret was preparing for winter by digging up from the garden and potting every plant that any expert in the history of flower encyclopedias had claimed could survive if it wintered indoors. When they entered she was hanging a wax begonia in a rope basket on a hook in the window wall. She was naked. A few dried remnants of the poison ivy rash still clung to her giant, provolone-like breasts and her massive stomach, giving her something of the look of a relief map. Her husband's friends stared at her, their jaws slack, their eyes glazed, for so long that she finally let the basket and pot drop to the floor to break their collective trance. What was perhaps most disturbing was that Roger's expression wasn't different from his friends'. If he had shown no sexual interest in her since the time when she had begun to swell, he had at least taken her for granted, never looking at her as though she were part of a freak show. She went into the bedroom and closed the door behind her and stayed that way through the night, not realizing until the following morning that the very fact of the closed door was a small milestone. In the morning she put on one of her tablecloths, stepped carefully over the various sleeping bodies that littered the living-room rug, took Roger's motorcycle key from his pocket without disturbing him and, with her pocketbook and the key in hand, left home.

    &#x218C; MANY people in her condition would have been disconcerted by the difficulty of a long ride on such a small and bumpy vehicle but Margaret had a very high threshold of pain everywhere except in her brain. An unforeseen result of the upbringing which had instilled in her the idea that females didn't actually exist below the neck except as an appendage for the hands, which were to be kept busy at all times. (One of her cousins had been more disastrously affected by this same philosophy and was given to rushing off to doctors with equal concern for hangnails, splinters or large lumps in the breast, being willing when she got to their offices only to say that something was hurting somewhere down there.)

Margaret had no clear idea of where she would go. She had little cash but she did have her checkbook and an indecent or decent, depending on one's point of view, supply of credit cards. She stopped for gas and to cash a check at the gas station in the village, where she picked up also a supply of road maps which she put in her bike bag and never looked at again. Her idea was just to get *away*. On the first night she slept in the woods off a highway in Dutchess County, eating wild berries when she got hungry. Unfortunately the berries were mildly poisonous so that by the following morning she had an acute case of diarrhea, a disease which would have been almost welcome were she at home, relieving as it did the constipation which was the normal iron cross of pregnancy. At this time, however, it had the effect of making her think in terms of destination.

There wasn't really anyplace she wanted to go. Except that in the months following her mother's death she'd thought for the first time since leaving it about the house and the street where she'd grown up. Of course she'd been back occasionally to visit her parents but it was the kind of place that didn't stay in your mind once your body was removed from it. A dull brownstone in a dim street of like houses, it had been little more than a spot to set out from to explore interesting places. Like the Back Bay mansion that had been her mother's childhood home and which her family had been forced to give up after losing its department store during the Depression. But that wasn't her own personal memory place to visit, really; the memory belonged to her mother.

Margaret's mother had been sixteen at the time of the Great Crash and seventeen when she met Margaret's father, a twenty-eight-year-old Boston Irish traffic cop who had prevented her from absentmindedly stepping in front of a large truck, thus setting up a symbolic foundation for the fantasy of salvation which would enable her to deceive herself for long enough to marry him, if not for many weeks longer.

Some families have a way of adjusting history so that they seem to have been more intimately involved in the great events of the day than they in fact were, the news stories of a period becoming the reasons for personal actions when in point of fact their relation was no closer than the morning papers. Even when there is a legitimate cause and effect sequence, the two on occasion become reversed. And so it was that in the minds of Margaret's mother's parents the two major crushing blows of an era were not only seen to be related but were somewhat strangely reversed, and years later a stranger listening to Margaret's grandmother discussing that period might get

13

the impression that it was some great floodgate Margaret's mother had opened when she married a Papist that had made it possible for the Crash to occur.

After their marriage Margaret's mother and father had moved to the ground-floor apartment on Beacon Street where they'd remained through Margaret's growing up and through her mother's suicide, and where her father still lived, able to sleep in the bed where he'd found his wife's body only because he was as much a stranger to his own feelings as he'd ever been to hers.

She'd been to Boston only once since her mother's death, and not inside the house at all, but it had occurred to her once in a while that she would like to see it again. Maybe to see if it looked any different, now that her mother was dead. Prettier or uglier. Bigger or smaller. Dead or alive. That was all. Curiosity.

The house at the Cape was different. It had been given to Margaret's mother's aunt as a wedding present some years before the Crash and was untouched when the rest of the family's possessions were lost. Margaret's happiest childhood memories were of summers at the beach with her cousins. She and her mother went for the season, the illnesses that had dogged Margaret's mother from the time she'd given birth always mysteriously leaving her for the duration; her father would join them toward the end of August, his arrival in that pristine Wasps' nest always somehow as spectacular as if a particularly monstrous tuna head had been washed up on the beach. Everyone else drew back into their skins just a little, and on the rare occasions when they were invited to tea there was a strange hesitation in the air, as though the hostess suspected it would be politic to offer him something stronger.

The fact was that he was a teetotaler, his only addiction being to tea. One of his favorite stories was about his first visit to a restaurant in this country, when he had been served a cup of pale tea with the tea bag still in it and had bellowed at the waitress, "What's this filthy rag doin' in me tea?" Like his other stories, this one had been received with an uncomfortable silence. It wasn't that there was anything exactly wrong with the things he said, it was just that somehow words that would have sounded perfectly all right on some lips sounded not quite clean on his.

The ruddiness of his cheeks, the loudness of his voice, the roll of his brogue—whatever it was that made his harmless anecdotes sound to them like dirty jokes—his initial reaction had been to become louder and heartier, as though he could break down their defenses so that when he subsided to his natural level of exuberance he would have become magically acceptable to them. Intimidated, he had failed to see that their defenses didn't control warmth but concealed the lack of it. And so, the cycle completed, his jovial offensive failing as it had been doomed to, he had given up and lapsed into a nearly permanent silence, taking on, in point of fact, the general aspect of that poor gray tea bag which had been his introduction to the culinary life style of twentieth-century America.

Maybe she would visit her father. She'd seen him only once since her mother's death—about a month after the funeral. He had taken her and Roger to Howard Johnson's for dinner. (Roger found her parents more tolerable than his own. His manner toward her mother had come as close to courtliness as any manner he'd ever had; to her father he was pleasant if condescending. Like one of the more benevolent uncles.) She'd been a little frightened before that last visit of how her father might be, but her fears had turned out to be groundless for he had undergone no visible change in that month, certainly no change comparable to the one after his forced retirement from the police force, when he had been in a deep and foggy depression for over a year. He had loved being a policeman even when he was pounding a beat and when they'd put him behind a station-house desk to make entries in his beautiful script each night he had loved it even more. He loved to write; even her mother had been unable to fault his penmanship. His fine Italian hand, she had called it, thus managing not to credit even that to his Irishness or his Catholic education.

It was her father who had flashed through Margaret's mind as she stood over the fallen begonia, being stared at by Roger and his old school ties. Nor was it the first time she had identified with him in this connection. She was her father's daughter, after all, and as far back as she could remember some of that tuna-head ambience had washed off on her. No one of her mother's family could imagine a child who, given the alternatives of speaking normally or picking up an Irish brogue, would choose the latter, while that was in fact what Margaret quite unconsciously had done. Nor was it easy for her aunts and uncles to see why a voice should be quite so loud, legs so long, a laugh so raucous, clothes on inside out so often, milk glasses knocked over so frequently, tables bumped into with such regularity, food chewed with such gusto as to give the unfortunate impression that pleasure was involved. Their children, her cousins, adored Margaret for reasons she could only understand much later on. For them her gusto had been the fresh breath blowing through lives which considering their wind-swept seashore ease were remarkably stale and dry. She thought up games that were enough fun to be well worth the trouble they got into for playing them. She made up ghost stories that held them in thrall. Until the boys began reaching their teens, she was the tallest of the cousins, and it was she who was called upon to retrieve kites from trees that no one else could get a foothold to. Her cousins were even fascinated by her father; their parents' attitude had conveyed the sense of him as a curiosity without passing on the negative quality of their absorption. When they visited Margaret (a cousin or two was occasionally permitted this treat but was seldom more than dropped at the front door) they were intrigued with something about the way Margaret lived, but Margaret could never understand just what that something was. Was it a strange quality to their possessions or simply their relative lack of them? Was it a special order to her life or the lack of order? Was it her freedom or the lack of those kinds of freedom that came with money, of which most of their parents had managed to re-accumulate a reasonable amount? Most likely it had to do with the fact that she had been given a great deal of independence from the time she was quite young. With a definite sense of how things were to be done for a child of her particular (fallen) status, Margaret's parents might not have permitted her to roam the streets of Boston on her own as early as she had. With either money or energy, her mother might have sent a nanny or gone along herself. Since they had neither, Margaret had freedom. Her father, when he woke up in the evening to have breakfast and go to work, might sputter some about the dangers to a young girl on the streets of Boston, but he was usually asleep when she left the house and her mother didn't have the will to stop her.

She crossed the border into Massachusetts and began riding east toward Boston. He lived still at the seedy end of Beacon Street, far from every other Irish cop in Boston but within psychological spitting distance of Roxbury, the implicit reminder that he was something more than his wife's family thought him. The street looked the same. Of course. It was only that she in relation to the street was different. She parked the motorcycle in front of the wrought-iron front rail and walked laboriously up the front steps. A young girl answered the doorbell, well maybe not so young but with the smooth, surrealistically rosy cheeks and round near-plumpness one associated with young girls from the old sod a week before they got married. Margaret stared at her blankly. The girl stared at Margaret blankly.

"Who is it, Maggie?" Her father's voice called from inside, causing Margaret great confusion because he'd never called her Maggie before and besides, why would he be asking *her* . . .

"I'm not certain, Mrrr. McDonough," the colleen purred gently. A gentle colleen named Maggie, her father had gotten to do for him. To do what for him? He was neat as a pin, cleaned up after himself constantly, and the three or four foods that he would eat he knew how to prepare for himself.

She stood paralyzed by hostility and confusion. She could not, would not explain herself to this stranger. This . . . could her father actually be screwing this girl? So soon? Cheeks so rosy, eyes so demure? How many months was it since her mother's death? Was it even half a year? No, not quite. It would be almost funny. Except that irony had its limits. Or should have. Some sort of statute of limitations to keep irony from spilling over into new graves. (Her mother, terrified of burial, had requested cremation; her father had disobeyed.)

She moved through the door; the girl drew back instinctively. She moved past the girl into the half-dark (as always) living room, where her father sat in his easy chair, reading the *Herald,* his feet up on the Ottoman, whose cover was newly embroidered.

*Fill in the missing item in the picture.*

Her father looked up and startled so hugely that the teacup in its little saucer on the drum table rattled. It was gratifying to see some tangible evidence of a guilty conscience; so little of what went on inside him was visible or had been visible in years. Buried alive, his emanations seldom reached them through the earth of his flesh. He had cried for a week when her mother died. "The poorrrr creaturrre, ahhhh, the pooorrr crreaturre," was what he'd said the whole time, never moved by the necessity to question what beyond the lack of money had impoverished her, or why he had brushed off Margaret when on her visit to Boston the year before she had asked him if they had to store such an incredible inventory of old sleeping pills when her mother was constantly asking why she should continue to live? It was unthinkable to him, a lapsed but rabid Catholic, that his wife should commit suicide. But in this context, what did unthinkable mean?

Aside from that week his last manifestation of feeling had been upon hearing of the death of John F. Kennedy and beyond that she could remember only small violent rages at the people upstairs for walking too hard and slamming doors. He had an obsession about slammed doors which Margaret had inherited, like so many other incomprehensible obsessions. When you thought about it, the genes were weighted against her on the matter of slammed doors since her mother was upset by *all* loud noises. She bit off one of her nails, a habit she always thought she'd kicked until she visited home.

"Is that you, then, Margaret?" her father said uncomfortably.

"Of course it's me," she said. "Who did you think it was? Kate Smith?"

His eyes went to the girl who stood somewhere in back of Margaret, then returned to Margaret.

"What brings you to Boston?" he asked. Not willing to acknowledge any tie between them strong enough to have made him the sole reason for her visit. The way his wife's family had felt about him, he felt about her, that was the truth of it. She'd always made him uncomfortable. If the inhuman standards of behavior they had set were unfair to him, that didn't mean that his daughter shouldn't have

19

naturally abided by them. From the beginning she'd been a disappointment to him, who'd assumed that Wasps were born toilet trained.

"I heard a rumor you had some kind of white-slave business going here, Dad," she said.

From behind her there was a gasp. The ruddiness of her father's face increased a thousandfold in the space of a second.

"Curb your tongue, Margaret," her father said.

Curb your tongue, curb your dog, curb your instincts, curb your humor, curb your appetite. *And don't slam the door!* But she was contrite in spite of herself.

"I'm sorry, Dad. You didn't give me a very warm welcome, you know, and your colleen didn't even want to let me into the house."

"I'm sorry," the girl whispered. "I didn't know."

She nodded without turning around. His angry color subsided. She had succeeded in putting him on the defensive, perhaps because of his knowledge that given his own way he would just as leave the colleen hadn't let her in to witness his quickly-found contentment. He belched a deep, easy beefstewy-belch, covering his mouth so that while his body might be racked by it, no sound would disgrace him. The containment theory of digestion etiquette; what didn't actually leave the body could not be proved to have ever been there. Every morning for as far back as she could remember he had locked himself into the bathroom for half an hour and farted fireworks that reverberated spectacularly throughout the apartment, a fact of which he seemed blissfully unaware. But that was the only audible sign ever that all the tea bags and all the meat and bread and potatoes had not taken a one-way journey to the center of his being where they would forever rest in peace.

"Maggie," he muttered, "this is Margaret."

"I'm sure I'm pleased to meet you," the girl said. Not actually curtsying.

"Did you know he had a daughter?" Margaret asked.

"Not living," the girl said, then put a hand over her mouth and stared at Margaret aghast, a victim of that peasant stupidity that let people believe that saying something could make it retroactively be true.

Margaret laughed.

"I mean," the girl said lamely, "I don't know wherrrre I got that idea . . ."

"I'm having twins," Margaret said, patting her stomach.

"Oh, how wonderrrful," the girl said, clapping her hands, her eyes filling with the holy tears of other women's weddings and childbirths.

"Twins," her father said.

She'd forgotten to tell him.

"You know me, Dad," she said. "Anything for a laugh."

"There are things you don't laugh about, Margaret," her father said.

"Mmmmm." Once she had asked him for a list of them but of course there was no paper long enough. That there were things you couldn't survive unless you joked about them was an idea utterly foreign to him, humor being linked as it was in his mind with drinking and the other vices.

She bit off another nail.

"I really think it's time you stopped biting your nails, Margaret," her father said.

"You always did," Margaret said.

Silence.

"Where's Roger?" her father asked.

"Home," she said. "I just left him."

"Left him!" Did her ears deceive her or was that an audible exclamation point? "What kind of craziness are ya tahhhking, Margaret?"

They'd thought she was lucky to get him, the bright white scion of a breakfast-cereal fortune, two years younger than she, a chain smoker who'd arrested lung cancer at the age of seventeen, painter and collagist whose greatest efforts now went into his titles (Madonna with Six Pack; Ivory Soap with Pubic Hair; Campbell's Soup Can from the Inside); still, they didn't know his stuff was dirty and he had a regular look about him that they liked, the look of a choirboy who will be arrested in ten years for multiple murders, and maybe that was what her father in particular had taken to, everything seemed to be safely inside. At least in the beginning. Even then he would pinch her hard or kick her in the shins under the table if they had an argument when her parents were around, coming attractions for his proclivity to hit below the belt. She'd found this strange in an objective way that amused her when she thought about it later on; all the things they saw about each other were strange or amusing and perhaps not entirely desirable and yet never before their marriage were they reasons to consider whether that marriage should take place. Once you decided to get married there was a kind of impetus that carried you through without leaving room in your thoughts for questions of mistakes. What was she to say now to her father, who thought change was the only serious mistake that could be made in life?

"I mean, he's home and I'm here," she said. "I left him home." Chicken. She was overwhelmed by self-dislike. The cowardice that other women coaxed and fertilized and periodically trotted out for the Good Housekeeping Seal of Femininity shamed her when she found it in herself. Why bravery, of all the things Margaret might have chosen to ask of Margaret?

"Anyway," she said, "I was in the mood to use the motorcycle and we couldn't all fit on it."

"Motorrrcycle," her father repeated numbly.

"Well," she said, "I guess I'd better go if I'm going to get there before dark."

Neither one made any attempt to stop her, or to find out

just where she had to be before dark, so she waved good-bye, clambered down the front steps and mounted her cycle.

❧ HER mother had been so frightened of being alone. (Loneliness was much more frightening than death, the absence of pain.) She needed her husband, however she loathed him, and it was this contradiction that had torn her apart every day of her life, destroying her self-esteem, making honest hatred of him impossible—indeed making all action impossible by the end, bringing in its wake a total external paralysis. If only ambivalence could have slowed down her mind as it slowed down her body. The only ambition she'd had for the last ten years of her life was to die before he did, never taking note that it would be possible to die ten minutes later. She wouldn't be left behind once more.

"Nobody *wants* to be left," Margaret had told her, and she'd answered that it was different for men. Why was it so different? Because men found other women right away. Ohhh . . . there was no possible satisfactory answer. Obviously the complaint had some reality to it, yet Margaret continually sensed that it wasn't the real part that was the problem. For her mother, men were part of that whole world of vulgar things whose very coarseness guaranteed their survival. . . . What coarse gesture had found him this lovely maiden to do for him? He hadn't the normal complement of widows, friends of his dead wife, themselves lonely, to begin inviting him to dinner, telling themselves they were only doing it to ease *his* pain. The one who'd tried

23

he had brushed off. She had despised him during his wife's lifetime and he wouldn't permit her to change her mind now. And verily he had found himself a dutiful young colleen who only wanted to serve . . . they also serve who only serve. Who hadn't known he had a daughter living. Did she know now for sure? Her father was a man with a deep-seated aversion to the truth. Painstakingly honest in all financial matters, the only man on the force not on the take in even a small way, he had the self-righteousness of the utterly honest man while in point of fact, his mind, when confronted with the simplest question with the most potentially painless answer, automatically, went through labyrinths to arrive at an answer which at best lacked relevance and at worst was the exact opposite of the real answer. Her mother couldn't tell a lie and had had no more desire than most to hear the truth so had retreated into silence over the years. But her father's special form of aphasia was so extraordinary that Margaret could easily envision a conversation between her father and the girl which began with the girl's saying, "Mrr. McDonough, I didn't know you had a daughterrr . . . that girrrl who called you Dad, she was your daughterr, was she?" and ended some minutes later with the girl not only uncertain of Margaret's identity but no longer sure that she'd heard him called Dad.

Where to now? She was hungry, she had to have something to eat, but then after that? There were the cousins . . . someone might still be at the house, they seldom really closed it before the end of October and the Cape was so beautiful in the fall. She hadn't seen any of the cousins since the week after her mother's death although they'd called her often when her mother was alive, and one or the other was always stopping off to visit on a trip to New York. Before. They didn't even know how ghastly she looked, so it wasn't that her appearance upset them, it was deeper than that. It was that with her mother's death all those traits of hers which they had for so long found exotic had been seen to be born not out of sheer Rabelaisian whimsey or some casual flair for the bizarre but out of a driving desperation not unlike their own but perhaps more acute. They felt cheated. As though, during a circus performance, someone had whispered that all the clowns wanted to play Hamlet, so that they'd been unable to enjoy the rest of the show.

After the funeral they'd gone back to cousin Hilda's house where Margaret had sat spaced out in a deep corner of the sofa rubbing her belly which was aching in some way that probably had nothing to do with the three-month-old baby, as she still thought of it, inside, while Roger had mocked them all, for her eyes only, by being excessively polite, and her father chanted his Poor Creature litany and aunts and uncles wafted through the room, embarrassed, these foreigners, by her failure to be embarrassed at the manner of her mother's death. Like a horse made skittish by the tension of its handler, she'd begun to make jokes, laughing nervously when they stared at her as she claimed that her mother had died of 1) cancer of the psyche; 2) indefatigable loss of the will to live; 3) medico-philia, a difficult ailment in which the contents of the medicine chest are seen to have greater appeal than everything else in the world combined. She'd flown home without Roger, who was in great good humor at being the Patcher Up, taking a taxi from the airport, telling the driver within five minutes of getting into the cab that her mother had just committed suicide, which gave him enough to talk about for the rest of the hour and a half ride. It was something she continued to do for months afterward, tell everyone she met, sometimes she had to stop herself from going up to perfect strangers on the street to tell them, very much in the manner that she would have felt impelled to tell them that the sky was falling if she had just come from the place where it was beginning to go and thus knew before anyone else. She carried with her a sense of disaster as immediate as lightning to someone standing under a tree. She made out her will and included provisions for the care of her child, if she and Roger should both die but it should survive.

She hadn't seen the cousins since that week although one or the other of them had called on the last day of each month of the few months since then, their regularity so obvious as to make her realize they were taking turns. Let them not once again be accused of negligence. Not that they'd actually been accused of neglecting her mother but the legacy of a suicide was a general accusation of neglect, barring the particulars of which no one could offer a self-defense and be exonerated. Who the hell had ever asked them for anything, anyway? What Margaret's mother needed they couldn't have given her, nor had she the right to expect it. Nowhere had Darwin made provision for a cold-water species which after seven generations of non-evolution produced a member who needed warmth to survive. Or who thought she did. The ambivalence of her claim being proven by the man she'd married who, on the surface so different from them all, was just beneath the skin and to the inner core a caricature of everything the Wasp, a caricature to begin with, stood for. Who initially strove to be what they thought he should be because it was what he really wanted to be in the first place, and only became grotesque in the striving.

She had some dinner and headed toward the Cape. There was at least an even chance the house would be empty in midweek at the tail end of September, and if it weren't, she could see who was there and then decide whether to stay. It had taken her many years to realize that she liked some of her cousins more than others. For so long she had thought of them as one glorious cousin pie which, cut open, produced people who were happy when she visited them. To differentiate between them would have been a form of criticism and it had never occurred to her, until one or two of them grew up and bolted to seed, that there were strong individual variations among them. Depending on who was there, she would stay or not stay. If the house was empty, well, she had the key, she had never taken it off her chain, and whether she would be able to bear it alone there, she couldn't tell in advance.

☙ IT was fairly dark as she crossed the canal and headed toward Sandwich. Sudden apprehension made her park the cycle off the highway about half of the ten or twelve miles there. She was exhausted and her bottom had finally reacted to its two-day punishment with soreness and itching. She should sleep in a bed where her weight could be distributed more reasonably. Yet the thought of entering the empty house in the darkness filled her with dread. When the tide was high the waves lapped at the sea wall with a noise that was soothing if you were happy, ghostly if you weren't. The house itself got musty after even a short damp spell. One of the cousins, years ago when they'd seen a movie called *Isle of the Dead* in which a coffin opened up and a dead woman rose from it, had made a joke about that coffin's lid being like the door of the house at the Cape when they first opened it in the spring, and the image, which had come fleetingly over the years, was strongly with her now. She half-sat, half-lay down with her head against a tree trunk, wishing she had something soft to wedge under her behind, barely able to raise it off the ground for a second or two at a time for relief. For a while she lay flat on her back with her head on the grass but it was hard and ants crawled down her neck and so she half-sat again. The whole movie took place at night in the mist, maybe because it was an isle. The woman who got out of the coffin had long, soft hair and her eyes were closed. The lid squeaked horribly but everything else was very quiet. Doors and lids. The first time she'd smoked dope after her mother's death all the pictures had been doors and lids opening endlessly in silent-movie time. Twice now she felt herself falling asleep and forced open her eyes. Then, finally, unconsciousness came.

She awakened in extreme discomfort, feeling that she couldn't move at all, and discovered that this was at least partly true because a young boy was asleep between her sprawled legs, his arms around her middle, his head on her breasts. She couldn't see his face but from his size she guessed him to be at least sixteen. He was wearing a sweatshirt and army pants. His boots, which had holes in the bottoms anyway, had been taken off, perhaps under the rules of some twenty-first-century etiquette that said you didn't go to sleep on strange ladies with your boots on. Next to the boots was a small stack of comic books and on top of the comic books was a sketchbook. Trying not to disturb him, she reached out for the sketchbook and let it flip open; every page was blank. She put it back again; the boy stirred. A clenched fist came up to his mouth, resting near it on her breast, the knuckles just touching his lips. There was something in his hand which, when his grip relaxed, she could see was a small, purple lucite box of the variety used to hold grass. It appeared to be empty. Occasionally his thumb moved back and forth along the surface of the box. His hair was fine and brown, down to his shoulders. She had a great urge to caress it and felt that under the circumstances he couldn't seriously object, but when she lifted one hand to his forehead she lost her balance and came close to toppling them both over sideways to the ground. He awakened and sat up, still in the narrow triangle made by her fat sprawled legs, rubbed his eyes without letting go of the box. He might be older than she'd thought; his hair had already receded somewhat. His face had that quality that makes people call some men of forty boys. It was a lovely, gentle sad face and she was moved by a strong desire to kiss his eyes.

He said, "Hi. I guess I fell asleep."

She smiled.

"What time is it?" he asked.

"I don't know," she said. "It must be nearly five. It's getting pretty light."

He nodded.

"Are you going to Sandwich by any chance?" she asked.

"I don't know," he said. "I guess so. I've been on the road." He smiled. "That's the best sleep I've had in a while."

"How long have you been on the road?" she asked.

He shrugged. "I dunno. All summer. Maybe longer."

"Don't you have to get back to school or anything?"

He shook his head. Nobody had to explain any more why he didn't go to school. It had cost her nearly a year of her life explaining in the fifties why she'd dropped out of her Sarah Lawrence scholarship and gone to work as a waitress in New York, but a few years later everyone had a whole new vocabulary to explain the boredom that had weighed on her like a physical presence, turning the very air of Bronxville into stone.

"My family has a house there," she said. "I'm on my way there now. You can come along, if you feel like it."

"Sure," he said. "I've got seventy-two cents."

"That doesn't matter," she said. "But we better sleep for another hour or two. It's a little early to buzz into Sandwich."

"My name is David," he said. She told him hers and was about to add that she was pregnant with twins but

29

changed her mind. David was watching her expectantly and it was finally borne upon her that he was waiting for her to adopt her previous position so that he could resume his. Thinking that she was too numb for it to matter, anyway, she did so; immediately, wordlessly, he took his place in what, for want of a more specific way to describe something that was presumed to sometimes exist, would have to be called her lap.

A combination of discomfort and a mild feeling of being aroused prevented her from going back to sleep, as David did immediately, so she amused herself with mental pictures of the various ways, all of them ludicrous, that he could actually get into her if he ever chose to try, and then, when those pictures ran out, by imagining conversations between the twins (whom she thought of variously as Amos and Andy, Gargantua and Pantagruel and Trick 'n Treat) during such a sexual congress, beginning with "Hey, what's goin' on here, Kingfish?" and ending with the twins' various attempts to define the identity of the intruder through the elastic barrier walls of the amniotic sac.

Finally David woke up and they started out, he on the motorcycle because her ass was in far worse condition than her feet, she trudging after him, assuring him when he stopped every few hundred yards that she wasn't ready to ride yet. Thoughts of Roger filled her mind, mingled with thoughts of this strange boy, so comfortable in her lap, so strange to the rest of her. Was he like other kids? How different were she and Roger from these kids? Was there really some change, deep as genes, that occurred in children born after Hiroshima, or was that just some bit of horseshit the liberal weeklies had picked up and would drop just when they had her convinced? The only thing that gave the idea currency was the fact that the kids themselves, the papers they put out and so on, seldom if ever mentioned it. Did David ever think about the bomb and if not, was it only because he was born knowing about it and so took it for granted? Or maybe because he never thought about anything? But if he never thought about anything, was it because of the bomb? Did Trick 'n Treat know about the bomb? If not, when would they find out? If they did, how could she possibly raise them? She, who didn't for a minute believe with her brain that the world would last another twenty years, yet persisted in planting trees that wouldn't come into full flower for nearly that long, in knitting sweaters because handmade sweaters lasted forever, in doing, in short, all those things that people didn't do who really believed in the end of the world? How with a straight face did you teach your kid the charm of manners, the virtues of abstention, the reconcilation to loss? Manners were symbols and there wasn't time for symbols any more; abstention might turn out in this century to be the virtue of the frigid and foolish; and loss, well, loss might be all there was left. Roger pointed out that there were excellent reasons not to have children; she agreed that this was so and stopped taking her pills, from which time she had become fond of referring to herself as an unintegrated personality.

She had expected Roger to be angry with her for being pregnant but all he'd said was, "Fine, fine. Keep you off the streets." By which it turned out he'd meant that it would keep her out of his way, since he would be in the streets more than ever, it being his notion that he had discharged, so to speak, any obligation he had to her in the way of friendship by creating some live company for her for the next few years. Roger, who'd thought he wanted another wife and should've just rented an orgone box.

DAVID parked the cycle in the lot next to the house. The key turned easily in the lock; the house was vacant but not stale, messy but not terribly messy, just enough to tell her that it was the younger cousins who'd been there last. Even the cousins were better here than at home, their training having taken better here simply because they couldn't be barred from their own homes, while in this house Great-Aunt Margaret reigned. Still, there were signs that it hadn't been Aunt Margaret who closed up the house. Dust on the beach bottles, sand on the floor, clamshells full of butts so tiny as to suggest some instant biological compensation by which everyone under twenty-one had been born with asbestos lips. Automatically she collected the fullest shells and brought them into the kitchen. When she came back she found David sitting in Great-Aunt Sabina's needlepoint-seat rocker, on which she herself had been sitting when Roger suggested that the weather being what it was, they ought to drive down to Virginia and get married.

"I never heard you say anything good about marriage," she'd pointed out. Nothing that suggested that his first marriage had been anything more than a bad joke. Nevertheless she'd lost track of the number of pink stitches she'd counted in the rose on the padded arm.

"Mmm," he'd replied. "Well you met me just after one. This is before."

And she'd gone with him. Why? She no more knew than she knew why she'd gone to bed with practically every man or boy who ever asked her, except that it usually seemed the easiest and pleasantest thing to do. So much easier than saying no. He was the first to ask her to marry, although she'd had no shortage of boyfriends in those prehistoric days when only Antioch and a few, tiny liberal arts colleges had a decent percentage of girls who put out at random. Actually, far from thinking of sex as a concession, she was always pleasantly surprised when someone wanted to get into her, having grown up with an image of herself as a provider of fun and games, as opposed to the more sensual forms of pleasure.

"I was sitting in that chair when my husband proposed to me," she told David.

"Where was *he* sitting?" David asked.

Startled, she asked what difference it made.

He shrugged. "What difference does it make where *you* were?"

"None," she had to admit. "I just . . . it's this house. It makes me think of things like that. Do you have a place like that, that sets you off on childhood memories and stuff?"

"I don't remember anything past last year," he said calmly.

Horrified, never doubting that what he said was true, she asked, "How about your parents?"

He said, "I saw them a few months ago."

"Oh," she said. "Well, I don't remember everything . . . but there are certain things. Certain places and times. This house has been in my mother's family—I guess I should say *they've* been in *it*—for nearly a hundred years. Those bottles . . ." lined up on the window sills, culled from the ocean, their sheen clouded by sand and water, many with ancient brand names still visible, different names becoming quaint with succeeding generations, "they were collected on the beach by my mother when she was a child, and my aunts and uncles, and my great-aunts and great-uncles and their parents. When I'm in this house I have a physical sense of history. Like being in a time tunnel."

He couldn't have cared less.

"My mother killed herself this past spring," she said. That grabbed him just a little. "And this summer I couldn't make myself come here. I didn't even know if I'd make it now. Maybe I wouldn't've if . . ."

"How'd she kill herself?" he asked with interest.

"Pills," Margaret said. "Hundreds of pills."

"Oh." Letdown. "The way you said *kill*, I thought maybe she did something violent."

Irritated, she started to tell him that the word kill didn't necessarily . . . then she stopped. Reminded herself that if things he said bothered her it wasn't because he meant them to but because he was at worst indifferent, at best, unknowing. Unlike Roger, who in a mood of yawning indifference toward her could still come up with the one remark most certain to drive her screaming out of her skin, this boy was not tuned to her or her skin or the things that could separate them.

"My father," she told David, "said she put herself to sleep, but I thought of that as a cop-out." A cop's out. "I figured it was that he couldn't face what she really did because he's a Catholic."

"But that's what she really did do, isn't it?" he demanded.

"I guess so. As a matter of fact, that was a very important part of it. She had a thing about sleep, she was crazy for sleep, she had the most terrible insomnia I've ever—"

He stood up abruptly. "Don't talk about insomnia."

"All right."

He walked around the living room, stopped to look through the window at the beach and the ocean.

"Is there anything to eat around here?"

"There must be," she said, and on the kitchen shelves she found chowder crackers, S. S. Pierce tea bags, S. S. Pierce marmalade, several cans of S. S. Pierce soups left from the cases Great-Aunt Margaret would have stocked at the beginning of the season, a few cans of S. S. Pierce fruits. After dropping out of Sarah Lawrence she'd taken an apartment on the Lower East Side of New York where her first Jewish friend had explained the meaning of *kosher* after she'd seen her hundredth delicatessen sign and immediately she'd nodded with recognition: *S. S. Pierce*. No one in her family had ever known what food was supposed to taste like and food had been her major discovery in those early months of perpetual excitement and wonder. Garlic, this incredible bud she'd first thought of as a fruit, so rich as to change the taste of anything it touched. Herbs and spices. At home there'd been salt, an occasional dash of pepper, parsley to decorate fish dinners and sage for the turkey stuffing at Thanksgiving, one little box of sage per lifetime. In New York she discovered basil and oregano and made tomato sauces so thick with them as to turn brown without meat. She found rosemary and used half a bottle to coat her first leg of lamb, along with garlic and a bit of flour, salt and pepper, the result being a thick and pungent crust that her roommate found inedible but she herself adored and ate between slices of bread the next day. She discovered chives and mangoes, avocadoes, Chinese cabbage and custard apples, none of them put up by S. S. Pierce, and came to know that all bread that wasn't white bread was not necessarily Italian bread. (Her father hated Italian food, in which he included Italian bread; none of it was allowed in the house.) She ground her own coffee beans and waited while an old man ground the cashews that would ruin her for commercial peanut butter forever. In restaurants she ordered tripe and sweetbreads and *kashe varnishkes;* after having kidneys in a French restaurant she lost a new boyfriend by attempting to duplicate them at home but ignorantly buying beef kidneys instead of lamb or veal.

She heated up two cans of chowder and served them to David with crackers. He didn't comment but she told him the store would be open in an hour or so and then she could get something else. As a matter of fact, if they were going to stay at the house for a while she might as well go to a real supermarket and stock up. He nodded.

"Do you *want* to stay for a while?" she asked.

"Sure," he said. "Why not?"

"I don't know," she said. "I didn't want to take you for granted." She smiled. "I mean, I don't want you to feel as if you can't take off if you feel like being alone or something."

"I don't like being alone," he said.

Why hadn't she been prepared for it, this simple admission of dependency? When she was his age saying you were lonely had been confessing to a social disease that might be contagious.

"Have you been alone all this—during all the time you've been on the road?"

"Most of it."

"I could never stand being alone until I got pregnant," she said.

"Pregnant?" he repeated.

"Sure," she said. "I'm pregnant now. Very pregnant. Can't you tell?"

"I thought you were just fat," David said.

"Well I *am* fat," she said. "But I'm not *just* fat. I'm going to have twins in a few weeks."

"Aren't you too old for that?" David asked.

"No," she said. "I'm not even thirty. I just look old because I'm fat." For this she had left Roger. The same old birdshit dropped from a different tree.

"Where's your husband?"

"At home."

"You separated?"

"Well, we don't exactly seem to be together."

"You going back before you have your babies?"

"I don't know. I haven't figured it out yet. I only left on impulse, a few days ago. I got mad and I got out on the bike and left."

"Did you ever think about going to a commune?" David asked.

"Sure," she said. "I think it's one of those things everyone thinks about nowadays."

"Someone told me about one in Vermont," he said. "I was thinking of heading up there . . . when I ran into you."

Why did he make her feel defensive? She was sure it wasn't anything he was doing on purpose. He'd been heading out on the Cape when they met, not inland.

"You can still go," she pointed out. And then, not wanting him to feel she was chasing him away, "I'll go with you, if you want me to."

"You want to?" he asked, but of course she hadn't thought about that yet, she'd only been responding to his need.

"I don't know," she said. "I guess so. I mean, why not? If I don't go home I have to go someplace else. Do you think they take babies at that commune?"

"Sure. Why not?"

"I don't know," she said. "Not everyone likes having babies around."

"At the communes they're supposed to love everyone," David said. "That's the whole thing with the communes."

"Have you ever been to one?" she asked. "While you were on the road?"

He shook his head. "A few times I almost did," he said. "But then I didn't feel like it."

Why not? For her the idea actually had enormous appeal. She didn't want to go back to Roger, yet. Couldn't go back. Couldn't face him in this condition. If it was true that Roger had a natural mean streak a yard wide and very purple, it was also true that her very appearance was an incitement to riot, a monstrous joke on him as well as herself, her visible willingness to be a moving target. A statement of need constantly filled and never fulfilled. Being fat was like being suicidal, there was that element of reproach that made people uncomfortable. And when Roger was uncomfortable he was nasty. Furthermore, it was a strange fact that while Roger's indifference might arouse her sarcasm, on any occasion when Roger was out-right angry or viciously critical of her, she became para-lyzed. Stopped speechless. As though magnetic force had pulled together their two complementary views of her and in the process, locked her tongue between. No, she wouldn't face Roger again until she loved herself so much that his view of her had become irrelevant.

"But do they have Blue Cross?"

"What?"

"Nothing," she said. "I was kidding. I guess we'd have to get a car, it's hard to see how we'd make it with the bike."

"What, do you have a lot of money?" David asked.

"No, I've only got about forty dollars, but I can cash a check up here easily. Everyone knows my family. And I'll trade in the bike. We should be able to get some kind of jalopy, and I've got plenty of credit cards for gas and stuff."

Aside from his allowance, Roger's family paid any large bills forwarded to them. They hadn't done so until he'd appeared at their home in Ardmore with his second rea-sonable choice for a wife. A few years earlier they might have entertained a less kindly view of a Sarah Lawrence dropout with a Roman Catholic cop for a father, but two years before that Roger had without prior notice brought home his new first wife, a colored dancer, and that single act had expanded their awareness of the possibilities to the point of making anything else he might do for the rest of his life relatively acceptable to them. Roger's wife had left him after only a year, her ego, though Roger claimed it had the size and strength of a California redwood, apparently unable to take the outrageous verbal slings and arrows that were the daily fortune of anyone living with him. His family had readily agreed to pay her alimony, and a couple of years later Roger had served up Margaret and ever since, as he was fond of saying, the checks had flowed smoothly from checkbook square.

Would Roger send her money if she asked for it? That would be like becoming a remittance man's remittance man. Roger's father liked her, flirted with her outrageously as a matter of fact, but she wouldn't like to ask him directly for money, would never do it unless the children's needs were involved. It had taken her quite a while to get adjusted to the idea that they were supported by Roger's parents; he'd complained of her lack of sophistication in this respect, pointing out that only people with no family money were supposed to be possessed of such theoretical qualms. But always until her pregnancy she'd made it a point to keep some kind of job, full time, part time, producing little dresses to be sold in Village boutiques, producing letters with carbons, food for hungry people (when she met Roger she'd been working in a Jewish dairy restaurant on Second Avenue; he had just abandoned sculpture for film making and was doing a documentary on an old people's day center upstairs from the restaurant), producing change from cash registers, her need to produce being laughed at by Roger, who subsequent to their marriage spent a year producing intestinal-looking collages of such a size and hideousness as to create an emotional ordeal for anyone who had to enter a room containing one of them. He filled their bedroom walls with them except that it wasn't just the walls because at points they were six inches deep, and when the walls were covered he suspended one from the ceiling over their bed so that whatever her eyes might light upon, if she happened to open them for a moment while they were making love, she became convulsed at the sight of some acid-green ruptured appendix, Day-Glow head-cheese or illuminated testicle descending, which convulsions, Roger took pains to tell her, constituted a singular improvement over her normal passive-reclining style of love-making.

Roger would readily send her money if he thought she didn't care. If it didn't occur to him that she might regard generosity as a token of love and concern. Roger was never stingy, except with his symbols. At the gas station that afternoon she agreed to exchange her motorcycle and a hundred dollars for a 1963 Corvair the owner's son had done some work on. She made out a check and called Roger collect from the station, asking him, in a disingenuously casual way, to deposit a lot of money in the checking account because she expected to travel around for a while. "Sure, kid, sure," he said. "I'll do that." And hung up before she could have second thoughts about what else she should tell him or wonder whether she wasn't being suspiciously cool.

David approved of her purchase in a mildly surprised way that made her realize that he hadn't assumed that just because she'd announced her intention of buying a car and left the house to do it, she would come home having done it or even having seriously made the attempt. Here again was that sense of radical evolution in less than a generation. Always there had been a disparity between what people did and what they'd meant to do but surely there had once been some more reasonable relationship between the two.

THEY slept together that night in the big bed in Great-Aunt Margaret's room. She had showered and made a bedsheet toga for herself and was reading in bed, the door to her room open, when David came upstairs and into the room, undressed and got into bed with her. She was suffused with heat and desire, dared not put down the book resting on her enormous white-sheeted belly—Great Aunt Margaret's *Compendium of Cape Cod Marine Life* —lest he see both in her face and be upset. What he wanted from her clearly had little to do with sex. Yet she could not take her eyes off him while he was undressing. He had a beautiful body, not at all the kind one associated with indecision or alienation. Broad shoulders, muscular chest, flat stomach and narrow hips. Sturdy, muscular legs. At what point, what age, had she become aware of the bodies of young boys? Maybe it was as recently as her pregnancy. When you were younger you liked a boy or didn't, and while there were obvious physical factors affecting one's attraction—one simply wasn't drawn, for example, to fat boys—she couldn't remember ever attaching importance to the looks of any body feature except the face. This pleasure now in watching young boys . . . playing Frisbee on the beach . . . walking half-naked along country roads . . . not even to speak of the specific frustrated lust this one was causing her . . . it was like some sort of coming attraction for senility. SHE WASN'T THAT OLD, GOD-DAMMIT! This was the century of the extended life expectancy, reality factors excluded. How could she feel so old, so young? Was it possible that some immutable factor

41

in the internal development of man would cause everyone to go through the same stages at the same ages as people went through them in the days when forty was a reasonable life expectancy? So that if you were thirty you were emotionally three-fourths through your interior life, even if you were going to live to be eighty? She shuddered, closed her eyes for a moment, opened them, tried to focus on the book. She looked at David; he lay on his back, eyes open.

"What are you thinking?" she asked him.

"I was wondering when you were going to turn off the light," he said.

She put the book on the night table but at that moment one of the twins, or maybe both of them, jumped under the bedsheet. They didn't move much any more, maybe they were too crowded now. A couple of months earlier there had seemed to be almost constant motion. Roger had watched her watching them and had taken out his sketch pad for the first time in years and had seemed to be drawing her, but then when she'd looked at the picture later, everything in it had seemed to be disembodied; her eyes were up in a tree, à la Cheshire Cat, and the twins were two tiny primitive beasts dancing in a forest.

"Soon," she said to David. "I want to watch the children playing."

"Huh?"

She pointed to her belly, thinking, I'm jealous of his beautiful body so I'm showing him what mine can do. The mound shifted.

"What's that?" David asked.

"They're playing ring-around-a-rosy or something," she said contentedly.

"I want to ask you something," David said. "You ever been to a hospital?"

"A hospital? You mean a mental hospital?" she asked incredulously.

He nodded. He was utterly serious. This youth, so strange that he might have been a chunk from the planet Krypton, for all he seemed to relate to earth, or what she normally assumed to be earth, *he* thought that *she* was mad.

"David," she said, "look." She pushed aside the toga to reveal her stomach, the stretch marks now barely visible in the dim light from the reading lamp. He stared at it with awe, obviously finding it more impressive in its clothed condition. "There are two babies in there," she said. "They'll be ready to be born in a few weeks, maybe less, and when they move around inside . . . when my stomach moves . . . watch now . . . there . . . see . . . ? When it moves like that, it's not something I'm doing because I'm crazy. It's *them*."

He watched as though hypnotized.

"If you want to," she said, "you can lay your hand on it. You'll feel them when they move."

He put his hand down on her stomach. The twins were still and she felt the momentary irritation of a stage mama whose child refuses to perform.

"Sometimes it takes time," she said. "If you wait you'll feel it."

Without moving his hand he adjusted his position so that he was lying on his side up against her; she raised her arm so that it cradled his head. Her heart beat wildly but her belly was motionless. When she looked down she saw that David's eyelids were closed and a moment or two later she realized that he was fast asleep.

☙ It was already dark when they arrived. The farmhouse looked very appealing—soft lights on throughout the ground floor, light spilling out onto the front porch, where bunches of horse corn hung from nails near the door and hundreds of pumpkins and winter squashes were stacked against the siding.

"Wow," she said. "I hope you like pumpkin pie."

He shrugged. She hung back as he started up the steps to the porch. He knocked and a moment later a skinny, black-haired woman with eyes like a Kaethe Kollwitz child opened the door.

David said, "Hi."

The woman smiled dreamily.

"Is Mitchell here?" David asked.

The woman shook her head. "He went back to the city a few weeks ago." Her voice was musical but the music was from another world.

"Oh . . ." He took a bit of time to consider this. "Can I come in anyhow?" he finally asked.

"Do you have anyone with you?" Margaret could have sworn that the woman had looked directly at her a moment before.

"Her," David said.

"Oh, dear, I don't know," the woman said softly. "I'll have to . . . we don't really have that much room, we've agreed that . . . I'll have to check with the . . ." She disappeared from the door.

*But it is dark,* Margaret thought. *And I am heavy with childs.* A sudden pitying image of herself trudging from

44

inn to inn looking for a bundle of hay. She'd needed to go to the bathroom for some time and now she felt a terrible cramp in her stomach at the thought of having to keep going. The woman returned with a man. A book-jacket kind of man, very slender with long, straight black hair, glasses and a pipe.

"Here they are, De Witt," the woman said.

He nodded gravely, raised his hand. "Welcome."

She felt another cramp in her stomach and decided to climb the stairs. Surely they would let her use their precious communal bathroom. With some difficulty, the cramps getting worse, she climbed the steps to the porch. Saw, without serious interest, that they were as stunned as her father had been at the first full sight of her.

De Witt said, "Welcome."

"Please," she said, "may I use your bathroom?"

"Of course," he said calmly. "Please come in. Both of you. Come in." They stepped back to allow her to pass through. David followed. She was vaguely aware of people in the rooms to the left and right of the hallway but was much too intent on getting to the bathroom to pay attention to them. De Witt pointed to the stairs and laboriously she climbed them, clutching at the rail with one hand and her stomach with the other. But she failed to relieve her cramps in the bathroom, although an enormous amount of liquid burst from her, and when she left it, she felt she couldn't manage to get back down the stairs. Blindly, instinctively, she headed for the nearest room and groped her way to a bed, panting with exertion. She stretched out with relief but was immediately seized with another wave of cramps. And then another. Her body was soaked with sweat and the tablecloth clung to her all over. She plucked it away from her arms and breasts, then her stomach, and was reaching to pull it up from her legs when another huge cramp seized her, convulsing her whole body into helplessness, wrenching out of her a scream that was expression of

45

nearly unutterable pleasure and nearly unbearable pain. Her body relaxed. With some difficulty, aware of a commotion on the staircase, she reached out and found a table light, which she switched on. Propping herself up on her elbows, she lifted the bottom of the tablecloth. Lying between her legs, swathed in a little blood and a great deal of some moist filmy substance, framed by excrement, with a head of dark wet hair and an umbilical cord the size of a transatlantic cable still leading to somewhere inside her, was Margaret's first child, a girl.

A voice said, "Oh, my God!"

With enormous difficulty she thrust herself to a sitting position and picked up her child, who immediately began to cry. Gratefully she felt strong hands behind her, propping up her back, heard De Witt's calm mellifluous voice giving orders . . . towels from the kitchen, newspapers . . . sterilize a pair of scissors . . . boil some rags, too . . . lots of newspaper . . . a mop, pillow . . . Margaret tried to bring the baby to her breasts but the cord wasn't long enough and so she let it lie on her stomach instead, its head on its side. It cried for a moment longer, a strange noise, at once furious and subdued, like a performance at the Fillmore with the amplifying equipment turned off. There seemed to be hundreds of people in the room. Still propping her up, De Witt stuffed more pillows in back of her, then withdrew. The baby stopped crying. Silence, overwhelming in its echoes. Then the first new spasms came and the baby began to cry.

"The scissors'll be here soon," De Witt said. "I'll tie the cord as soon as the placenta's born."

"What about the other one?" Margaret asked, holding the baby on her heaving stomach, stroking its wet downy head.

"Other one?" De Witt repeated.

"Didn't David tell you it's twins?" she asked through the contractions.

"David and I didn't get to any of this," De Witt said, smiling broadly.

She smiled back but the smile was cut short by another contraction. Breathing became difficult; her fever, which had subsided, went up again and she began panting. Someone beside the baby was crying, a woman or a girl, but Margaret couldn't take the trouble to find out who it was.

"Someone help her hold on to the baby," De Witt ordered. "Get the dirty blanket out from under her." The calm of his voice was a miracle in itself. "Rip it if you have to, but get rid of all that crap and get down some newspaper." Somehow it was done. Someone put a white cloth over the baby on her stomach. "You hold on to that one," De Witt said, "and I'll get the other one when it comes out." The height of schizophrenia, this combined feeling of supernatural power and utter helplessness. She could do anything but what could she have done without him? A moment or so later one huge convulsion crowned the head of her second child, the rest of whom came out into De Witt's waiting hands with very little labor, wet but without a trace of blood, soundly asleep, still in the middle of the original wet dream, trailing her own thick, wet umbilical rope, another girl. Kneeling beside the bed so as not to stretch the connection between them, De Witt held the new baby upside down and spanked her bottom. She cried and he turned her back upright, holding her against his sheet-covered chest. She stopped crying immediately. The placenta birthed, plopping down between Margaret's thighs like a battle-scarred jellyfish. Someone said they should fry it and eat it but De Witt said that while Mira could live with the fact that most of them were meat-eaters, he thought that cooked human placenta would really freak her out, and even in her current condition Margaret found a second to be grateful to Mira, whoever she was, for being a vegetarian. He wrapped the second baby, who had no real hair yet, only a light down on her head, and hand-

47

ed her to someone kneeling beside him, then cut the cord from the second baby and covered the spot with a piece of wet cloth someone handed him. On Margaret's stomach, still crying, the first baby was turned over and her cord cut and covered. Margaret lifted it up to her breast then De Witt laid the other one on her other breast. The first one, still crying, flailed her arms frantically and in so doing scratched the cheek of the second one, leaving a surprising red mark on it.

"Oh, dear!" said the musical voice of the woman from the front door. Mira, maybe.

"They scratch themselves sometimes," De Witt said tranquilly. "It's nothing. Someone get me a manicuring scissors."

Margaret smiled but she was upset by the mark. The only thing that prevented her from being more upset about it was her tiredness and the continual crying of the first baby.

"Maybe I can nurse her," she said to De Witt.

"There won't be anything there yet," he said. "But see what she does."

"Do you believe in fate?" Margaret asked worshipfully.

"I believe in myself," he said firmly.

"Well I believe in you, too," she said, "but that's not what I'm talking about. What if I'd landed someplace else?"

"Most of the farms have someone who can deliver a baby," De Witt said.

"I can't believe they're like you," she said.

"Better tend to this one," De Witt said.

He held the sleeping baby while she brought the crying one to her nipple, squeezing the nipple and letting it brush the baby's lips. Nothing came out, but the baby's mouth immediately opened around the nipple and firmly bit it. The crying stopped. The nipple stayed in the baby's mouth and De Witt told her that some were born knowing how to suck while others took time to learn. She held out her arm for the other baby, who slept on her breast without once opening her eyes.

✒ SHE named the girls Rosemary and Rue, in reverse order of birth, and someone said that plant names were so beautiful. Margaret didn't bother to say that Rosemary wasn't after a plant but after her favorite cousin because then she would have had to explain Rue. De Witt had a table brought into the already cramped room, which the previous occupants had insisted upon turning over to Margaret, and he improvised a double cradle by nailing two crates to the top of it, then lining them with hay and sheets. Rosemary slept through the night but Rue was up so much that Margaret simply kept her in the bed, letting the baby suck her breast, now oozing some watery stuff that wasn't milk but which Rue seemed to like, anyway. By early the next morning the angry line on Rosemary's cheek had nearly disappeared.

✒ MARGARET gave De Witt a check for two hundred dollars to cover some of their expenses and to buy for her some of the things she needed from town, asking him also to find out if David needed anything. He would also send a telegram to Roger for her, saying that the girls had been born and she was staying at the farm for a while. Mira went with De Witt. Mira was De Witt's wife. The woman at the door. Margaret was profoundly disconcerted by Mira although she wasn't sure why. Perhaps it was the contrast between the unchanging, haunted eyes and the serene smiling mouth. (Roger's mother was like that, her eyes never changed no matter what the rest of her face was doing, although the basic expression in that case was different; however weak, frightened or agonized Roger's mother might become, her eyes were always *watchful*.) Perhaps it was the seductive voice combined with the cropped hair and the convent-like, floor-length, osnaburg smock. Or maybe it was just her manner, a Mother Superior already on her way to the better place. She called Margaret *dear*. She called everybody dear, including De Witt, something in her manner suggesting that she was Maria Montessori and the rest of the world was her Italian slum. What had a man like De Witt seen in her?

"Yes, of course," Mira said, glancing over De Witt's shoulder at Margaret's list.

When they'd left, she lay in bed, tired but comfortable. She had deflated substantially—whatever the twins had weighed, she must have lost another twenty or thirty pounds of water and other stuff so that she again looked like a human being, albeit a soft, fat and somewhat asexual one. Her breasts were swelling and hardening with the new milk, or colostrum, or whatever, and since the twins' appetites were not yet keeping pace with the supply, Margaret frequently overflowed onto the sheet, which by afternoon had acquired a mildly sour smell which she actually found pleasant but which she suspected other people would not.

David came in to see her, a little shyer than he'd been that first time she found him in her lap.

"Hi," he said with that endearing grin he had that was

really half a grimace and half a question mark. "That was great timing."

She smiled.

"I mean it," he said. "They wouldn't have let us in. They didn't mean to take any more people, they don't have that much space now."

"Good," she said. "I'm glad it worked out."

He wandered aimlessly around the little room, seeming to look at nearly everything but the twins—Rosemary asleep in her crate, Rue asleep on Margaret's breast after feeding.

"Did you see the babies?" she asked.

"Sure I saw them," he said. "They're right there."

"Do you think they're pretty?" she asked.

"I don't know." He came closer, sat down on the side of the bed, stared at Rue, whose head nested against the underside of Margaret's breast as she slept. Then he looked briefly at Rosemary in the box.

"This one's prettier," he said, head gesturing to Rue.

"How can you say that?" Margaret asked. "They're practically the same and if there's any difference . . . anyhow, you're just saying it because she has more hair."

"Mm," David said without interest.

Margaret shifted the baby to the sheet so she could lie on her side, but as she did so, the pressure on her unmilked breast made it squirt milk.

"Oh, Christ, I'm leaking," she said. "It's just as well. I'm so full it hurts." David stared at the wet breast. "Mother's milk," she said playfully. "Want some?"

With utter seriousness he reached out a finger, touched her nipple, licked the finger.

"It doesn't have any taste," he said.

"Cocoa Marsh hadn't been invented yet," she said. "Anyway, it's probably not the real milk. Some other stuff comes out first."

He was thoughtful.

"What are the other people like?" she asked him.

He shrugged. "They're pretty old. Like you, maybe. De Witt's wife is all right. Then there's this girl . . . I'm supposed to go looking for kindling with her now."

A small pang at having been replaced in David's heart without actually having reached there in the first place. That he found Mira nice she wouldn't even think about.

"Don't let me keep you," she told him.

"I don't really feel like it," he said.

"How come?" she asked.

"I don't know," he said. "I think she's a phony. She's got this phony acid name."

"What?"

"Baby Butterscotch." He grimaced.

"Is she pretty?"

"I don't know, I guess so. But I think she's a phony." Without seeming to be thinking of what he was doing he reached out the same finger, touched her nipple again, sucked the finger for a moment.

"David?" A girl was at the door, a pretty girl with a soft voice and hair the color of butterscotch.

Margaret smiled in what she hoped was a benign fashion. The girl smiled back.

"I'm sorry," the girl said. "I just wanted to know if—"

"Don't be sorry," Margaret said. David didn't look at the girl. "Would you like to see the babies?"

The girl nodded eagerly but seemed hesitant about actually coming into the room.

"Come on in," Margaret said. "They're both sleeping."

The girl glanced at David, who was looking out the window. Then she tiptoed into the room and over to the cradle.

"Oh, she's beautiful!" Baby Butterscotch exclaimed softly. "They're both *soooo* beautiful."

It was the first time anyone had said to Margaret the thing people used to say about babies in the old days, and only now could she admit how she had craved to hear it. Margaret's heart went out to Baby Butterscotch, who was certainly not a phony at all, just a lovely girl with the right instincts, but David fixed on the girl a gaze at once harsh and remote.

"Aren't they really?" Margaret said. "Their names are Rosemary and Rue."

"Oh, those are beautiful names," Baby Butterscotch said. "Really beautiful groovy names." She stood quivering with pleasure and admiration, seemed about to reach out to touch Rosemary but unsure that it was all right to do so.

"You can pick her up if you want to," Margaret said, and was about to add that the baby's head should be held so it wouldn't wobble, but Butterscotch had already happily picked up the baby, supporting her head, cradling her, running her lips over the baby's downy head. Finally she looked up and smiled at Margaret, the author of her pleasure.

"God, I love babies," Butterscotch said.

"How old are you?" Margaret asked.

"Eighteen," Butterscotch said. "I used to babysit a lot. Not just for the money, I mean I *liked* it. I used to think that was all I wanted, you know, to get married and have babies and have a house and a car and, you know, the whole suburban bit. It seems ridiculous now when I think of it." She rocked the baby as she spoke.

"Why?" Margaret asked.

"Well, you know," Butterscotch said, "it's just the whole suburban bit, that's not my thing. My parents . . . I mean the whole nine to five bit . . . meeting the commuter train and putting in the flowers in neat little . . . well, the flowers, that's okay I guess . . . but what I mean is, that whole routine, that life style . . . can you see me?"

David said, "I can."

The girl's eyes filled with tears. Gently, sorrowfully, she

lowered the baby back into the crate, gazed at it for a moment, turned back to David. Her expression was tragic. She seemed about to thank Margaret but then decided against it—after all, such a small gesture might prove to be another unwitting step toward damnation. Her body sagging with defeat, Butterscotch turned and left the room.

Margaret watched David. If he felt any satisfaction at having destroyed the girl, his face didn't show it; he looked about as emotionally involved as if he'd just ordered a BLT down. Roger never attempted to conceal his satisfaction after having put Margaret down in some cunning new way; his smile would become benign and expansive and his posture, as he moved around the house, briefly changed from caged beast to lord of the manor.

"I wonder," she said, "what Roger is doing now."

"Roger?" David repeated.

"My husband."

"Where is he?" David asked.

"At home," she said. "In the suburbs." *My husband's name is Roger, we live in Realestatesville and he sells Rorschachs. Or vice versa.* "He's a film maker."

"You miss him?"

"I don't know. We haven't slept together since I got pregnant, practically."

"Are you allowed to?"

*Are you allowed to? By that Great Obstetrician in the Sky?*

She nodded. "There are men who like it better that way." *Remembering Howie Ard, the Pregnant Lady Freak she'd slept with once around her fourth month, who'd begged her to keep in touch.*

David took another lick.

She'd thought about Howie for a long time, trying to decide whether she had reason to feel rejected at his nocturnal admission that he had no interest in seeing her after the baby was born. She'd thought of Howie before she thought of Roger, when the doctor told her she was having twins; Howie would go wild, was her thought.

They'd met at a party given by old friends of Roger's in a huge loft on Broome Street full of inflatable furniture and representational paintings which had repelled and upset Roger; when they were in school together this friend had been the most far-out of his painting friends, and now the guy had deteriorated into someone cranking out this traditional garbage. In Roger's lexicon the word *traditional* was invariably followed by the word *garbage*. For him the only thing the past had to offer was money, a philosophically difficult situation for Margaret, to whom tradition meant the house at the Cape and beach bottles and a fire burning all day in the hearth at the aunts' and uncles' houses on holidays. She and Roger had had one of their most bitter arguments when somewhere near the beginning of their marriage he'd insisted that what all the pleasant things represented by the cousins and the past really came down to was that the cousins had been richer than she. Margaret had refused to let it go by although she had let other far less reasonable arguments go by. It was unbearable to her to have the pleasure taken out of those particular memories and it was unbearable to him, a permanent thorn in his paw, that she should remember the past fondly. He claimed that he had parents who were no worse than most and a filthy rich childhood and if he hadn't enjoyed being young, nobody could have. If she didn't remember how miserable she'd been it was because she was a mass of repression. She'd asked if it wasn't equally possible that he was repressing the times he'd had fun and he'd called her a dumb vapid cow and said he was going to buy her a block of salt for Christmas.

Roger had never been addicted to the small amenities like introducing her to other people they met, and in the months of her pregnancy he seemed to have developed a specific resistance to letting anyone know they were related, so that she was pretty much on her own at parties unless someone paid attention to her, at which point Roger might materialize from nowhere and tell her he was ready to leave. Now as she sat in a suggestively shaped, round rubber chair, a man plopped down in back of her, grabbing her hair.

"You have magnificent hair," he whispered in her ear. "I bet you're pregnant. Sell me your hair."

"Oh, no," she said quickly. Her hair was the only thing about her that had Roger's unqualified approval. It hadn't been cut since she was twelve and came down to her waist, between auburn and chestnut in color, thick and silky in texture. On their first date they had gone to a party from which Roger had taken her at an extremely early hour with the words, "I'm taking you home now, I have an overwhelming urge to come in your hair." To Howie she said, "I couldn't do that. Why don't you buy a wig?"

"Real hair wigs are prohibitive," he informed her. "And there's no guarantee they come from pregnant women, I could be cheated easily."

"How did you know I wasn't just fat?" she asked.

"As a truffle is to the nose of a truffle hound," he said solemnly, "so is a pregnant woman to my whole nervous system. Is your husband here?"

She nodded.

"Are you very close to him?"

"I suppose so," she said. "In a strange kind of positive-negative way."

"Show him to me," Howie said. "Show me the lucky bastard."

The lucky bastard was in a far corner of the room, surrounded by the four beautiful wives of four other artists, with one or more of whom he would undoubtedly be in the sack before the evening was over since he had to be getting it someplace.

She pointed out Roger to Howie.

"The stupid bastard," Howie said. "How can he bother with those skinny broads?"

"He doesn't like fat women," Margaret explained. "For that matter he doesn't seem to appreciate pregnant women, either."

"Come wiz me," Howie whispered in her ear, "and I weel show you what iz it to be apprezhiated."

With a readiness astonishing to herself, for she had been married to Roger for more than five years and had been unquestioningly faithful to him in that time, she hoisted herself out of the rubber chair and followed Howie out of the loft to his apartment in Washington Square Village.

"How come you live *here?*" she asked him.

"A specific response to specific needs," he responded mysteriously as they rode up the elevator.

It was a good-sized apartment for a bachelor, furnished beautifully, but in a conventional—nay, super-bourgeois, manner that was somehow surprising in a person of Howie's otherwise unconventional tastes. Soft blue wall-to wall carpeting, a deep blue velvet sofa, colors of rose and gold in the drapes and chairs. There were no paintings but a large number of enlarged, well-framed photographs hung on the walls. Howie went into the kitchen to make drinks and as she inspected the photographs more closely she found them all to be of pregnant women: a pregnant Jackie Kennedy, a pregnant Colleen Dewhurst, a pregnant Jeanne d'Arc after the painting at the Metropolitan, a pregnant Happy Rockefeller, a pregnant Venus on the Half Shell, a pregnant Sophia Loren and several ladies of equal pregnancy if not equal renown.

Howie came back with the drinks. "Let's go into the bedroom," he said. "That way you won't have to get up again."

Obediently she followed him into the bedroom where a

six-foot-high photograph of a pregnant Eleanor Roosevelt dominated an interior that was otherwise straight Marjorie Morningstar. Howie set down the drinks and carefully pulled back the yellow satin quilted bedspread, then beckoned to her to stretch out next to him.

"A pregnant woman," he said, running his hand along the mound that had barely begun to specify itself, "has different needs than an ordinary one. I shouldn't say needs, I should say desires, because basically a pregnant woman has no needs, she's the most complete, un-needy person in the world, but what she wants . . ." His voice was low and hypnotic, like the man on the astrology forecast records. "What she wants is comfort. The part of her that grooves on dirt and discomfort and being miserable is submerged. Tradition and pleasure are in the ascendancy."

They sipped at their drinks.

"This is delicious," she said.

"I invented it for my wife during her pregnancy," he said. "My ex-wife. She was pregnant when I married her. I should've realized it couldn't last."

"Maybe you should've married an elephant," Margaret said.

"It has lemon and honey in it," he said, "which is why the appeal to pregnant women. I won't tell you more because it's part of my total plan to lure you back." He put down his drink, leaned over her, kissed her ardently while massaging her belly.

"How come you care so much?" she whispered, already pleasantly excited, putting down her drink and encircling him with her arms. "I mean, what is there about us?"

"Arrogance," he whispered back, kissing her neck, drawing up the skirt of her flowing maternity dress and pushing down her pants so that he could fondle her stomach without interference. "Pregnant females are the most arrogant fucking creatures in the world . . . You can't touch 'em . . . All you can really do is keep trying."

"I don't feel arrogant," she said truthfully.

"Sure you do," he told her. "You just haven't thought about it. If you reflect for a while . . . c'mere, sit up, I'll help you get your clothes off . . . if you think about it you'll realize that you have a certain good feeling these days. You're sort of satisfied with yourself, right? You don't sit around worrying about what you should be doing because you have this sense that whatever you're doing is good enough. And you're right! It is! It's magnificent!" He took the barrette out of her hair so that it fell loosely down her back and over her shoulders. Naked and happy she reclined. For the first time since she'd begun to put on weight she felt no shame, no desire to hide under the covers. Once or twice in her third month Roger had still made love to her but he had made it quite apparent that he was using her very much as he would have used a knothole if that happened to be the most readily available place for him to come, the result being that she had experienced just about as much pleasure as a knothole would have in the same circumstance. Now, feeling like a marvelous jewel for the first and last time during her pregnancy, she made love with pleasure, and if she still tended to be submissive rather than active, that seemed to be perfectly all right with Howie, who had, after all, said that what she was doing just by being pregnant was so magnificent that there was no need for her to be doing anything else.

Not two weeks later she had gotten the call that her mother was dead.

⋙ "So how come you haven't been sleeping with him?" David asked.

"With my husband, you mean? I only said *some* men like pregnant women. I didn't say he was one of them."

"So who've you been sleeping with?"

She started to point out that she hadn't said she'd been sleeping with *anyone,* but stopped herself. David had a shit-detector astounding in one so young and so detached.

"It was only once," she told him. "A few months ago."

"How come?"

"I was afraid of getting too attached to him. He only liked me because he had this thing for pregnant women."

"How do you get attached to people?" David asked.

She stared at him, not having the vaguest idea of how to answer, not even sure what the question was. It was almost like a straight request for lessons, yet that couldn't really be it. How could you *not* get attached to people? She got attached to everyone, even people she disliked. She liked David and De Witt and Baby Butterscotch and she loathed Mira, yet already in some unbearable way she was attached to Mira just as much as to the others. A part of the same jig-saw puzzle.

"I don't know," she said. "It's just something that happens. I'm extremely attached to Roger, even if we haven't made love in half a year and even if I'm mad at him. Even being mad at people . . . probably you wouldn't get mad at people if you had no attachment to them."

"Is *he* attached to *you?*" David asked.

There it was again. She smiled. "I guess so. I don't

60

know. I'm not sure." Why did her sense of irony seldom enter directly into her speech when she was with David? Because it was such a superficial part of her that she knew it wouldn't even register through his armor? He waited. "I guess we'll know by whether he shows up here. De Witt is sending him a telegram for me, with the address on it."

"What did you say in the telegram?"

Unwillingly (although at first she wasn't sure why) she told him. "I just said I was at this farm with some other people, some girls and boys and some married people, and I had the twins."

"So if he comes," David said slowly, "you won't really know why. Whether he's curious, or he feels like meeting the other people . . . or he's attached to you."

She took a deep breath. "David, tell me about yourself."

"There's nothing to tell."

"How old are you?"

"Nineteen."

"Where do you live?" she asked.

"Here," he said.

"Where did you grow up?" she asked.

"In the suburbs," he said (with a flickering smile).

"Which one?" she asked.

"What difference does it make?" he said.

"None, really," she admitted. "It's only that you're a very mysterious person to me. I'm trying to sort of solve the mystery by finding out something specific about you."

"There's nothing to find out," David said. "That's the thing. My father kept talking about being a dropout but there was nothing ever there for me to drop out of. Nothing. Ever."

For one moment she hoped violently, physically, fearfully that Roger would drop everything the moment he got her telegram and come up to be with her. Then Rosemary awakened and needed to be fed and she reminded herself

61

that De Witt would be coming back before long, and then a minute later Rue, too, awakened, and her mind was filled with their needs.

🖎 DE WITT and Mira returned in late afternoon, when the sun was already down—so early, a warning of even shorter days ahead. They had split Margaret's shopping between them; everything De Witt had gotten for her was perfect and everything Mira had gotten was slightly wrong or worse, right down to the children's kimonos, which she'd gotten fewer of than Margaret had requested because she was sure they could dig up some old ones around the farm from the other kids, and which she'd bought in six-month size instead of three-month because she'd realized upon seeing the size of the latter that they wouldn't do for more than a month or so and she'd been certain Margaret wouldn't want to throw away her hardearned money on things the girls would outgrow so soon. I am rich, Margaret wanted to say, and furthermore, you skinny witch, I am supported by my husband's parents, and furthermore I spent my childhood in clothes from the cousins always too big or too small or just wrong, and if you weren't a . . . but De Witt was in the room, prying the crates off the table and replacing them with padded wicker laundry baskets . . . and Margaret was afraid to anger him by speaking sharply to his wife. Maybe she wouldn't have done it anyway. Something in the other woman there was that made it inappropriate to even discuss such matters as infant clothing with her, much less get nasty over it.

Also Margaret was tired. It was a pleasant tiredness because here in the midst of these people, most of them friendly and solicitous, there was nothing she had to do but take care of her babies' immediate needs and that required very little energy. So her tiredness, which in other circumstances might have left her angry and upset, left her instead still and calm, elevating her anger to a philosophical level. A tentative one. It was a When I Come Down from this Mother-Birth-Tired Trip I think I'll Hate You kind of anger, almost pleasant to entertain. How could De Witt have married this creature? True, Mira wasn't ugly. When Margaret catalogued her features—a high, blank forehead, stupidly huge, dark eyes, a long straight nose, thick lips, all set in a heart-shaped face that was just about as suitable as a Valentine for looking at three hundred and sixty-five days a year—having finished this list, she had to admit that if one did away with the derisive adjectives, a beautiful woman was being described. What was the thing in Mira's face that negated the rest of it? Margaret wasn't normally reluctant to grant other women their good looks. Nor did she think it was an automatic balance to her instant worshipful love for De Witt, because it had begun when Mira appeared in the doorway, pretending to see only David. *How could De Witt,* she started to ask herself again, but stopped, because the question implied some knowledge of De Witt that made him incompatible with Mira, yet she really knew nothing about either of them. She sensed about Mira that the woman's serene surface could easily crack to reveal hysteria just beneath; she knew about De Witt only that he had a knowledge of childbirth and retained, to understate the case, an impeccable calm in emergencies.

"De Witt?" she said. "Can I ask you something?"

"Mmm," De Witt said.

But what could she safely ask him? To some extent the

farm represented a new life for anyone who came to it, and when people began a new life it was impolitic to ask what they'd done in the old one.

"Have you ever delivered a baby before?" she finally settled upon.

"No," he said. "I've wanted to but the chance hadn't arisen."

"How long have you been here?"

"Two years."

"Have the others been here just as long?" Margaret asked him.

"Not most of them," De Witt said. "Carol and Jordan were friends of ours and I wrote to them when I'd finished getting the place to a point where it could be occupied, and they came a while later, and then Paul and Starr were friends of theirs, and then I happened to hear from Dolores, who was a close friend from years ago . . . we were married for a brief time, actually . . . and she was looking for a place and came up toward the end of that first winter. The kids we picked up all at once, not Butterscotch, she just wandered in one day, but the others . . . they're in Canada now but they'll be back in a few weeks. Anyway, they were part of a political house up near the Canadian border and while the six of them were away, all the others got busted for possession, and one of them was a friend of a friend of Starr's and asked if we could take them in. That was last spring. They worked with us through the summer but they got . . . restless before harvest and took off. We'll put them to work when they come back or we won't let them stay. Then there've been others . . . the winter is pretty rough here, some of the others just couldn't take it."

Margaret was silent, her mind blown. *We were married for a brief time, actually.* Dolores. Which one was Dolores? Had she met her yet?

"Are you going to stay through the winter?" Mira

asked. Her manner was solicitous but Margaret felt that her intentions were not.

"I don't know," Margaret said. "I haven't made any plans."

"You don't need to," De Witt said.

Margaret beamed at him.

"What about David?" Mira asked.

"What about him?"

"Well, I mean, will he be staying here with you?"

"I thought he was staying with all of us," Margaret said, but then for De Witt's sake added, "I met him on the road. He was the one who told me about this place."

Mira nodded. "He knows Mitchell. Do you happen to know how he knows Mitchell?"

Margaret shook her head.

"Do you know if *he* plans to stay through the winter?"

"I don't know. We just happened to meet and come here together. He's free to do what he wants and I'm free to do what I want." She was really lying here in a bed, a baby sleeping on either side of her, describing freedom to someone who'd been living in a commune for two years?

"What he wants," Mira said, "is to sleep in this room with you."

"Fine," Margaret said calmly. "What bothers you about that? Aesthetics or morality?" Whoops. She was playing Roger to Mira's Margaret. Maybe that was what bothered her so much about the other woman—that she was a fun house reflection of all the hypocrisies in herself that Roger had made her ashamed of.

"Oh, dear," Mira said, "I see I've offended you. I didn't mean to do that."

*Like hell you didn't.*

"It's just that Paul and Starr have given up this room for you," Mira went on sweetly, "and we were just wondering whether they should think of the new arrangement as permanent."

"I'm sorry," Margaret said, truly contrite, "I didn't realize . . ."

"There's nothing to be sorry for," De Witt said. "Butterscotch gave them her room with the double bed she didn't need anyway, and she's going to sleep on the cot in Dolores's room."

"And nobody minds?"

"And nobody minds." He smiled at Margaret in a manner which, if it had been her own husband smiling at some other woman, would have been upsetting to her, but Mira registered calm.

"I have a favor to ask of you," Mira said—as though the previous conversation hadn't taken place.

*The moon? The stars? Leave immediately?*

"Yes?"

"The children are so anxious to see your babies." She was positively winsome. "Do you think they might come up now? They've been asking all day."

Margaret laughed. "Are you kidding? People've been in and out of here all day, saying hello and everything."

"I know, but I thought the noise might bother you, you know how children are."

"Sure," Margaret said. "Of course. They won't bother me at all."

"Oh, I'm so grateful to you," Mira gushed—as if it *had* been the moon and stars she'd requested and Margaret had given in. She left to find the children.

"These should do for two or three months," De Witt said, tapping the wicker baskets. "We don't have to think past then, for now."

Margaret thanked him. "Does it really not matter?" she asked. "That I don't know what I'm going to do?"

"Not to me, it doesn't. Especially since you're paying your own way. To someone who worried ahead, it might."

"Don't you ever worry at all?" she asked.

"Only about being bored," he said with the utmost seriousness.

An extremely self-possessed child, a girl of somewhere between the age of seven and ten, Margaret could never tell children's ages, appeared at the door, trailed by a younger one of indeterminate sex with long hair, big eyes and a heart-shaped face. Mira's children. But De Witt's, too.

"Mira said we could see the babies now," the older one said to her father. De Witt nodded and they came in. They went to one side of the bed, then the other.

"Is he sleeping?" the little one asked, standing on tiptoe to see.

"Yes," Margaret said.

"It's a girl, you idiot," the older one said. She turned to Margaret. "How come they're both girls?"

"It just happened that way," Margaret said.

"I'm Lorna," the girl said.

"Who's that?" Margaret asked her.

"That's my brother," Lorna said. "Baba."

"Hi, Baba," Margaret said.

The little boy smiled at her in a beautiful sunny way and Margaret decided it would be possible to overlook his resemblance to his mother.

"You know you have a beautiful smile," Margaret said to him.

"Could you tell he was a boy?" Lorna asked.

"Sure," Margaret said.

"Everyone thinks he's a girl," Lorna said. "When we go into Brattleboro people say isn't she cute? Isn't that deeeesgusting? Nobody at the farm says it but I still think he looks like a girl, don't you, Baba?"

"Lorna," De Witt said, "go see if your dinner is ready."

"Mira's making it," Lorna said. She turned back to Margaret. "My mother has to make our dinner all the time because we're vegetarians. Not Daddy, but me and Baba and Mira, except bacon is Baba's best food, isn't it, Baba?"

"Lorna," her father said. "Go down now and see if dinner's ready."

"Maybe you can come back early in the morning," Margaret said. "They'll be awake then."

Lorna left, trailed by Baba.

"De Witt," Margaret said uncertainly after a moment, "I guess there's no one exactly in charge here . . . but if there were, it would be you, right?"

He nodded.

"I don't even know the ground rules."

"You will."

"I know, I know," she said, "but I mean meanwhile if I do something that seems perfectly all right to me and it just happens to upset you . . . or Mira, say . . . or everyone . . . how will I know?"

"You'll know. After the outdoor work is finished we'll pick up again with regular meetings, at least a couple of times a week, to get things off our chests, confront each other with gripes and so on, so they don't become major."

"Meanwhile, if there's something I should be doing that I'm not doing, you'll tell me?"

"I'll tell you. We schedule very closely. We tried it the other way, waiting for people to feel moved to feed the chickens and milk the goats and so on. It doesn't work. Ask the chickens and goats. Half the chickens died when no one felt moved to give them water for three days. All the duties are rotated but it seems to me that being a new mother is about all the duty anyone should have for a month or two. It seems to me Starr's baby was a few weeks old when they came last year and she didn't share in chores for a while. I'll take it up with the others."

"This business about David sleeping in here," she said

. . . fools rush in . . . "I guess he can bring in an old mattress or something. I wouldn't have thought it would bother anybody but Mira seemed . . ."

"Don't worry about it," he interrupted. "Mira became celibate a couple of years ago. It's a religious thing and in theory she accepts other people's sexuality but in practice it's difficult for her sometimes."

*We were married for a short time, actually . . . Don't worry about it, Mira's a celibate . . .* Was he crazy or was he into some very advanced form of sanity?

"As far as the others go," De Witt continued, "I imagine David's sleeping in here'll bother a couple of the young girls." He smiled. "Nobody else."

"I don't think he's ready for young girls," Margaret said. "It's not that he's particularly attached to me. Actually he's suspicious of everyone. Maybe he's a little less suspicious of me because he's known me a little longer." She laughed. "Like four days." Was that possible? Less than a week? "De Witt, do people come and go from here a lot?"

"Sure," De Witt said. "Especially the younger ones. They don't even feel it when they move around, most of them have no sense of being rooted anyplace. If you talk to them about roots they'll quote the Fuller line about man being born with feet, not roots. If you say that applies to our bodies but not necessarily our minds they'll look at you blankly or maybe quote some vaguely Eastern line about the oneness of body and soul." He smiled in a melancholy way. "A lovely thought but certainly not true in all cases . . . mine, for instance."

"Do you feel as though living in a setup like this changes people?" *Because I really feel the need to change, to grow up, although I don't know exactly what I mean by that.*

De Witt shrugged. "People who're susceptible to change seem to change with any new experience. The others . . .

most of them will tell you they've changed, too. And there're people who say that if you think you're different then you are."

"That's the New York thing, isn't it. People who seem absolutely crazy going around telling you how crazy they used to be before they had therapy."

"When I was practicing psychoanalysis in the Midwest," De Witt said . . . so that was it . . . "I found that one of my greatest difficulties was in learning what kind of *personalities* my patients had, as opposed to what kind of conscious or unconscious problems. Once I treated a young woman so depleted by melancholy that she could barely talk. After months of trying to understand what was getting in the way of her functioning I happened to walk into a party where she was having a political argument with someone. Her voice was so strident that almost all other conversation had come to a halt. And I discovered from the conversation of the people who'd brought me that this gentle, depressed creature had the reputation of being one of the most vicious, witty, argumentative women in Oak Park."

"But she was really different when she was with you."

He nodded. "If anything, the other part was the fake but that isn't quite so either. The fact is she saw herself in a different light in my office and so she behaved differently."

"Did you feel," Margaret asked after a moment, "when you were practicing psychoanalysis, did you feel that you got real results?"

"My rate of cure," De Witt said, "was somewhat lower than when I was practicing chiropractic in Los Angeles."

SHE hadn't been hungry since the children were born. Three times a day someone brought her a tray with food. There was always a glass of fresh goat's milk and some fruit—an apple or peach or some preserved berries —and then there was homemade bread and some eggs or cheese, or an occasional piece of unidentifiable meat or stew surrounded by vegetables. She ate what they brought with pleasure and craved nothing in-between. Gone was that driving hunger that had plagued her through pregnancy, or even the restless noshing need she'd often felt before.

She found herself also to be quite free of sexual desire, even as the days wore on and the soreness from her delivery disappeared. At odd moments she might still look at David's naked body (he had brought in the mattress and slept on that when the twins filled up the bed) with something akin to nostalgia. Or her mind, during one of De Witt's reminiscences (he had been, it developed, a lawyer in Hays, Kansas, a C.P.A. in Vincennes, Indiana and a real-estate broker in San Francisco, all apparently without benefit of license) might suddenly pan to a picture of herself and De Witt tumbling in the hay someplace, or talking very intently on the staircase from *Gone With the Wind*, but she was free of lust. Partly it was that the experience of birth had been so earthshaking . . . or whatever was the personal equivalent of earthshaking . . . SHE was the earth and SHE HAD SHAKEN . . . and what could she do for an encore . . . ? But beyond that there was the sense of herself as part of a closed circuit. David might touch it

71

but not he nor anyone else could become a part of the charmed circle comprised of herself and the twins. Her sexual needs were satisfied by fondling them and by having them suck at her breasts. *They* didn't care about the condition of her body, her stomach flabby with lost volume, ridged with stretchmarks which resembled nothing so much as strips of mauve grosgrain ribbon sunk into her flesh; her breasts still stretched to near-blue translucence; her thighs stretched too, though not so greatly. Before they were married Roger had once said that he liked her fat legs because of the way they could grip him, but it had been easy for him to say, then, when her legs weren't really fat and only her thighs bordered on the generous.

The thought of Roger's seeing her naked was enough to make her physically ill, if she let herself dwell on it, although she couldn't conceal from herself the wish that he would care enough to visit them for a few hours. A couple of times each week she received mail addressed to her, as opposed to both her and Roger, and the forwarding address was in Roger's handwriting, but beyond that there was no word. Once she dreamed that she passed a room and looked in and there was Roger, sitting in bed, an arm around each of the twins, all of them looking beautiful and happy, and in the dream she kept saying over and over, "Such a beautiful father, such beautiful girls," and somehow in the dream there was the feeling that it was *he* who had given birth to them, but her waking fantasies were of a less surrealistic order, with Roger coming back and falling madly in love with his daughters and a newly glamorous wife.

THE second week she wrote a postcard to her father telling him about the birth of the twins, using the farm's post-office box as a return address. Then she went downstairs for the first time.

They'd already had their first hard frost at night; everyone was working with a pleasant urgency because winter would soon be setting in. One end of the long trestle table in the kitchen was piled high with green tomatoes; at the other end Baby Butterscotch and Carol were separating potatoes, putting the good ones in crates for storage in sand, peeling and cutting the imperfect ones to be cooked right away or put up in jars. Carol and her husband were both potters but Jordan was a painter, a printer and a photographer as well. Carol's older girl, who was about five, was standing on a stool, drying dishes as Lorna washed them. Carol's year-old baby was curled up in an old blanket in one of the potato crates, fast asleep. Mira was sitting in a rocking chair, coring and slicing apples; her eyes were half-closed and she was smiling. Dolores, very tall, very thin, with braided black hair and a long, finely drawn face, was packing sliced peaches into Mason jars which were, in turn, put into a big sterilizer. Dolores was a weaver. She'd come to Margaret's room once to say hello but it had seemed to be a difficult thing for her to do. She had that ambiance that always made an instant slave of Margaret—very kind and at the same time very withdrawn. Starr was placing winter squashes on newly built shelves at the other end of the kitchen; someone had told her they would prefer the kitchen's warmth to the cellar's cold. Her three-year-old boy was handing her the squashes from a bushel basket; her baby was strapped to her back by a piece of canvas, sleeping. Starr was a gifted batikist and seamstress. From time to time the women spoke but Mira was never involved in the conversation.

On a cork bulletin hung some notices. A schedule of yoga classes. Some picture postcards. A price list for the New England Co-op. A huge, beautiful, country-psychedelic chart showing planting and harvest dates for the various vegetable crops, as well as which brand and type of seed had been used and someone's neat comments on whether each was satisfactory. Aduki beans, black beans, green beans, beets, broccoli, cabbage, carrots, corn, cucumbers, eggplant, garlic, lettuce, onions, peas, potatoes, pumpkins, spinach, summer and winter squash, tomatoes, herbs. A November duty schedule was also posted, with Margaret's and David's names at the bottom. It covered jobs like cooking, baking, cleaning, sowing of the winter cover crop, wood chopping and hauling and other outdoor jobs. Margaret's name had BABIES printed after it; David was scheduled for woodcutting and work on the barn.

She wandered into the common room, a small pleasant place full of old rugs overlapping each other, cushions, and here and there a battered rocker or armchair. It would have been drab had not some artist—she saw now that Paul's name was signed in the corner—covered the walls with nymphs and glades and art nouveau sunrises. She was about to go back to the kitchen when she noticed David's sketchbook on the hearth in front of the fireplace. She looked through it and found that David had done some drawings in and around the house. With great technical facility he had drawn the fireplace, the treadle sewing machine in the crafts room on the other side of the living-room arch, the porch, the barn, the Corvair. There were no people in the pictures but their draftsmanlike quality suggested that was just as well. She found herself remembering a postcard she'd bought years before and still had somewhere at home, a Van Gogh portrait of a chair. An ordinary but gracefully carved wooden chair with a green and gold striped upholstered seat. Holding in its lap two golden books and a small lighted candle in a stand. Rich blue lights hit the wood of the chair; the rug was in warmly mottled autumn colors; the background was a meltingly beautiful green. But the chair was the important thing for with its mellow wood, its arched back and its slender arms curved in to a point where they seemed almost to embrace the candle, it conveyed an intensely human life, an unbearable warmth and longing. And then there was Roger's work, which invariably conveyed strong feelings—be they largely hatred and pain. In his drawings and sculpture it was more the hatred that came through; it had taken film to document his pain. At the time she'd met him he'd been working with a small group of experimental film makers who'd set up facilities on the Lower East Side. She could still remember every moment of his first film, the one made in the old people's recreational center; not just the faces but the very angles of the room, the chess pieces, the foreign-language newspapers, had fairly reeked with pain.

What was so different about David's pictures? About David, who could admit with equal casualness that he didn't like to be alone and didn't know how to become attached to people? Had he anaesthetized himself to pain and accidentally to pleasure as well? He gave no hint of any event in his life so traumatic as to cause deliberate insulation against feeling. In fact he'd suggested the opposite, that the suburban incubator in which he'd hatched and expanded to full physical size had been so devoid of color and incident as to barely exist. Was it that very emptiness he mirrored? Or maybe he'd just cleaned out his own head with acid; other people, after all, had risen above narrow stultifying backgrounds. Maybe the worst thing about the suburbs was that unlike the slums they didn't leave you anything tangible to fight against, deprived you of the chance to build up a useful energy of rage. She replaced the notebook, listened at the bottom of the stairs for a moment for noise from the twins, then went back to the kitchen.

"What're they doing in the barn?" she asked.

"They're practically building it from scratch," Starr said. "They put on a new roof and now they're insulating it and then they're going to partition it into lots of rooms."

"So you can have more people?"

Starr laughed. "So the ones who're here already don't kill each other."

"Oh, dear." Mira opened her eyes. "I wouldn't say that."

"You didn't," Star pointed out irritably. "I did."

"We do need more space for meditation and so on," Mira said.

"Oh, sure," Starr said sardonically, "we need lots more space for meditation."

"You're being provocative," Dolores murmured.

Starr stomped out of the room.

"We're really anxious to share what we have with more people," Mira continued placidly. "There are people who have wanted to be with us but couldn't because of space, or schools. We're going to equip one of the rooms as a schoolhouse and try to incorporate."

"Also," Carol said, "they bug De Witt now when they see him in town. Lorna's supposed to be in school in town, she was there last year but she took a lot of crap, not just because she's hard to take but also because she's a natural target for the kids who're hostile because they picked it up at home. The kids here are nothing like the Brattleboro kids, 'yknow, Brattleboro's always had some city influences, even before there were all those schools."

"And of course there are the others, too," Mira said, as though someone would accuse her of an ego trip if she

76

talked about her own kid for two minutes. She hadn't reacted at all to Carol's saying her kid was hard to take.

"There're really a lot of groovy people who'd have come in the past year if we'd had even a legal excuse for a school," Carol said wistfully. "I met this woman over in Rindge, I was crazy about her, I never knew anyone so easy to talk to . . . she wasn't happy where she was but she had two kids around ten and twelve, she couldn't go to a place with no school. I lost track of her, she moved again, but I thought about her all winter."

"How is it in the winter?" Margaret asked, puzzled by the loneliness in the other woman's voice. Carol might have been an abandoned suburban housewife, for all the comfort she seemed to take from being surrounded by adults.

"Ohhhhhhh . . ."

"It's great!" Starr said, hauling in another bushel of squash. "Plenty of snow, plenty of work, plenty of fucking and plenty of fighting."

Carol smiled sadly. "She thrives on it."

"Which of it?" Margaret asked.

"All of it," Starr said, grinning. "Especially the fucking and the fighting."

⚜ BUT for now the life of the farm was like a brightly woven fabric whose individual threads might tangle but seldom really knotted. Anger flared but was quickly dissipated in hard work. There was a steady rhythm to their days and Margaret found herself caught up in it long before the time when she was obliged to join. One of the reasons being that if she was idle for too long, when the twins were both sleeping, say, her mind wandered back to Roger in Hartsdale and then she became miserable and confused. She had related to Roger in recent years mostly as victim so that having removed herself from that status she had no way of understanding her relationship to him.

Other than magazines (De Witt subscribed to *Fortune*, *Mother Earth* and the *Wall Street Journal*) the reading stock was limited, tending to be heavy on Norman Brown, Herbert Marcuse, Adelle Davis and Castaneda and light on anything that could be called pure pleasure, literary or otherwise. But how much difference did it make what you picked up to read when your eyes generally closed after half a page? They worked hard and slept soundly. The craftsmen had only evenings to work on their own projects and they were often too tired; the downstairs lights were out by nine or ten. None of the sleeping rooms had shaded windows and they all awakened early. In the mornings the responsibility for the young children rotated. Other jobs were continuing ones—building and insulating, wood chopping, canning and preserving. Each day one man was responsible for bringing in the day's supply of wood for the cook stove in the kitchen and the fireplace in the common room, and starting the fires in each. The upstairs had one wood-burning stove in the central hallway but in the interest of conserving wood, neither that one nor the ones in the common room and crafts room would be used until December or January, when the house would otherwise be unbearably cold. Each day one woman was responsible for cooking, one for cleaning up after meals and one for baking for the following day. By the third week of November the shed was three quarters full with dry split wood and the completion of the barn before the first heavy snowstorm was the major concern of everyone.

David occasionally got annoyed at Margaret because she couldn't stay awake to hear his phonies list for the day but even he admitted that he was sleeping better than he ever had. He was working very hard. He never volunteered to do anything but did what he was assigned to do without complaints. Once or twice she asked him how he felt about the work, about the farm in general, but he shrugged off his questions as though she were some particularly dumb psychiatric social worker trying to turn him into a case. They spent very little time together, awake.

THE first real snow came. It had covered the ground and laid heavy fringes along the bare branches and evergreens by the time they awakened. It was still snowing as they finished breakfast, large light flakes that drifted down and settled in for the duration of winter.

"Oh, God!" Carol groaned. "I keep trying not to panic but it's really here."

"It's so beautiful," Margaret said. She'd faced the winter with a surprising equanimity, maybe because she was in a new place. "How can you mind it?"

David sat beside her at the long table. Silent. He seldom spoke when anyone else was around. The babies, having been fed and changed, were asleep on the quilt in the corner near the heat stove. Every child who could walk had been bundled up and sent outside for the first snow. In another corner De Witt sat with his coffee, his chair tilted back against the wall. She'd noticed he had a tendency to do this when there were more than two or three people in a room, push back his chair and become an observer.

"It makes me think of dying, that's how," Carol said. And in point of fact she had switched from her usual red

79

sweater and jeans into a black sweater and black pants. "Or maybe as if someone's trying to bury me alive. I ache all over."

"You always ache all over," Starr muttered.

"That's not true!" Carol said, tears in her eyes, although it was certainly true that she often ran off to the chiropractor in Brattleboro for some ache or pain, particularly if Jordan had snapped at her about getting fat, or Starr was mad at her about something or the baby was demanding. Carol's fear of the baby's demands, in particular, was very upsetting to Margaret, bringing up as it did memories of her mother's perpetual refuge in symptoms.

Dolores said, "The first time I saw snow I thought I was in heaven."

"That's the same thing as being dead," Carol said, letting herself be distracted from Starr.

Dolores laughed. "I don't think so. I grew up on a cattle ranch in Texas, y'know, very dry and barren."

Carol nodded. "I know."

"My mother ran away when I was very little, back to Chicago where she came from. She couldn't take the life down there. For years we never heard from her."

"You never talked about your mother," Carol said wonderingly. Few of them actually did. If you knew anything about their past it was because something filtered in from the outside world. Butterscotch's mother showed up in a gold-colored Cadillac with M.D. plates. You found papers lying on a table that showed Jordan as a party in the bankruptcy proceedings of a printing business. Dolores's second husband showed up with a Florida sun tan, tight-fitting, baby-blue, knitted bell bottoms and the ambience of a gangster. Dolores, peacemaker, weaver of ponchos in blacks, grays and tans. Whose third try, De Witt had told Margaret, had been in a lesbian community. A magical person, the kind of person that every bagel baby

80

on an acid trip thought she was going to be when she came back.

"When I was about nine or ten she finally sent word that she was there and she wanted to see us but she couldn't face coming back. My father got plane tickets and took us up there the next day. My brother and I. We hadn't been out of Texas in our whole lives. When we landed in Chicago it was snowing. I'll never forget it. At the moment we landed I made up my mind that when I grew up I'd live in a place where it snowed."

"Maybe it was because you were going to see your mother," Carol said.

"How come your father would take you up there after what she'd done?" Starr asked.

"That's just the way my father is," Dolores said.

"My son-of-a-bitch stepfather," Starr said, "if you *sneezed* the wrong way he'd never talk to you again."

"What was your mother like?" Carol asked Dolores.

Dolores just shrugged.

Outside the kids were rolling, sliding, trying unsuccessfully to pack the dry powdery snow into balls. Even Lorna looked happy. Margaret felt an odd urge to go out and roll and scream with them.

"My father always hated the snow," she said. "The super didn't clear it fast enough so he always ended up doing it himself and complaining the whole time. He hated any kind of exercise." Why was she talking about him in the past tense? Maybe because he'd never bothered to answer her postcard announcing the twins. Couldn't he even have sent his colleen—maid—whatever—to pick up a card? Something appropriate, with flocking and a pink satin bow? *Sincere congratulations on your untimely freak birth?* "The snow is so clean here," she said. "In the city it gets so filthy."

"How'll Mira get to the ashram in this?" Carol asked no

81

one in particular. Mira, into some particularly rigorous form of yoga since an acid vision a couple of years earlier, attended services once a week which involved more than an hour of driving each way even in the good weather. No one bothered to answer.

"Why couldn't we be one hour out of Boston instead of two or three?" Carol asked plaintively.

"Oh, shit," Jordan said.

"It's easy for you to say oh shit," Carol told him. "You don't hate car riding!"

Carol's whining was beginning to get to Margaret, who was afraid that it was a preview of her own feelings of boredom and isolation during the winter months ahead.

"Doesn't Brattleboro have a lot of things to do?" she asked.

"Ohhhh," Carol said, "not really. I mean there's nothing really there. A couple of movies. Stores. One or two restaurants. That's it."

"What else do you need?"

What else might *she* need? Sex. Sooner or later she would surely get interested in sex again. It was almost comforting to know that her sexuality was buried for now but it was horrifying to think this situation might continue indefinitely. Mira had pretty much renounced sex, except as a means of procreation (but not to be enjoyed in any event) when she went on her yoga trip and whether that contributed to her objectionable piety or vice versa, the whole syndrome was appalling. De Witt had a girlfriend in Brattleboro who'd lived briefly at the farm but had been driven out by pressure from Mira, although Mira was supposedly understanding about De Witt's disinclination to become a celibate vegetarian. Both Starr and Dolores had told Margaret that once Mira had been a really beautiful sexy woman, but De Witt never referred to their life together.

"I dunno," Carol said. "More of something. Or better. I get so *bored*."

"Don't you make a lot of your pots in the winter?"

"Yes, but I thought that we were trying to get away from that whole bit when we came here, that whole pressure of constantly having to *produce*."

"I'll tell you what Carol wants," Starr said. "Carol wants to lie on her back and have a bunch of buttons, a Feed Me button, a Fuck Me button, a Make Me Happy button, one for everything so she never has to do it herself. YOU'RE A PAIN IN THE ASS, CAROL, Y'KNOW THAT?"

Margaret smiled; Starr's furies were always relaxing to her. She waited for Carol to argue that Starr was being unfair but instead Carol nodded dejectedly.

"You're right. I know you're right."

"And *you're* a fucking ballbuster," Jordan said to Starr, suddenly coming to his wife's defense, "but do *you* know *that?*"

"You think any woman with guts is a ballbuster," Starr flung at him. "Isn't that true, Paul?"

"Leave me out of this," Paul said.

"Out of WHAT?" Starr exploded. "Out of EVERY-THING! That's what you really mean, isn't it. Leave you alone, don't bother you with arguments, don't bother you with your kid, don't bother you with LIFE! You're worse than *she* is because at least she *wants* to be happy if someone would only do it for her!"

"My God," Margaret said, "I thought you were the one who *liked* winter." She laughed but she was uneasy; if she'd always cared about people, here at the farm there was an urgent quality to her caring. There were very few people in her real world now; each was precious beyond belief.

"I LOVE winter," Starr said. "What I can't stand is being dragged down by deadheads."

"You're frightening me," Margaret said, surprised to hear herself admitting it. "I keep thinking you're going to get mad at me next."

"Why would I get mad at you?" Starr asked.

"I don't know," Margaret admitted. "I just . . ." She was on the verge of tears, for crying out loud. She smiled. "You sound as if you hate everybody, so why not me?"

"Hate?" Starr looked genuinely puzzled. "I don't hate anybody. You mean Carol? I LOVE Carol, Carol's my soul sister."

Paul laughed. "It's like my mother's old joke," he said. "With that for a friend you don't need an enemy."

"Fuck your mother," Starr said.

Paul laughed again. "Right on."

"I'd think that by now," De Witt spoke from his corner for the first time, "a lot of the free schools would be in full swing."

"So?" Starr said.

"So I was just thinking," De Witt continued, "that maybe when the roads are cleared a couple of people might want to take off and look at a few of them, get some idea of how they're run, and so on."

"De Witt," Carol said, "I love you."

"What about the kids?" Starr said suspiciously. "Would we have to take the kids?"

"I don't see why you should," De Witt said, "unless the others . . ."

Margaret and Butterscotch said it was fine with them if the kids stayed. Mira, her eyes closed as she sat in the rocking chair, said nothing.

"How about you, Mira?" Starr asked.

Mira opened her eyes. Starr explained the question again, as though to a deaf person. Mira said she thought by all means the children should stay.

"Fine," De Witt said, "I'll find out what steps we have to take to make a school legal."

THE younger group came back from Canada. Butterscotch was pleased to see them and baked a cake to celebrate their return; they treated her with friendly condescension, someone fit to keep the home fires burning while they manned the barricades. They looked very much alike, the four boys and two girls. All around twenty years old, uniformly tall, handsome, healthy looking. David displayed no interest in any of them, although they were so close to his own age; when she questioned him, he said he wasn't into their phony revolution bag. She asked whether it might not be better to be in a phony bag than in no bag at all and he stomped out of the room, brushing shoulders with one of them as he went. They seemed not to notice him or anyone else as they trooped toward the kitchen for a meal, ignoring Mira's gentle protests that lunch wasn't ready yet.

"Do they talk to anyone?" Margaret asked De Witt.

"Not much," De Witt said. "They're suspicious of us. They feel the odds are that at least one of us is CIA, probably me."

"Doesn't that bother you?"

He shrugged. "In the long run it doesn't matter. Trust can change, too."

"Why would the CIA bother with this place?"

De Witt smiled. "I can't think of any good reason, but maybe the CIA can."

It kept snowing. Carol and Starr got tired of waiting for it to clear and took off in Carol's Volks after De Witt had plowed the dirt road for them.

Rosemary was sleeping through every night and Rue was just waking up once for a feeding and then going back. Margaret gave a lot of attention to Starr's and Carol's kids, none of whom seemed to mind in the least that their mothers were gone.

She began doing yoga exercises every morning with Dolores and Mira.

The younger group built an igloo in the woods beyond the farm. "They're on a survival trip," Butterscotch explained. They slept in it for two nights and then decided to spend the winter with some friends in the movement in Key West.

When she thought about Roger it was most often to wonder idly who he was screwing, or how many at a time. Occasionally she questioned the nature of their relationship: whether it was more good than bad (probably not); whether there were reasons aside from parenthood to continue it (probably not); whether Roger would mind if she were to write him she was going to stay at the farm permanently (probably not). She didn't actually think of it as staying at the farm so much as she thought of it as staying here with De Witt. This brought up a lot of other questions, like the difference in her bonds to the two men; why she was more relaxed with De Witt than with her own husband (that was an easy one, really—De Witt accepted her as she was while Roger, at best, accepted her in spite of what she was, whatever *that* was); whether those qualities of hers that Roger detested were about his problems or hers (maybe both; all the things he said about her always sounded terribly right, but why had he married her, then?); whether she could be happy indefinitely without that complicated tension that made life with Roger at once so difficult and interesting (probably not). At this point, where to progress meant to plan or at least to anticipate the future, she always backed away from her thoughts into the present.

Carol and Starr came back from their investigation with Carol's friend of the previous year from Rindge and her two children, who'd become so unhappy where they were that they'd decided to help set up the school at the farm. Carol's ancient Volkswagen had died trying to get out of a snowbank in Maine and they all arrived in Hannah's jeep, which was pulling a small trailer. Everyone was pleased, not only because Hannah and her children were attractive and likable but because they'd brought their own living quarters with them. Hannah had a snowplow on the front of her jeep which, combined with the tractor plow, made a short job of clearing the snow from enough of one side of the barn so that a long side of Hannah's trailer could nestle against it. Hannah made one request, that they plow in such a way that she could get out at any time. Otherwise, she explained, she would feel claustrophobic.

"I was hoping you'd really settle here," Carol said, looking very upset.

Hannah laughed. "Who knows? Maybe you won't feel that way in two months."

"I know I will," Carol said vehemently. "It's not just you I dig, it's your kids."

HANNAH's children were, in truth, delightful to have around. A girl and boy of twelve and nine, respectively, Daisy and Mario both seemed possessed of unusual poise and assurance. Agreeable to each other as well as to the rest of the children, all of whom were younger than they, they seemed to fall into a natural leadership, so that immediately after their first lunch at the farm, for example, instead of the younger kids hanging around while the grownups chatted, they all followed Daisy and Mario out to the barn to set up a basketball hoop that had been transported in the trailer along with the Berksons' other possessions, which were minimal. Hannah had a thing about ownership and had decided at some point in her life that she would never again own any more than she could fit in her little trailer along with its tiny bathroom, Pullman kitchen and four bunk beds.

"When I walked out," she said as they drank tea, "I didn't feel as if I was giving up a Park Avenue duplex and the good life. I felt as if I'd been carrying around a sack of fancy silver and china and antiques on my back for ten years and suddenly I'd straightened up and thrown it all off. I have no use for *things,* only for people."

Everyone nodded understanding. Margaret nodded too because she could see what Hannah meant. Hannah's eyes were beautiful—huge, brown, limpid—and there was about her none of that aggressive piety that made you want to disagree with people even when you knew you weren't wrong. Still . . .

"I know what you mean," Margaret said slowly, "but

it's not so simple. Things aren't just things, they can be tied up with people, with the past." There was nothing Roger wouldn't sell if someone happened to offer him a price for it, even though he never needed the money.

"That's just what I mean," Hannah said. "Who needs it?"

"Sometimes I do. Not here, maybe, or at least I haven't thought about it yet, maybe because I still have a home someplace else . . . But sometimes . . . My parents had a very bad marriage."

Hannah laughed sympathetically. "Whose didn't?"

"I know that sounds off the track, but what I wanted to tell you is . . . after my mother died last year my father sent me a package of her stuff, personal stuff. I guess it was too painful for him to have it around. Anyway, there was a bunch of old letters I'd never seen before." The ribbon had fallen apart as she'd tried to untie it. "They turned out to be letters my father had written my mother just after they were married. His mother was very ill in Ireland and they thought she was going to die so they sent for him but then she hung on for months and meanwhile he wrote my mother these letters. And the thing is, they were very beautiful." Her eyes filled with tears; ashamed, she brushed them away. "I mean, they were very *tender*. There were feelings in them I'd never even thought of him as having toward her because they were buried by the time I can remember back to." *By my birth, by her life, or by an unfortunate combination of the two.* "They made me feel much more sympathetic toward him." *For a while, anyway.* "They gave me a sense of caution about what it's possible to lose."

"Letters are different," Carol said after a pause. "They're a part of yourself."

"What about jewelry, then? Or photographs?" Why couldn't she let it go?

"You see?" Hannah said. "You're doing it already. Getting all weighted down."

"I like old things," Starr said.

"Me, too," said Carol, but with some reluctance, as though she were afraid of offending Hannah.

"Not me," Hannah announced. "If I had my way there'd be a Design Research store in every town for me to move in and out of."

"But that's the contrast factor, obviously," De Witt spoke from his corner for the first time. "Feeling weighed down by your husband's ornate possessions, so to speak."

Hannah's eyes narrowed even before Margaret had had time to note the undertone in De Witt's words. The narrowed eyes, recently so large and limpid, changed her appearance entirely, making her very much the mother cat.

"I'm not into that Freudian shit," she said.

"Then take it on a simple obvious level," De Witt said calmly. But it was obvious that he wasn't bothered by the possibility that he'd upset her. Some antagonism was there that she hadn't seen in him before.

"I don't think I'll take it at all, thank you," she said, casual again. "I think I'll take a walk and see what my kids are doing." She stood up and stretched, waited for Carol and Starr, who followed her happily out of the house toward the barn. De Witt stared after them moodily.

"Aren't we lucky to have such marvelous people coming in!" Mira exclaimed sweetly.

Dolores glanced at De Witt. Neither said anything. David began whistling softly. Dolores smiled broadly at De Witt. Butterscotch began clearing the remaining dishes from the table.

"Why is everybody so quiet all of a sudden?" she asked.

De Witt stood up abruptly. "Does anyone want to go to town?"

"But it's Thursday, dear," Mira said.

"Mmmm," De Witt said, "but my toothache is coming back and I think I'd better try the dentist. Margaret? Are you ready for the outside world?"

"Almost," Margaret said, not really ready but feeling as though he wanted company.

"If you go," David said to her in an obvious, challenging manner, "I'll go."

"Fine, fine," she said. "I'll let you know when I decide." *So you can get the handcuffs.*

"On second thought," De Witt said, "will you excuse me? I think I'd like to be alone for a while." He bent down and kissed Margaret's cheek. "You don't really mind, do you, Margaret?"

"No, of course not," Margaret said. "I didn't really—"

"We're having our first school meeting," Mira said. "Hannah's going to talk about—"

"If I'm not back on time," De Witt said, "start without me."

THE meeting was open to everyone, of course, and everyone came; only De Witt was missing. The common room was packed with adults and kids to a point where it seemed that it would be difficult to accomplish anything, but then Daisy and Mario led the kids into the kitchen to make popcorn and the pressure eased. There was an air of expectation and camaraderie, probably connected to the newcomers' arrival. The petulant expression that so often ruined Carol's face had been replaced by a lively smile as she sat at Hannah's feet and listened to the other woman's stream of stories and funny anecdotes about places she'd been. The school where the children had been before Rindge was called the Fountain and Hannah explained that she'd called the nominal leader of the school the Fountain Head because he was really a fascist in hippie clothing and they all laughed, feeling lucky not only to have someone new just as winter became serious but to have acquired someone so delightful and interesting. David just glowered at Hannah in a way that reminded Margaret that De Witt wasn't back yet. Carol suggested that since De Witt wasn't there and Hannah was the only one with actual free-school experience, she chair the meeting, but at that moment De Witt walked in and apologized for being late, explaining that he'd been talking with a lawyer about the legal steps necessary to make the school official. Papers would be coming through shortly.

Silence. A school was an awesome enterprise. Everyone knew what a school should *not* be but how many of them, De Witt asked, had any particular idea of what it *should* be? A place where learning was available, someone said. Of course there were two kinds of learning, the kind you could get from books and the kind you got from apprenticeship, learning to do something. Someone said the latter kind was the only real learning, the rest was just mental exercise, words, words, words. Even if that were true, Margaret said, mental exercise had value. It could take your mind off yourself in a way that physical exercise couldn't, since almost anything physical you could do left you time to think at the same time. And then she sat back, confused by her defense of academia.

Hannah was amused. "I don't mind thinking about myself. I'm not running away from anything."

"I don't think Margaret was suggesting frantic flight," De Witt said immediately. "She was suggesting that if your mind's active it's best for it to have something to relate to actively. Ideas, philosophies, politics, whatever."

Hannah laughed. "How old are these kids we're talking about? What'll we give them, Nietzsche?"

De Witt flushed. Margaret had never seen him so rattled. "The same thing applies to young kids, obviously, it's just a question of the level you're going to teach on."

"I'm not teaching my kids to run away from their own heads at any level," Hannah said.

"It's difficult for me to understand," De Witt said, "how anyone who lives in a trailer can be smug about other people running away."

Hannah stood up. "You've been hostile to me since the minute I walked in here," she said angrily.

"Wait a minute," Carol scrambled to her feet. "I don't understand what's going on here. Nobody's hostile to anybody, are they, De Witt?"

"No, of course not," De Witt said.

"If you are, tell me now before I settle in," Hannah said. "I don't stay where I'm not welcome."

"You're positively welcome here," Carol said frantically. "Everyone was just talking about how great it was having you here, you and your kids."

"Not everyone," Hannah said.

"What would represent an appropriate sign of welcome?" De Witt asked.

"I have a feeling we're getting off the topic," Margaret said uneasily. She felt vaguely responsible for the discord, an echo of childhood when so many disagreements between her parents might never have arisen if she hadn't brought them some need of her own, some problem to solve.

"Right!" several people said.

"I hate it when people I love fight with each other," Carol said tearfully.

"Will there be required classes, or what?" Dolores asked. "And who'll teach what?"

Silence while they all tried to shift gears.

"We might begin," De Witt said, "by making a list of those people who're willing to teach and what they're willing to teach."

"And getting a list from the kids of what they want to *learn*," Hannah said.

"But what if there's no one to teach them something?"

"No problem," Hannah said. "Someone learns it and keeps ahead. That's the way we did it at the Fountain and it worked pretty well. Mario had a thing to learn some Latin so I just picked up the textbook and got enough to stay a couple of weeks ahead of him."

"Truly a remarkable woman," De Witt muttered, softly so that Margaret thought only she herself heard.

Carol was appointed to be secretary and they began a list of subject offerings. Dolores signed for weaving, Paul for printmaking, and Carol said she would take the younger kids each morning for encounter and improvisation. Margaret said she'd like to do clothes-making with the two older girls and Hannah asked why only girls, didn't they want to keep out of those cultural bags? Margaret said she'd be delighted to teach clothes-making to Mario or any boy who was interested, she'd just assumed. . . . And Hannah, with an extremely winning smile, said she hadn't meant to jump on Margaret, it was just that she had a bug about kids being stuck in pigeonholes. When she was a child her consuming passion had been for math and she'd been made to feel eternally guilty about this, it meant she wasn't feminine, while for six years she'd been forced to take flute lessons, which she loathed, all because of . . . Margaret said she understood perfectly and didn't mind at all. This was true, but she didn't look at De Witt.

They ended up with a huge variety of possible subjects, far more than there would be kids to take them, it seemed. Hannah would do cuisenaire rods, Butterscotch would bake cookies with the little kids, De Witt would set up a greenhouse and do botany and indoor gardening. Would

94

David like to do painting? No. But Jordan would do photography.

"What about reading and writing?" Mira asked.

"Most of it you do yourself," Hannah said, not unsympathetic. "If there's one lesson in the free schools it's that you have to educate your own children."

"I wish I had more skill," Mira said humbly.

"I'll work with you, it'll be all right." Hannah's manner was nearly seductive. "If your kids dig me, I'll work with them. Don't set up roadblocks in your own mind."

Mira smiled at her radiantly.

"What if her kids don't dig you?" De Witt asked.

"If her kids don't dig me," Hannah said, "then I hope it'll be because something about me really bugs them. Not because some chauvinistic bastard turns them against me."

"Maybe it'll be both."

"What is it with you two?" Carol wailed. "Here I bring back this great person . . . I've never seen you be so hostile, De Witt, I've never seen you this way at all, you're always the *healer!*"

"It's true, De Witt," Starr said. "You haven't been nice to her."

De Witt was silent. He seemed terribly vulnerable and Margaret longed to squeeze his hand or give him some supportive sign. Hannah was silent, either genuinely injured by his attitude or enjoying the others' defense of her. Or both.

"That's true," De Witt finally said. And to Hannah, "I apologize."

Hannah beamed at him, bounced over and gave him a big kiss on the cheek. "I accept, and I apologize if I bugged you. I even understand why I bugged you, so let's forget it!"

Carol, tears in her eyes, said, "You're both so wonderful. This is the first time I ever had a good mother image and a good father image going at the same time!"

To David that night, as she lay on her side nursing Rue, Margaret said, "How come you don't want to do anything in the school?"

"You don't need a reason for not doing something," David said fiercely. "You need a reason for *doing* it."

"Do you like Hannah?"

"Don't be dumb."

"You don't like her."

"Why should I?"

"You don't need a reason for liking someone," she suggested tentatively. "You need a reason for *dis*liking them."

"Ha ha."

"Is it because she's aggressive?" Prepared to give him a lengthy reasoned defense of aggression, a history of its suppression in women—most recently, herself.

"What does that mean?"

"Aggressive? You know what it means, David. Domineering. Takeoverish." Strange words for a defense, Margaret.

"*You* don't like her, that's *your* problem."

"I *do*," Margaret protested. "I just can see why someone else might not."

"Bullshit," David said. "You're just afraid to say you don't like anybody. You think you'd get kicked out of here or something."

It was so patently unfair and so true at the same time.

"I tend not to dislike many people," she said. "I think it has to do with being an only child, you're lonely a lot of the time and you place more of a value on each person you meet."

"You're not a child, you're a grownup," David said. "That's just a lot of bullshit."

✒ HANNAH told De Witt she had a couple of marvelous biology texts and teaching aids in the trailer that he might like to look at if he was going to do botany with the kids. He said he'd very much like to see them and after lunch they went back to the trailer together. Margaret, half an eye on the clock anyway because she was rising bread for the next day, noticed that they were there a long time. When he came back he had two books and a box of teaching cards.

"I really think I was doing Hannah an injustice," he said.

"Mmmm," Margaret replied, knowing she should be glad to hear him say this.

"There's a tendency, when you meet a woman like her, to be, well, frightened off. But it doesn't make sense because that whole strength thing is only a front. Underneath she's just as soft and frightened and needing as anyone else."

"How could you tell?" Margaret asked, not bothering to conceal her jealousy from herself now.

De Witt laughed. "She told me. I mean, she admitted it."

*Now it's my turn to laugh.*

"The funny thing," De Witt mused, "is that I had an ar-

gument with Linda yesterday almost exactly about that."
Linda was his girlfriend in Brattleboro. "She said I
couldn't stand it when a woman was independent and
didn't need me. I guess she was right . . . She was very bitter, actually. As a matter of fact, we split up."

"You and Linda?" Mixed feelings. Pleasure and antici-
pation of pain.

He nodded. "She did it, actually. She said I was sap-
ping her strength by forcing her to need me."

"Everyone wants to be needed," Margaret pointed out.

De Witt smiled, rumpled her hair. "Of course," he said.
Then, "Do you know that you're a very lovely girl—
woman—Margaret? And I'm very fond of you?"

Pure pleasure.

BUT during the next couple of weeks he spent all
his free time with Hannah. Talking, talking, talking, whenever you saw them they were talking animatedly together,
or rather mostly Hannah was talking and De Witt was nodding, commenting. She looked very animated and beautiful. Her whole body moved when she spoke. Mira's initial
cordiality toward Hannah disappeared to be replaced by a
cold, formal appreciation for her efforts to get the school
started.

De Witt, with a forged teaching license from Ohio, was able to get a Vermont license. Carol, who had a primary grades license from New York although she'd never taught, also had one. School got off to a fumbling start the week before Christmas. Carol asked if maybe they shouldn't wait until after Christmas as long as they'd waited this long but Hannah convinced her that Christmas was just another American consumer myth. De Witt said that he dug Christmas as a midwinter pagan rite and they compromised to the extent of killing two of the geese and having a royal feast with candles and a tree, but school had already begun. Monday to Friday. Mornings, mostly, except that provisions were made for the kids to be on call in case they should be visited by some nosy bureaucrat. They were all a bit paranoid on the subject of being closed down by some petty cog of the bureaucracy, and kept expecting once they began, although they'd seldom worried before, to be surprised by hostile inspectors. They followed carefully the state prescriptions for bathrooms and kilowatts and each day someone was responsible for supervising the children in a thorough cleanup. (The supervisor usually ended up doing the cleaning rather than get into an authority trip with the kids.)

JORDAN was away on a selling trip and for a while you always saw the three of them together, Carol, Hannah and De Witt, unless it was just Hannah and De Witt, but then De Witt and Hannah seemed to have had some kind of falling out because suddenly it was just Carol and Hannah. Margaret tried in various sly ways to get De Witt to talk about it, but the most he would say was that Hannah's trip was too heavy for him. He remained extremely polite and pleasant to Hannah but she began to be sharp with him and critical of his classes and the next thing they all knew, it had been decided by Daisy and Mario that they didn't really dig the way De Witt was approaching the botany class and wanted their materials back so they could do the work under their mother's supervision.

Margaret and David took silent walks together on the road that led through the farm and out a mile or so to the highway. The snow-whitened countryside was very beautiful and she found herself wishing she could identify more of the trees and shrubs, so once she brought along a paperback tree guide but David refused to be drawn into speculation over which leafless tree was which. She put away the book in the pocket of the old Mackinaw De Witt had loaned her. Aside from these walks, or brief outings with the twins, she stayed indoors. Gradually the twins stayed awake for a little more of each day. She found it possible to just sit and watch them lying on their backs, looking at their swaddled toes or playing with their fingers, but if David saw her doing this he glowered and she felt guilty.

At the beginning of February Margaret went into Brattleboro for the first time with De Witt on his weekly trip. The twins were a little more than three months old. The first thing she did after leaving De Witt was to weigh herself on a drugstore scale; she'd lost every pound of her pregnancy weight. She'd known all along she was losing a lot but without a scale or full-length mirror it had been difficult to say how much. In an orgy of self-congratulation she bought purple eye shadow, pink lipstick, three sweaters, two pairs of pants and a ski jacket so she could return De Witt's coat. (As soon as she'd left the store she took back the ski jacket, finding herself desolate at the thought of giving up De Witt's symbolic protection.) Also two flannel nightgowns and some long underwear. Having put all of which in the parked jeep, she bought a snowsuit and stuffed bear for each of the twins, some heavy blue wool to make a sweater for David, a mohair shawl for Butterscotch and for De Witt, on last-minute on-the-way-out-of-the-store impulse, an incredibly soft rust-suede tobacco pouch. Purchased while assuring herself that she would now of course have to buy something for Mira, which she somehow had failed to do before it was time to meet De Witt back at the truck. It wasn't much past four but it was already quite dark.

"De Witt," she said as they drove out of town, "I'm embarrassed. I bought you something . . . not a big deal, I mean, I just felt like it, but the thing is I didn't get anything for . . . hardly anyone else . . . and now I won't have a chance and, oh God I sound like an idiot. It's just this little thing but all of a sudden it seems as if I can't . . ." She broke off helplessly.

"Maybe you'd like to give it to me now," De Witt said.

"Oh, yes!" Gratefully she dug around in the paper bags in the back and pulled out the pouch, wedging it between his hands and the steering wheel.

"Mmmmm," De Witt said, "That's marvelous. So soft. Lovely. Thank you, Margaret." He gave her the plastic pouch he carried with him and asked her to transfer the tobacco. In its unburned condition the tobacco had a pleasant fruity smell; she did it slowly to make the job last longer. "All right," De Witt said, opening his window wider to tap the pipe outside, "now fill this up for me." Carefully, feeling as though some high honor had been conferred upon her, she began filling the pipe, taking a few strands at a time, pressing them down, but then she suddenly became aware of the sexual nature of the act . . . *of the present itself* . . . the softness of the pouch, the whole thing . . . a soft suede proposition . . . she was full of distaste for herself. What a sneaky fumbling way to tell someone you were horny!

Horny she was again, that was for sure. It had crept up on her slowly. Subtle accommodations to her celibate state, like trying to be asleep before David came up to the room so she wouldn't betray her need to him. Dreams that Roger was giving her a shampoo. Memories of losing her virginity on the beach near Gloucester, except that nostalgia transformed the coarse grains of Gloucester sand into something resembling talcum powder, and fierce little Tony Lopanto into a ballet dancer in the manner of Jacques d'Amboise.

Oh, to be a member of some earthy primitive tribe where the simplest symbol would suffice to get you laid! Twirling a bead! Baking a tart and laying it at someone's feet! The lack of formal symbols only served to make you self-conscious about the contrived ones. Why did she have to know what she was doing so she'd feel rejected when it didn't work? Why should she assume she'd be rejected, anyway? With the exception of Butterscotch he'd made love to every woman at the farm at one time or another. Mira. Dolores. Carol and Starr had both needed him at bad times during their marriages, and he'd been there to fulfill their needs. Why not her? *Why not me, De Witt?*

"De Witt?"

"Mmmm?"

*Think of something.*

"When you think about the future, do you ever think you'll stay forever?"

"No. I never think that about any place."

"I used to think it about every place. Until I left."

"I couldn't survive that way," he told her. "To me the thought of being in one place forever is the thought of living death."

She'd lived in more than a dozen places before she met Roger and half again that many times since, but each time she'd moved she'd been paralyzed for weeks, for all intents and purposes. Once she'd accused Roger of moving just for the pleasure of seeing her go into shock. She hadn't mentioned that she'd moved more often before meeting him but it had seemed different then because her real life hadn't yet begun.

"My God, you're not planning to go soon, are you?"

"No."

"Good. The thought of being here without you or Roger is frightening." Whoops. She'd said what she meant. But De Witt nodded, seemed to find it easily understandable. *Then do you know maybe De Witt what it's like to want to be filled up?* A phrase she'd once taken for a metaphor, the kind of thing no one ever felt except via Maxwell Anderson.

"I sometimes think of how much I'd miss you if *I* left," she said. "But I never thought about *you* leaving."

"Well that's fine," he said. "Because I'm right here. Aren't I?"

"Mmmmm." *You, me and the pouch. Talk, Margaret, make a cold shower of words.* "De Witt? What's Mitchell's thing with the farm?"

"You mean why he lets us use it and pays the taxes and so on?"

"Uh huh."

"Well, first of all, he has some pretty good tax breaks going, but if he didn't he could still afford it. He's rich."

"Are you close friends?"

"I wouldn't say so, no. We met a few years ago at a party. He already owned the farm and he was sort of flirting, you could say, with the idea of intentional communities . . . but he himself couldn't conceive of living in one on a full-time basis. His businesses wouldn't allow it and even if they did, he's not really suited for it."

And De Witt was suited for anything as long as he didn't have to do it for too long.

"What makes someone suited for it?"

De Witt puffed at his pipe; the fruity smoke wafted past her cold nose. "Oh, lots of things. Some pleasure in physical work, I suppose. Which Mitchell doesn't have, as a matter of fact. He's very much a city person, business, lunches, theater, cocktails before dinner and grass after, when he comes up in the warm weather he takes out a chair to sit on while he reads the Sunday *Times*. But let's see, more importantly, the ability to accept some degree of organization . . . maybe you know that before we came into this Mitchell had let his oldest daughter and some friends take over the farm for a year or so, you know, a bunch of kids who thought of anarchy as an everyday way of life, the place was an incredible wreck inside of six months . . . so, there's the ability to submerge one's own personality just enough to permit others to express theirs, which you could say is almost the same thing as the ability to compromise. The ability to recognize that the world we came from was also something less than perfect. Aside from my own specific necessity to escape . . . some legal unpleasantness in Los Angeles . . . you can't divorce the idea of a place like the farm as an escape, a refuge, from its other attractions. It isn't Utopia and Utopias always exist in contrast to some outside stress, anyway. Many of the people who would flourish in a setup like this also flourish in the business world, the city, whatever, so that their intellectual perceptions of that world—"

"Good grief!" she interrupted. "Talk about intellectual perceptions! It sounds as though you sit around intellectualizing about the whole thing all the time." *For Christ's sake, Margaret—goading him just because you're horny.*

He didn't seem irritated though. "Not all of it. I think about the whole business a lot, though. It demands some conscious effort, you know. If it didn't I suppose I would have gotten bored with it a long time ago."

"Still," she persisted, "you're making it sound very abstract." She glanced out the window; the highway was lighted only by the reflection of the banked snow. She couldn't tell where they were, felt desperately frustrated at the idea that they might be nearly home.

"That's only because I'm talking in generalities. If I talk about specific people I can tell you things that aren't at all abstract. I can talk about Alice, for example, who left the spring before you came. A bright aggressive woman with a mind too restless to be harnessed. She spent her first four months at the farm memorizing the contents of the *Organic Gardening Encyclopedia,* then planting time came and she left because she couldn't accept the rigid scheduling. It seems it reminded her of her childhood. She got into constant arguments with Mira, who was in charge of schedules during that period, and finally she just took off one night. Then there was—"

"Were you fond of Alice?"

"Yes, you could say that. I enjoyed talking with her, we had some very good conversations."

"You mean you didn't fuck her?"

He laughed. "I didn't say that."

*When is my turn?*

He opened his window again, knocked out his pipe on the side of the truck, handed it to her. She looked around outside. On the otherwise deserted road she saw a neon sign. As they approached she could read it—LAUREN-TIANS MOTEL . . . Vacancy . . . *Ici on parle français*. De Witt turned the jeep into the driveway and parked in front of the office. He leaned over and kissed her forehead lightly.

"I'll be right out, Margaret."

So she hadn't had to ask outright. He'd understood. But in a *motel?* The last time she'd seen the inside of a motel she'd been hitchhiking home to Boston from college and had gotten a lift from an extremely attractive middle-aged man in a robin's-egg-blue Cadillac who'd begun by lecturing her on the dangers of hitching when you were an attractive young girl, almost suspiciously bought her a steak dinner somewhere in Connecticut, the burden of his conversation being that he didn't approve of this sort of thing at all, and by the time they'd reached New Haven, where his wife and three beautiful daughters, whose pictures he'd shown her during dinner, were awaiting his return from a business trip, he was trying to decide at which of two motels he'd be less likely to run into one of his buddies who did this sort of thing all the time.

De Witt came out, led by a small barrel-shaped man whose feet pointed away from each other and who waddled in the fashion one would thus expect. The man led them to one of the rooms, opened the door, turned on the light, and said, "Voilà." Never looking at them the whole time. Margaret went in while De Witt moved the jeep.

*It could have been worse, Margaret.* The plastic philodendrons could have had plastic flowers on top of them. The chenille bedspread could have been pinker, the green walls darker. She took off her coat, refrained from looking for a quarter for the TV set, sat down in the armchair and closed her eyes. She heard De Witt come in and lock the door.

"De Witt," she said without opening her eyes, "I feel stupid."

"I don't see why."

*First of all because I feel as if you're just doing this on my account.*

"I dunno," she said. "A motel, for Christ's sake."

He laughed. "I was thinking of privacy."

"Oh, my God, the twins!" She opened her eyes. "I haven't thought about them since I left."

"That's as it should be." He'd taken off his coat. He was wearing his sexy black turtle-neck sweater. He stretched out on the bed and beckoned to her. "There're plenty of people taking care of them, they don't need you right now." His eyes pulled at her.

"Don't you think I should just call?"

"It's difficult to see what purpose that would serve," he said gravely.

"I could tell them I'm on the way home." Yicch. She stood up but didn't go to the bed. She felt like a great jackass, not at all sexy. "I could say you noticed I was horny so you took me to this motel for a short . . . it'd be great. No one would believe me. Living at a commune and getting laid in a motel with plastic philodendrons."

"Why are you putting up barriers, Margaret?"

*Gazing at you, I hear the Muzak* . . . but she moved toward him, nervously turning off the light on the way. Groping. Sitting down on the edge of the bed. He ran his hand up and down her arm lightly.

"De Witt?" she asked nervously. "Do you really feel like screwing me or is this, like, part of your job?"

"Now you're being ridiculous," he said, pulling her gently toward him.

Panic. "De Witt! Please!" Whispering because it was dark. "I can't stand the thought of being someone's obligation."

"What a terrible view you have of yourself," he said, caressing her hair, her breasts, kissing her forehead, her nose, her cheeks, her chin. "You're not my obligation, Margaret. You're my very good friend whom I love." He kissed her lips and she found herself getting drawn in, quite in spite of her mind. "I don't know what's wrong with me," she whispered as he pulled up her sweater and eased it gently over her head. "I feel like a criminal." He kissed her breasts, sucked gently at her nipples. David! She should've brought David with her to town, then this criminal thing couldn't have happened! De Witt tugged at her slacks and she lifted her backside to make it easy. "I must be practically a celibate by now, it's been so long . . . eight months . . . My God!" He kissed her pubic hair, fondled her thighs. Since she was sixteen years old she hadn't gone eight consecutive months without getting laid. "Do you think maybe if you get laid when you're very young and never again maybe the membrane grows back by the time you die?" He parted her legs and began to gently massage her. "Mmmmmmm," he said, "you feel wonderful." It felt good to her, too, when she thought about it, but if she didn't think she forgot about it. What the hell was wrong with her? Was it her concern about being a charity patient? Or was it guilt, and if so toward whom? David, who didn't want her? The twins, who'd never know the difference? Mira, who was off someplace on transcendental cloud number nine? Mechanically she got under his clothes, fondled him, licked his ear, caressed his buttocks, did everything she could think of that she was supposed to do. He got out of his clothes and slowly, gracefully got into her. Stroking away masterfully. Everything was just right.

**WHAT THE HELL WAS WRONG WITH HER?** She clung to him tightly as he came, no closer herself than if they'd just walked in the door. They kissed lengthily. Finally he rolled off her. On his side he peered down at her, caressing her belly. Her belly was still flabby and stretchmarked but he wouldn't be able to see that. Maybe he wouldn't even care; he seemed not to notice her more gross characteristics.

"I don't know what's wrong with me."

"There's nothing wrong with you, Margaret." He tried to part her legs to get his finger back into her but she resisted. He wanted to satisfy her and she didn't want to be satisfied.

"De Witt. I know I'm acting like an idiot. I don't know what it is. Maybe the whole situation. Why couldn't we do it in the barn or something?"

"It's pretty cold. And I thought you'd feel safer here."

Safe. "But the atmosphere!" Of course if you were really in the mood you didn't notice the atmosphere. But she *had* been in the mood, or at least she'd thought so. "It's not that, De Witt. I know it's not that. Maybe it's the kids, I keep thinking about them." *The truth is I keep thinking about anything at all I can think of to avoid thinking about what's happening here, whatever that is.*

He turned on the light, gazed at her tenderly. "Are you telling me that you want to go home?"

She nodded. "I know I'm being revolting and I'm truly sorry I let you pay for the room but I'm—"

"Margaret," he said sternly, "you've got to stop all this self-criticism. You are a lovely woman, and in a particular situation at a particular time, you felt a particular way. Another time you might feel quite differently. Now get dressed and I'll have you home in a flash. Okay?"

She nodded without looking at him.

❧ IT had begun to snow but the roads weren't coated yet. They rolled home without passing a single car, the silence broken only by an occasional shift of gears or one of them coughing. Everyone had finished dinner. Mira accepted De Witt's accelerator-trouble explanation with a celestial smile and gave them each a bowl of soup and some bread. David wouldn't look at Margaret or speak to her. Rosemary had had a full bottle and gone to sleep for the night; Rue was awake but not cranky. They put her on the rug in the common room where she could see the hearth fire as well as the various people. Everyone laughed because she began to cry as soon as she saw Margaret. When Margaret came in or out of a room, David left it.

Later, when Margaret had gotten Rue off to bed—under piles of baby blankets because the upstairs was now terribly cold with only the wood-burning stove in the hallway—she debated whether to go down again to join the evening huddle around the fire and try to make David meet her eyes, or to stick it out in the cold, get into bed in one of her new flannel nightgowns and try to make some sense of the jumble in her head. She put on the blue nightgown then unbraided and brushed her hair. She'd gotten laid in pigtails. In a motel. What happened in a motel by definition couldn't be completely good; it was like saying you could sustain real life in a test tube. But if her failure hadn't been a failure but a success, the success of having refused to be a full participant in the swinging motel age, why was she depressed? Oh, screw . . . she couldn't go to sleep like this. David was perfectly capable of crawling under the covers and warming his feet on someone he wasn't speaking to but she would be up all night, tense and worried. She went downstairs. The women were huddled around the kitchen stove, talking about the school. The men were at the table, talking about a craft cooperative. De Witt and Paul had recently become concerned with the problem of becoming more financially independent of Mitchell. Maybe even buying the farm, if he should ever decide to sell it, as he'd hinted he someday might. One possible way, they felt, would be to establish a cooperative that would function on a more steady basis than the guild shows that gave craftsmen without steady outlets their only chance to display. David was with them but when she came into the room he walked out. De Witt beckoned to her to come and sit next to him but she shook her head and went back to the living room, which was empty. She stretched out on the rug in front of the fire; a moment later David's feet appeared before her eyes and then the rest of him plopped down next to her.

"What'd you do to your hair?" he asked accusingly.

"Nothing," she said. "I took out the braids."

"I never saw you leave it just loose without even tying it," he said.

"So?"

"Nothing." He took some of it in one hand and stroked it with the other.

"Where were you all day?" he asked.

"In Brattleboro," she said.

"What were you doing?" he asked.

"Shopping," she said.

"What'd you buy?" he asked.

"A lot of things," she said.

"Like what?"

"Like some make-up."

"Make-up! Since when do you wear make-up?"

"Once in a while I put it on. For fun." A criminal of cosmetics.

"What else?"

"Some stuff for the twins."

"What else?"

"A couple of presents for people."

"Who?"

"What difference does it make?"

"I wanna know."

She sighed. "I bought some wool to make a sweater for you."

"What else?" No change of expression.

"A shawl for Butterscotch."

"What, are you queer for her?"

"No, idiot," she said. "I'm queer for you."

He stared at her with unmitigated disgust. "I don't believe you."

"So you don't believe me. So I'll slit my wrists." She got to a sitting position and tried to stand up but he was holding on to her hair.

"Anyway," he said, "you smell as if you've been fucking."

She stared at him helplessly for a long time. Then, unable to confess or to lie, she pulled her hair out of his hand and walked upstairs in what she hoped was a dignified manner. Still warm from the fire and the interrogation, she took off her nightgown and crawled under the covers. Not two minutes later David came in, slammed the door, got undressed, got under the covers, and without preamble climbed into her ready and eager body. She began coming from the moment he entered her and didn't stop until he, too, was finished.

STARR had fallen madly in love with a fifteen-year-old boy, who was a student at the Putney School, and was spending a great deal of time away from the farm. Paul, looking as though he'd been hit by a ton of Styrofoam bricks, wandered around the house aimlessly when he wasn't taking care of the children, until Hannah took him and the children in hand and got him functioning again. The argument between Starr and Paul that had preceded Starr's falling in love had been over the question of whether Paul was a good and/or devoted father. Starr complained that he might as well have deserted them as her own father had abandoned her and her mother, for all the love and warmth he gave them. Carol and Jordan had both taken Paul's part in that argument, asking Starr what for Chrissake she wanted from the poor guy, who was always perfectly decent to his kids, the result being that Starr wasn't speaking to either of them although she was on polite remote terms with her husband. Jordan was making it with Butterscotch. Carol took great pains to let everyone know that this was just fine with her because she'd really had it with men for the time being anyhow and was thinking of getting into women. Or mescaline. She did have to be careful when she talked to Hannah, whose feelings against both drugs and lesbians were very strong and a source of amusement to Dolores. Carol did still spend a great deal of time with Hannah, although she began to be upset not so much by Hannah's ideas on women and drugs as by Hannah's comments on motherhood. It was Hannah's opinion, for example, that any woman who intended

113

to work after having babies would do the kindest thing if she drowned the babies first, a view which caused Carol guilt and pain and terrific confusion because she wasn't absolutely certain that Hannah was wrong. Carol tended to be indifferent to babies and children and some of the worst scenes during the winter were over her reaction to their noisiness and needs. Aside from the fact that she got very remote when her own kids were demanding, Lorna made her crawl up the walls.

A whole mystique arose around the trailer, who visited Hannah and when. De Witt and Dolores were the only ones who never did for any reason. Hannah didn't consider that anybody really liked her who wasn't willing to pay court in her own domain. Margaret still felt very ambivalent about Hannah but in this period after her unadventure with De Witt, when she found herself somewhat shy with him, she often dropped by the trailer for an hour or so of conversation.

If the farm was a refuge from one's previous life, the trailer was a refuge from the farm: bright (everything in it was white, bright blue, orange or a combination of those colors); neat almost beyond belief, considering that three people spent a lot of time in it; not an inch of space unused, from the floor area between the bunk beds, with its thick rug over foam rubber that Hannah called "my sofa," to the ceiling over the cooking area, whose every inch was covered with screw-in canisters holding stores of wheat germ, whole grain and soya flours, dry milk, apricots, nuts, molasses, safflower oil and a mind-blowing collection of vitamins and healthful herbs ranging from desiccated liver through lecithin to seaweed. Hannah gave her kids most of their meals at the trailer, where the regime was a purer (and more expensive) form of Adelle Davis than was observed in the big house. (Hannah said that they read from *Let's Eat Right to Keep Fit* every evening at dinner the way some people read from the Bible, and it was part of her charm that she could be quite serious about this but also know it was funny.) Hannah tended to be very sharp in her comments on the people at the farm which was discomfiting because you wondered what pointed comment she was making about you when you weren't there. On the other hand it gave Margaret a distance from the goings on which she sometimes felt she needed.

For as she'd settled in, becoming really at home on the farm, her tendrils had spread to the other people there, attempting to replace what she'd lost. She had left behind the person in the world she was closest to as well as most of her friends, who were largely his friends, Roger having expressed early on a distaste for the kind of women she was attracted to so that her once close friends she'd eventually begun to see only a couple of times a year for lunch. After her arrival and during the harvest season she'd found almost everyone friendly in a casual way and had assumed that once the heavy labor was done there would be warm, winter-fostered intimacy. But the complications in the others' lives, the fluidity of their marriages, militated against the kind of solid friendship she'd looked forward to. If Carol and Starr came to her for a chat it was invariably to moan about some immediate crisis in their lives, there being prevalent the mistaken notion, perhaps, that Margaret's life had ceased to be in crisis when she left her husband. Dolores and Mira, for different reasons, were too remote for easy intimacy. David told her she was full of shit every time she tried to talk to him and while she was as fond as ever of De Witt, she was full of guilt about her greater pleasure in sex with David and could hardly talk to him about her emotional needs when she'd rejected his attempts to fill them. So there was Hannah, whom Margaret would surely one day bring herself to confide in, but who meanwhile had a marvelous collection of stories.

"When I told Eddie to fuck off, don't you see, Mar-

115

garet, I was saying it to my whole life, not just to my husband. To everything in my life that was lousy, which is to say everything but my kids. I didn't know what I was going to do next but I knew I wasn't going back where I came from because that was no less a death than the other kind." She'd been ill. She'd drunk a lot during that period anyway and one day she'd gone on a fast to prove a point to her husband and that would have been okay except she kept drinking. At the end of two weeks she'd been taken to the hospital with hepatitis, infectious mononucleosis and one destroyed kidney. For the first few days it was touch and go but then she'd rallied. "They started bringing me stuff to read, all these magazines I subscribed to that'd been piling up around the house, and I started reading, only the thing I did now that I'd never done before was, I got very selective. For seven years I'd been reading every goddamn magazine I could lay my hands on. *Vogue, Glamour, Time, Life, Newsweek, Harper's, Cosmopolitan, Better Homes and Gardens, Atlantic,* the *Times,* the *Voice,* the *News, The New Yorker, Prevention. Prevention* I got because Eddie's maiden aunt who was a health food nut gave me a subscription. Before I was sick it hadn't made any more of a dent than any of the other shit I was reading. Now I realized it was the only damn thing in the pile that made any sense, and what I'd done was, I put his aunt in this bag and I was afraid of jumping in because I labeled the bag *NUTS.* So I really got into *Prevention* and I started getting *Organic Gardening* and a lot of the other back-to-nature stuff and then someone brought me a copy of the *Whole Earth Catalog* and in some way that crystallized this plan that'd been coming into my head. Not that it had the stuff on trailers, but it was this whole idea of independence, which is really where it's all at, of being able to do for yourself so you won't be victimized by the Machine, or the Man, or whatever. Self-regulation, self-control, self-motivation, self-education, the whole thing. Setting your own house in order. Creating your own environment. Controlling your own destiny."

Controlling your own destiny. It had a quaint ring if your brain had been even briefly sandpapered by the implications of the moon, the tides and the military-industrial complex.

"How did your husband feel about all this?" she asked.

"Feel?" Hannah repeated scornfully. "Eddie didn't *feel* anything. He *thought* maybe I was making a mistake. He *thought* maybe a woman shouldn't be alone on the road with two kids. He *thought* maybe we could start by setting in order our lovely eighteen-room duplex full of Aunt Isabelle's ivories and Uncle Thad's chess pieces and Great-Aunt Mathilda's glass collection. He *thought* maybe you couldn't erase the past, you could only learn to live with it, and I thought maybe the only way to erase it was by refusing to live with it, and that's what I did, and it worked."

A triumphant crescendo followed by silence.

"How often do the kids see him?" Margaret asked.

"Once or twice a year if I happen to be around New York."

She started to ask how he felt about that but then remembered Hannah's statement that he had no feelings.

"And I'll tell you something else," Hannah said defiantly, "it doesn't mean shit to them. He's no further away from them than when we all lived in the same place and his mind was always on his stocks, anyway. He thought his kids were just two more growth stocks."

Margaret thought of Roger, who had two children he'd never seen and no interest at all in the stock market.

"What's the matter?" Hannah asked.

"I was thinking about my husband," Margaret said.

"What about him?"

"Well, that he's never seen the girls . . . they've never seen him. They wouldn't know who he was if they saw him, I guess. They probably think De Witt's their father or

David, or God knows who." She laughed to dispel the sadness she felt at this. "Maybe they don't even know I'm their mother."

"They know you, all right," Hannah said.

"I guess I know that," Margaret admitted.

"Personally, I don't think the father ever has the same importance to a child. A lot of the Freudian literature has it that at a given age they grow away from the mother toward the father, you know, someone pushes a button or something. I never saw it in my own kids. What I think really happens is that a lot of half-ass Radcliffe girls read some Freud and then when their girls reach the age of six they say, okay, kid, time to go through your daddy stage, so they push away the kid and naturally the kid has to go someplace for comfort."

"What school did you go to?" Margaret asked uncomfortably.

Hannah smiled. "Radcliffe but it's irrelevant . . . the only thing it did for me was to retard my education for another four years. Anything I ever learned I learned in spite of some school system."

Margaret nodded. She knew how Hannah felt about schools, a lot of it carried over even into their little school, where the way other people were teaching her children was a constant source of argument between Hannah and those others. Daisy and Mario now seldom took classes with the others, doing most of their work with their mother in the trailer. Her own school memories involved boredom but little pain; she vaguely remembered having been happy to go off to school every day, if only to be out of the bleak, silent house she lived in.

"School's not what's on your mind, though," Hannah said.

"No," Margaret said, "I guess Roger's on my mind. I have very mixed feelings about Roger, but I really want

118

him to see the twins. I want him to be . . . I guess I want him to love them. It seems very important to me."

"I'll tell you one thing," Hannah said. "It's better for them not to even know he exists than to have him drop in and out of their lives or not give a shit about them."

ON the eve of Margaret's thirtieth birthday an old friend of Hannah's came by with some Newsreel films and they sat in the common room watching the Richmond Oil strike, that unique and lovely strike where the workers had for once understood that when the cops broke your strike you got radicalized. Then there was a film about People's Park, interesting because the pictures showed the utter destruction of the Park while the narrator talked triumphantly of the people's victory.

Someone turned on the lights and there was Roger, leaning against the archway, hands in his pockets, as though he'd stood in that same doorway a thousand times before. He was looking around but not with any apparent anxiety about finding her. He'd shaved off his beard and moustache so that the fine, almost delicate, lines of his face showed once again. Her heart leaped when she saw him but she didn't move. Not toward him, not away from him.

"Who's that?" Carol asked.

Roger's eyes met Margaret's. He smiled in a desultory way. She smiled back, trying to remember how she looked, trying to see if Roger was seeing how much better she looked. She started to get up and go over to him but stopped herself. Confused.

119

"Hi, Roger."

"Hi, Maggie."

Roger himself was looking somewhat drawn, maybe because of the beard but probably not just that. He'd looked this way when they met so that for all his verbal machismo her heart had gone out to him. Only later had she become aware of the universal quality of her reaction, that Roger, who under normal circumstances was quite attractive to women, had to fight them off physically when he looked like this. He claimed, as a matter of fact, that it was this situation that had created his mistrustful attitude toward them, that he'd become attractive to women only after, as he put it, the kiss of death had been planted on his forehead when he was seventeen. His mother said this was Roger's fiction, that girls and women had adored him from infancy, with his beautiful gray eyes and curly blonde hair and sassy tongue, and that from those tender years he had been suspicious of everyone. Nobody had ever been able to explain this satisfactorily, that a child treated so well from infancy should be so mistrustful and dissatisfied. Actually, though, Roger was only mistrustful if you were trying to please him, as though he'd decided very early in life that anyone trying to do so was trying for reasons of convenience, not love, and if this were true it seemed adequate reason for his dissatisfaction. Or so she'd sometimes thought in a sympathetic moment.

People began to get up and stretch and mill around. David was sitting next to her on the floor. Watching her. He didn't get up. De Witt and Mira were standing on the other side of the doorway from Roger, also watching her. She went to them.

"This is Roger," she said vaguely, hoping De Witt would remember her husband's name because Roger didn't like to be introduced as my husband.

De Witt nodded.

"We've been hoping you would come," Mira said tranquilly. Margaret wanted to kick her in the shins. Roger said nothing. David was drawing designs on the rug with his finger.

"Do you want to see the girls?" Margaret asked.

"I see them," Roger said, nodding toward Hannah. "That one's not too bad."

"Oh, dear," Mira said playfully. "No wonder Margaret left home."

Roger stared at Mira for endless yards of time, a capacity of his Margaret envied. De Witt suggested to Mira that she put up some tea and Mira went quietly.

"Where are my daughters?" Roger demanded now—as though she'd been holding out on him.

She led him upstairs. De Witt and Paul had built a sort of bunk-crib arrangement against the wall, two sections with a removable divider in between. In the dim light from the night lamp they could see the girls, each curled up in her own compartment, facing the other through the wooden divider, looking, with their identically beautiful baby faces and furry blue pajamas, like two sides of a Rorschach blot.

Roger, she begged silently, *please don't say anything bad about them,* but when she looked at him she saw there was no need to say it for he'd been disarmed. He stood quite limp with wonder at what he had wrought.

"What are they like when they're up?" he asked after a long time.

"Rue's very lively," she said. "She's more active. She stands up already if she's got something to hold on to, and she cries if she doesn't get what she wants. Rosemary's quiet, sweet, she hardly ever cries. You can put her someplace and she'll sit there and look and look and never cry. Not that Rue's bad-tempered, she just . . . wants what she wants." This was something that occasionally troubled her, the possibility that she was preferential to Rosemary. She loved them both, was fascinated by both, thought

121

them both beautiful, yet there was in her feeling toward Rosie that extra desire to give, to please, that one had only toward those who asked little. It was probably one of the most basic rules to human nature, that protective feeling toward those who didn't think to protect themselves, to call on the kid who didn't raise her hand, and so on, yet she thought it might be unfair.

"Good for her," Roger said emphatically. "Only an asshole wants what he doesn't want."

It wasn't what she'd meant but of course Roger knew that. She could feel him waiting for her to begin one of her losing arguments but she didn't feel like it. What she was feeling was a combination of curiosity and relief; curiosity at her own mixed reaction to Roger's arrival, relief at his reaction to the twins. For in all the times she'd thought of his coming, it was always in terms of how he would react to *them,* never in terms of whether he would be loving to *her.*

On the other hand, it *was* somewhat flattering that he'd come. After all, the days when you could walk out on your husband and picture him in a state of abject misery were past; he could have love and/or care at will, so that his having sought her out could be interpreted as a specific need for *her.*

*If he comes you won't really know why. Whether he's curious or he feels like meeting the other people or he's attached to you.*

She wondered what David was doing now.

"I missed you, Roger."

"Oh? What'd you miss more? Getting laid or getting insulted?"

"Oh go fuck yourself. There're people here who can do both."

They smiled at each other. She was happy because her response had come so easily, unlike the old days when he'd always had to goad her into expressing her nastier thoughts. Roger was happy because he enjoyed resistance.

Years ago he had told her what she was sure was his own made-up plot of his supposedly favorite novel of all times, the name of which he claimed to have forgotten, but it was about a man and wife who fought side by side in a war and then went home and made love. The wife was eventually killed on the battlefield and the husband never remarried because he never found a woman who could fight like that.

"Tell me about it," he said, easing her back toward the bed.

"I don't feel like it," she said.

He kissed her warmly and warmly she responded to him.

She said, "The door is open."

"Isn't that the way you do it here?" he asked in her ear, licking it.

"It's not the way I do it," she said, shivering.

"With who?" he asked.

"No," she said.

He started to unzip her jeans but she forced herself past him and closed the door of the room. Roger took off his sweater, lay down on the bed, watched her. She had a vague feeling that there was something to be settled between them but she couldn't say what it was.

"What is it?" Roger asked.

"Nothing." She turned off the light.

"For Christ's sake," Roger muttered, "when you looked like a hippopotàmus with clap you walked around the house naked all day, now you look like a human being and—"

"And I'm acting like one," she said defiantly, afraid to tell him she felt shy.

"You're acting like a fucking idiot!" he shouted, "That's what you're acting like!"

Rue began to cry. Roger leaped to his feet and turned on the light in one motion.

"What's wrong?"

"You woke her up."

"Big deal. What is it, the first time in her life she woke up?"

"She often wakes up crying, especially to loud noises."

Roger picked up Rue and cradled her in his arms.

"How'd you know how?" Margaret asked, pleased and startled.

"That's a dumb question." He hummed and rocked Rue in his arms. Watching, Margaret felt cosy and excited, eager for Rue to go back to sleep so they could make love. Somewhere in her parents' photo album there was a picture one of the uncles had taken, of Margaret's father cradling her in his arms when she was a baby. His face, his whole body, bespoke love and tenderness. When had it changed? When the realities of herself as an imperfect human being had emerged, dimming his hopes of self-justification through fatherhood?

"I guess I'll have to feed her." She took off her sweater.

"Ssssshhh," Roger said, his back to her.

"She never goes back to sleep without being fed," Margaret whispered irritably. Slowly, still rocking, Roger lowered the baby into the bunk bed. Silence.

"You were saying?" he asked triumphantly.

"Nothing." She smiled, giving him his moment. He sat down on the edge of the bed, looked at her breasts, fondled them.

"You still nursing them?"

"Rue. She won't drink from a bottle. Rosie had a bottle last month for the first time and wouldn't bother with the breast any more. It's a little easier this way, they'd get terribly swollen before."

"Lie down."

"I was eating all this terrible stuff, and extra vitamins out of Adelle Davis so I'd have enough milk. Not everyone has enough for twins." Did he know that she was bragging?

He peeled down her pants, stared at her stomach, tracing the now-pale ribbony ridges, leaning over and kissing them tenderly.

"I thought you'd be . . . I thought you'd hate the marks," she whispered. She'd feared he would be repelled because she'd sensed more than once behind his cultivation of ugliness an attempt to exorcise some power it held over him.

"On the contrary," he murmured, lovingly stretching her groin to see where the marks ended, kissing them, "they give you character. You could use some on your face." The night they'd decided to get married he'd insisted on making her up as an old lady so he'd know what he was getting into, then informed her it would take her face about twice as long as most people's to get interesting. She'd asked him then in utmost seriousness whether he'd ever considered marrying someone twice his age instead of just a couple of years older and he'd replied with equal sobriety that he'd considered just that but had decided it would be more fun to find some bland-looking young girl and help her age prematurely.

Margaret giggled. She giggled because she had married Roger and that was a funny thing to have done.

Later, when they'd made love with fantastic pleasure and she had lain in bed sleepily wondering why it couldn't be that good all the time if you just lived together like two normal human beings—that must be the answer, it wasn't normal to have fantastic pleasure in regular doses—she drifted off into sleep and Rue woke up in howling indignation at having been tricked back to sleep earlier. Thinking Roger was asleep, she put Rue between them on the bed and lay on her side to nurse. Then she looked up and met Roger's eyes. He caressed the baby's head, moved closer

125

so that his body cradled the baby's back as Margaret cradled the front. Margaret and Roger looked at each other without smiling. A crystal moment she would always remember. A moment of awesome peace. Of *tangible* contentment. When she moved Rue and turned onto her left side, Roger cradled *her* back instead of the baby's. Briefly they all fell asleep but Margaret was awakened by the tightening of the sandwich whose filling she was, and then she put Rue back in the crib. When she returned to the bed Roger had rolled over to her side. She went around and got in on his side but it was an old peculiarity of hers, not to be able to sleep on the right-hand side of the bed, so finally, wide awake, she decided to go downstairs and make some tea. She put on Roger's long scratchy brown sweater that was on the floor and opened the door. David was curled up on the hallway floor, his eyes wide open. Oh, Jesus! David!

"David," she whispered, "what are you doing, for crying out loud?"

"I thought you wouldn't want me to come in," he said.
*No shit.*

"You were right, but why didn't you stay downstairs on the couch or find someplace in the barn?"

"It didn't seem fair," he said. "The whole thing didn't seem fair, that all of a sudden I'm shut out of our room." He was hugging himself, his hands caressing the soft blue wool of the sweater she'd finished for him just a few days before.

"Come on downstairs with me," she said, at a loss. "I'm going to make some tea."

"I don't know," he said doubtfully. "I'm pretty tired."

"Oh, come on," she urged, tugging at the sweater. "It won't take long."

He stood up and they went downstairs, where she put up water for tea.

"How come you're wearing that?" he asked.

126

She looked down at Roger's sweater, which came about a third of the way down her thighs. "It was just the closest thing to grab." Ridiculous to be put in the position of feeling guilty that you slept with your husband. "The baby woke up. I didn't feel like going back to sleep."

"Did you tell him about me?"

"No, David. I didn't."

"Are you going to?"

"Not unless I have to, I guess."

"What does that mean?"

"It means that if I have a choice of telling the truth or lying and having Roger know I'm lying, then maybe I'll tell the truth."

"But if you can lie and get away with it you will." A certain moral loftiness in his tone.

"Sure." The water began boiling and she put in some tea, wishing that tea bags weren't *verboten* at the farm because of the chemicals in the paper. "It seems like the least I can do."

David said, "Sometimes I don't understand you."

Margaret said, "This is because of your extreme youth and my advanced age." Two poles with a distance of eleven years between them.

David said, "You're not so old."

"You don't think I'm old?"

"I like women of all ages."

"I'm so glad to hear that, David, because the fact is that tomorrow's my thirtieth birthday and I was fearing you would reject me."

"But instead *you* rejected *me*."

"I didn't reject you," she told him. "My husband just showed up."

"Did you know he was coming?"

"Of course not. I would've told you."

"Why did he come?"

She shrugged. "Maybe he missed me . . . or maybe he

127

was just curious." She smiled but David didn't. He couldn't remember their conversation of months before. Why did she? It must have to do with the importance other people had for you. Yet David was acting as though she *was* important.

"David, you know that I'm fond of you and that's not going to change just because Roger's here."

"What *will* change?"

"Oh, God," she said, "I really have no idea. I find it hard to think in terms of the future." *And so do you most of the time.*

"The future," he said bitterly. "Where I'm going to sleep tonight, is that the future?"

It was a question at once reasonable and impossible. She hesitated, his urgency about the present briefly contagious.

"Would you like me to get a blanket and sheet and make up the couch for you?"

He shrugged. How long had he been on the road and how often had he slept on grass, on gravel, on somebody's floor? But of course he'd made it clear from the beginning that he expected more of her. She made up the couch and grudgingly he stretched out on it without taking off his shoes. She pulled off his shoes and covered him. She turned off the light and sat on the floor near him, stroking his head, wondering what would happen if Roger woke up. Trying to figure out how David had managed to make her feel guilty about neglecting him instead of betraying Roger. Maybe she wasn't betraying Roger? Maybe it was what he wanted? No. More likely it didn't matter in her own deep down balance book what Roger wanted. If you were of that generation which having repudiated the old values still carried them around tattooed in your vital organs like some IBM cards of guilt, registering old ladies helped across the street, litter not picked up, husbands abandoned, young boys screwed, then it didn't matter what your explanation was or what your views of the future, it only mattered that you were the devil's handmaiden. The guilt was there, it simply hadn't made itself felt, yet. David's eyes were open, wakeful. Challenging her to make him sleep. What could she tell him? The things she could say that might make him feel better would all be lies.

"If he leaves tomorrow will you go with him?"

"No," she said. "I don't think so. But I don't think he'll want to, either."

"What if he does?"

"I don't know, David. I hardly ever know what I'm going to do in advance." No. That wasn't the right thing to say. "I can't imagine that I would just walk out of here and leave you and never see you again, if that's what you're thinking."

He glowered at her.

"You're not being fair," she said. "You know that I'm crazy about you."

"What does that mean?" he asked.

She hesitated. "It means I'm all involved with you. I like you and I care about you and I've been all wrapped up in you for a pretty long time."

"You've been wrapped up in your *babies*."

"Yes, but in you, too." Not in a hundred percent different ways. But maybe you know that. You know it and it doesn't mean shit to you.

He wanted to make love to her but she couldn't let him. She sat on the rug and leaned up against the couch.

"I'll have to go up soon."

"You said you'd stay until I fell asleep."

"Are you going to stay up all night, then?"

"How'm I supposed to know?"

Fair is fair.

"Maybe tomorrow we could set you up in the barn," she said. "In the room next to the one Butterscotch is using." And Jordan.

"You're trying to get rid of me."

"If I was trying to get rid of you," she pointed out, "I wouldn't be trying to figure out how to make you comfortable."

"I was comfortable where I was," he said.

She sighed. "I know that, David, but it's not fair for you to . . . I mean it's not my fault Roger showed up."

"It'll be your fault if he stays."

"Not necessarily. He could stay to bug me."

"You mean you don't want him to?"

"I didn't say that. I don't know how I'm going to feel. All I'm saying is that what he does doesn't depend on what I want." Any relationship, if it exists, being inverse.

"What if you had your choice right now? Would you have him stay or go?"

"Right now . . . I guess I'd have to say stay, David. His daughters are here, you know, he's never even seen them before. How could I want him to go?"

"What if they weren't here?"

She stared at him, her mind a temporary blank. "What do you mean? Of course they're here, how can I . . ." *How can I want to know the answer to that?* This was her whole life they were playing around with as though it were some kind of game plan.

"All I'm saying is if it didn't happen that you became pregnant, and you did what you did, came here and so on, and we were all going along pretty much like we were except you had more time because no babies, and then he showed up—how would you feel?"

No, that wasn't it; she was wet wash being put through the mangle of an old-fashioned washing machine.

"I guess I'd have mixed feelings, like now."

"What would you need him for if you didn't have this crap in your head about kids and parents?"

"It's not crap."

"It *is* crap." Fiercely. "My parents got divorced and it didn't make a fucking bit of difference in my life."

"Mmmmmmm."

"I mean you can tell yourself some shit about how I was a boy scout when they were still married and this terrific change came over me but that's what it'll be, a load of shit."

"How old were you when your parents got divorced?"

"Eleven." Sulky.

"Did they get married again?"

"Yeah."

"Did you live with your mother and her husband?"

"Yeah."

"Did you like him?"

"Mitchell? He's all right. I mean he's a prick but he's a nice guy and he's got plenty of money and they travel all the time so they weren't on my back."

Pause to digest. "David? Do you mean the same Mitchell who owns the farm?"

"Yeah."

"Why didn't you tell me that?"

"What difference does it make?"

"I don't know but it does."

"Bullshit." Fierce again. "All this is bullshit because you don't wanna answer what I asked you before."

"That's only partly true."

Silence.

"You were getting balled anyhow, so you didn't need him for that."

She smiled. "Maybe I like the kind of written guarantee that I'll always get balled."

"Marriage doesn't give you that. Half the married people I know don't ball."

"They told you."

"They don't have to tell me. I can look at them and tell myself. Mitchell balled my mother more before they were married than after. You think I couldn't tell?"

Silence.

"There's a permanence to the idea of marriage," she said feebly. He snickered. "I mean, I'm not saying it always works, but there's a certain security to the idea of it, of always being with the same person, for better or worse, and all that stuff."

"You make me sick with your lies."

*That, David, is because you're thinking I'm lying for your benefit while in truth I'm lying for my own.*

Silence.

"All I was saying, David, is that a place like this you feel as if the whole thing could split up any minute, people coming and going, for me that's a very shaky feeling." Shakier than going to parties with Roger and wondering how I'll get home? "All right, so a lot of it is baloney. I admit it. So I can't answer your question."

"Which question?"

She wanted to shriek something unintelligible. He'd left her in the mangle and then walked away from it.

"About what binds me to Roger. Besides the kids."

"Forget it," he said. "You answered that already."

"I did?"

"Sure. A lot of bullshit binds you to Roger, that's what."

"I'm going upstairs now."

"That's okay. I don't need you here. You or your bullshit."

THE twins slept late and so did she. Roger was still sleeping when she took them downstairs. The couch had been stripped and David wasn't around. Only Dolores and Butterscotch were left in the kitchen—and Dolores's new lover, a young girl with long black hair and the eyes of a fawn caught in the headlights who never spoke to anyone but Dolores and then in a whisper.

"Is it all right to talk about David?" Butterscotch whispered as Margaret gave Rosie her bottle, put her in the playpen and sat at the table to nurse Rue. She nodded.

"He took off early this morning," Butterscotch said. "I think he's upset."

"Where did he go?"

"He wouldn't say."

"Did he say when he'd be back?"

"He wouldn't tell me."

A moment of fear. David has gone. David is hitching another ride on the potholed highway of life. Who will pick up David next? Another old lady? An older old lady than me or a younger old lady, like maybe twenty-eight? Hey! It was her birthday! She hadn't thought of it until now. You could make out a case for disaster; briefly it freed your mind of symbols.

"He did say he'd be back, though?"

"When I asked he just said why wouldn't he be, as though he was pretending he didn't care about your husband."

Margaret nodded. "We talked late last night but it

133

doesn't seem to do any good. It's very difficult . . . Roger's still asleep," she added irrelevantly.

"I sleep much better than I used to, better than I've slept since I was little," Butterscotch said, "but Jordan doesn't fall asleep until it begins to get light."

"I guess I'll go see how De Witt's doing with the goats," Dolores said. "Leila's having trouble with her udders." She left, followed by the girl.

"No matter how busy we are all day," Butterscotch said softly, "he doesn't go to sleep while it's dark. It frightens me because I always think he's so strong."

"Maybe that's when he gathers his strength."

Butterscotch smiled gratefully. "That's a beautiful way to think of it."

Hannah came in now, having given her kids breakfast in the trailer. She poured herself a cup of coffee (not allowed in the trailer) and sat down.

"I'm exhausted," she announced. Her friend who'd brought the films had slept in the fourth bunk and apparently he snored. In the middle of the night she'd dropped down her pillow on his head and he hadn't awakened but had slept badly and, blaming her for this, had gone off early in high dudgeon. Hannah giggled. "No more films." She didn't seem upset that her friend had gone off angry with her.

Roger came down and asked where the girls were. Margaret said they were in the playpen, pointing to the other room. Roger went looking for them.

"He's making up for lost time," Hannah said softly, something in her tone inappropriate to a woman who kept her kids away from her husband for three hundred and sixty-four days a year.

Roger came back holding Rue. "Rosie's asleep in the playpen," he announced, sitting down with Rue on his lap. "How about some breakfast?" He was looking at Hannah

134

as he said it but Margaret got up to make some eggs after noting that Hannah smiled demurely.

"Who're you?" Roger asked.

"I'm Hannah."

"I'm sorry," Margaret said. "Roger, this is Hannah and this is Butterscotch." She broke three eggs into the pan, brought Roger a cup of coffee. He was bouncing Rue on his knee; she seemed to accept him without question.

"You really dig your kids, don't you," Hannah said.

"They're fantastic," Roger said. "No one ever told me they'd be like this."

Rue lunged for his coffee and he pushed it away but then dipped his finger into the cup and let her lick it.

"Coffee's terrible," Hannah said, solemn but twinkling. "Aside from giving you false energy it robs your body of B vitamins."

"No shit," Roger said.

"No shit," Hannah said.

There was a pause. "All right," Roger said. "No more coffee, baby."

Hannah smiled sweetly. Margaret gave Roger his eggs.

"You and me," Roger said to Hannah, "we can have a cuppa, huh?"

"As long as we're perfect in all other respects," Hannah said.

Margaret bit her lip. She was experiencing that feeling of dread which had lost its familiarity in recent months. Maybe it was this she'd been anticipating when she'd refused to let herself be purely glad that Roger had come. She sat down at the table but it was like having to watch your own execution, a ritual which once you'd forgotten it, couldn't be resumed again so easily. She took Rue and wandered into the sewing room, letting Rue down on the floor to play while she hemmed napkins for a while. When she wandered back into the kitchen, only Roger and Hannah were still there.

"They think they're ready for anarchy," Hannah was saying. "That's because they don't know what anarchy is."

Roger nodded. "The idea of self-government is foreign to Americans." He seemed quite serious, not at all condescending. He really liked Hannah. For the first time since meeting her, Margaret was able to feel a simple, direct dislike toward the other woman. "Self-government is a form of self-control, self-limitation. It goes against our whole grain. We're supposed to go after what we want, not question whether we really need it."

"Well said," Hannah murmured.

"I feel qualified to discuss this at length," Roger went on, "because I'm an absolutely typical American in that respect."

Hannah smiled. "You're young. There's time for change."

"I'm very young," Roger agreed. "I'm two years younger than my wife, as a matter of fact."

"I'm three years older than your wife," Hannah said.

"Good, good," Roger said. "That's promising. Anyhow, the problem is, I don't really want to change. I have yet to be convinced that I'll benefit in any real way from changing."

Hannah, who might in other circumstances have been repelled by Roger's confession, was quite charmed by it, said that at the moment she couldn't see where there was any crying need for change.

"But here I find myself in this place you say is full of half-assed anarchists," Roger persisted.

"I wasn't talking about this place," Hannah said. "I was talking about the last place. Here the problem is quite different, from what I can make of it." She glanced at Margaret, seemed about to go on, stopped herself.

"What's the problem here then?"

"Well . . ." She was still hesitant but she was going to

136

force herself. "This place seems to be full of people looking for the father they never had. Ready to turn over their brains and free will to the first fake wise man who promises to take care of them."

Margaret was stunned, although she wasn't sure by what—this simple new version of their lives with De Witt or Hannah's assurance that it was all right to voice it. De Witt, who had assumed leadership so reluctantly because without any leader the whole thing didn't work!

Roger laughed. "That doesn't describe my wife."

"I didn't mean—" Hannah began.

"My wife will turn over her brains to *anyone,* fake wise man or not."

Hannah laughed. "Margaret, you're not going to let him get away with that, are you?"

"Sure," Margaret said, standing up, faking calm. "Why not?" Then left the room quickly before the façade could crumble. Went out on the porch, then down the front steps although it was freezing cold out, a cold gray day in March, and she was wearing only a light sweater.

*Why not? Because you were out of the habit and it was a good habit to be out of.* Margaret the shit-eater. Making fun of her had been like something Roger did instead of working. And her readiness to accept his mockery had been based not on saintliness or good will but on some crazy idea of the way she was *supposed* to be. Some lopsided notion of femininity maybe not invented by her but certainly fully acquiesced in. Not that she was ready to disclaim the whole notion; it was only that in recent months she seemed not to have worried much about what she should be. She had worried about her sex life, about whether she was a good mother to both girls, about whether she was doing her share. About what she was *doing,* in other words, instead of about what she *was.* And now back came Roger with his yardstick and she wasn't in the habit any more and *fuck you, Roger, that's all, fuck you! Even when there is justice in your remarks you never make them in the interest of seeing justice served!*

She wandered over to the barn where Paul and Jordan were holding down Shirley while De Witt cleaned her udder, which had become so distended that it dragged along the ground and had picked up some surface infection. Now, as De Witt spread bacitracin on Shirley's teats, Margaret went around the stall picking up the tiny, neat pellets of goat shit and tossing them out the little window into the pen. Shirley rammed Jordan angrily as soon as they all let her loose.

Afterwards Paul and Jordan went back to the house and Margaret asked De Witt if he would take a walk with her. Gone was the uneasiness she'd felt with him in recent weeks; in the crisis of Roger's arrival De Witt's presence was purely reassuring to her. All but an inch or two of snow was melted from the meadows and the road was clear but for a thin layer of ice that would turn to slush when the midday sun warmed it. In another two weeks, De Witt said, the mud would be so deep that the little kids wouldn't be able to walk through it and even the adults would have difficulty. She wrapped her arms around herself to keep warm.

"Roger and Hannah seem to be getting along fine," she said, and laughed uncertainly.

De Witt glanced at her but said nothing. She shivered. He put an arm around her and she put an arm around him. She began to cry. They kept walking.

De Witt said, "Do you know that you never talked about Roger at all?"

*"Really?"*

"Really."

"I don't know why," she said. "I mean . . . I talked about him to David but I guess David asked me questions about him. Roger . . . Roger is a very interesting person," she finished lamely.

"I don't doubt it," De Witt said.

They walked some more.

"We've been married for almost . . . more than six years, actually." *So what?* "He's an artist . . . I must've told you that."

"Nope."

She laughed. "I always dug artists. I don't know why."

De Witt laughed. "I think you dig everyone, Margaret, unless you get turned off."

"That's true," she admitted. "I guess I'm not very fussy."

"Why do you put it that way? As though there's something wrong with liking people."

She thought about it. "I guess because I feel as if it's not as though I like them because I'm a good person, charitable or something, I accept them mostly without thinking about whether I like them, but out of my own *need,* y'know? Not out of goodness."

"What's wrong with that? You think it's unusual?"

"I dunno, it's just . . . I had this neighbor, for instance, in Hartsdale, this suburb where we lived . . . Celeste . . . she was a pain in the ass really, nobody could stand her, none of my other friends, neighbors, and so on, but it took me a long time before I even realized she was supposed to bug me, that it was okay, I mean, because I *liked* having her drop in, especially before I knew anyone else, because Roger was always taking off and I didn't know anyone, and I was lonely, that's the thing. I wasn't tolerating her because I'm a tolerant person."

"Sure you were."

"Oh . . ." But she wasn't annoyed, she was pleased. She kissed his cheek and he squeezed her. They were almost at the main road. They walked into the corner of the woods

where the kids had built their igloo, which was only beginning to melt because it was heavily shaded by pine trees.
They peered into the igloo. A bed of pine needles made it
look inviting but the roof was dripping in twenty different
places. They returned to the road, arms around each other
again.

"Do you want to go back?" De Witt asked.

"Not really," she admitted.

They began walking along the side of the highway.

"I'm a little worried about David," she said.

"He wasn't around this morning."

"He took off. He's angry with me because Roger
showed up. He said he'd be back but I don't know . . . if
something better turns up . . . of course I should *want* him
to go if something better turns up."

"Maybe you know nothing better than you will turn
up."

She laughed. "You always give me such nice motives."

"You always give yourself such poor ones."

"Do you really believe that? That David can't do better
than me?"

"Yes. I really believe that."

"Doesn't want to, you mean?"

A little white sports car went past, stopped and backed
up. The woman driving leaned over and opened the window; FM rock blared out at them.

"Wanna ride?"

De Witt looked at Margaret, laughed, said, "Sure, why
not?" He grabbed Margaret's hand and they ran to the
car, but it was hard to get in because the front seat was occupied by a car seat in which sat a large baby screaming
over the music. The driver got out and they went around
the car and got into the back where a somewhat older
child was singing over and over again, "Turn off the
music, it gives me a headache, turn off the music, it gives

140

me a headache." The woman turned off the music and for a moment the car was absolutely quiet.

"Am I far from, like, Brattleboro?" the woman asked.

"Once you get on 91, less than half an hour."

"How far am I from 91?"

"About ten minutes."

"Are you going, you know, to Brattleboro?"

"No. We're just going a little ways down the road."

"Is Brattleboro a good town?"

"I suppose it depends on what you're looking for," De Witt said.

The woman laughed nervously. "What I'm looking for is some decent grass, if you really want to know."

"Sorry."

The woman laughed again, that uneasy, grating laugh. "You probably think I'm a narc."

"I don't think anything," De Witt said. "I think this is where we get off."

"But there's nothing here," the woman said, so piteously that Margaret felt for her.

"Mushrooms," De Witt assured her. "We're collecting mushrooms."

"Where are you from?" Margaret asked as the woman pulled over to the side of the road.

"Would you believe Elmhurst?" the woman said. She turned on the car radio again and the baby began crying and the older child said, "Turn it off, it gives me a headache."

They got out and began walking back to the farm.

꿍ᔑ DAVID came out of the barn to accost them.

"Where've you been?"

"We took a walk."

"Some walk."

"Where've *you* been, David?" De Witt asked gently. "We were worried about you."

"I was sleeping at the end of the barn," David said. Bristling. He fell into step with them except he walked just slightly behind, as though he were afraid of giving De Witt access to his back. As they neared the house, Roger opened the front door. "Where the hell've you been?"

"I took a walk," she said.

"Do you always walk out of the house and leave your kids to scream their heads off?"

She was stricken; it was true she hadn't given them a moment's thought when she left.

"If you'd been here with them for the past few months," De Witt said calmly, "you would know what she did when they cried."

"Where the fuck do you get off butting into this argument?" Roger said.

"I'm sorry," De Witt said, "I feel very close to Margaret. We're like brother and sister."

*Attempts at incest having more or less failed.*

"Isn't that touching," Roger sneered, turning his wrath then to David. "How about you, cousin? You have something to say, too?"

David didn't.

"Where are the girls?" Margaret asked.

142

"They're upstairs with Hannah," Roger said. "You're damn lucky she was here."

"Mmmm." Hannah had never looked twice at the twins before but if you left your kids alone there was always someone around to take care of them. That was it, she'd taken it for granted until now, never thought how lucky she was to be there instead of alone in the house in Hartsdale, having to hire sitters if she felt like going someplace herself while Roger was tripping off to the Lower East Side.

"Is she putting them to sleep?" Margaret asked.

"How the hell do I know? Go up and find out."

"No, that's all right." She smiled. "I'm sure Hannah can manage them very well."

He stared at her fixedly. Her smile became strained but she forced it to stay there. Their eyes were locked.

"Which one of these jokers is fucking you, Maggie? Or is it both of them?"

She stood her ground but her insides caved in.

"Don't let him put you on the defensive, Margaret," De Witt said. "Ask him what he's been doing with *his* time."

"What I don't see," Margaret said, "is why everything has to end in the same place. A second ago we were talking about the children."

"And children have nothing to do with fucking."

"Not in the context that we were talking about. Whether I can leave them in the house with other people."

"Without a word."

"When they were tiny I never left the house at all."

"And now they're teenagers."

"Now I sometimes take a little walk or something."

"You were gone for more than an hour."

"So I took a big walk," she said, concealing her doubt and letting only her irritation show. "You were here, weren't you? Other people were here. I knew they'd be all right."

Hannah came down announcing that the children were

both in their cribs, Rue was sleeping and Rosie was playing quietly, something in her tone suggesting that some special Hannah magic had been required to bring about this miraculous turn of events. Hannah waited and Margaret suddenly realized she was expected to say thank you for doing me this huge favor but she wouldn't say it because it would be a point for Roger and she knew what Roger did with his points. She announced that she, too, was going to take a nap and went upstairs, brushing past Hannah without a word.

She gave Rosie a kiss and stretched out on the bed, wide awake, with no thought of napping. Waiting for Roger to come up and rant at her some more. So that when he did come and begin ranting, she had a curious sense of displacement—as though she were screening a replay. He paced around the room saying pretty much what he'd said before only in sharper language and she stared at him as though he were a caged animal in the zoo, his anger no more caused by her than the animal's would be. *That* was it. That was what she was seeing that she'd never seen before: her own irrelevance to Roger's moods. Living together, just the two adults of you, it was easy to fall into that cliche—being mad *at each other*. And since so many of Roger's complaints about her mirrored her complaints about herself—her genuine or faked incomprehensions . . . her sometime fat . . . her suppressed anger . . . her need to mother—it had been easy to believe that these qualities angered him. Bearable to understand that his anger masked a dependence that made him need her to be a better person to fight against, i.e., to lean upon. Yet she was the same person now as she'd been before; why had those qualities which had disturbed Roger so much failed to irritate De Witt, who surely saw them as clearly as Roger did? Was it simply the lack of that chafing bond? No, because then the insanity of Mira, to whom he *was* tied, would have disturbed him more than it did. De Witt's vision was different, he didn't see other people as the reasons for his problems. Which brought her back to her final irrelevance, because the tides of Roger's anger had about as much to do with her as with his mother's menstrual cycle or the traffic patterns in Philadelphia. Less, probably.

He stopped. He stared at her.

"What's happened to you, Maggie?" His anger had evaporated; so it was true that it had been by mutual consent. "Don't you care about me any more?"

"I did last night."

"Just having sex, you mean?"

"I don't know if it was just that."

"Maybe I'm obsolete, now that I gave you your babies that you wanted."

"Then why would I like sex?"

"Maybe you just like sex with anyone."

"Maybe."

He looked out of the window. "I gave up smoking after you left."

"That's great."

"I had a sore throat and I got scared and I said to myself what kind of fucking stupid game am I playing, smoking the cigarettes and remembering the old throat thing, and I stopped. Just like that."

"Maybe it was good for you, too," she said. "Me going away."

"Maybe." He walked around the bed, looking down at the twins for a while, looked back at her. "You're not in love with someone else, are you?"

"The phrase gets in my way," she said. "The closest answer I can give is that I think there are a few people here I sort of love."

"De Witt?"

She nodded.

"That kid?"

She nodded.

"Who else?"

"A couple of the women. Starr. Dolores."

"You're not screwing around with women, are you?"

"No."

"How about the others?"

"I tried once with De Witt but it wasn't too good, I don't know why, I was full of guilt and my mind just . . . I don't know."

"And the kid?"

"David."

"All right. David."

She hesitated. "I came here with him. I met him on the road after I left. He knows the guy that owns the farm, it's—"

"De Witt doesn't own it?"

She shook her head. "He's a friend of De Witt's. He's David's stepfather, as a matter of fact. He's rich and he owns it but he only comes once in a while. I've never met him."

Roger laughed. "David's stepfather."

She nodded.

"So," he said, "you and little David are making it."

"I guess you could say that. We were. It didn't begin that way, I mean, you know the condition I was in, and anyway, it wasn't what he was looking for. He wanted someone to take care of him, you know, even now . . ." But she stopped herself. Even now half the time David didn't come. He would make love to her and she would come and come and then his erection would disappear and he would lie quietly inside her, and sometimes they would fall half asleep that way, but she couldn't tell all this to Roger, it would be disloyal, and besides it might be used against her or David at another more hostile time. "What I'm saying is, he's a very sad kid, very needy . . . He's upset that you've come and he can't sleep in this room."

146

"That's too fucking bad about him."

"I know, Roger," she said patiently. "I'm not asking you to let him."

"Am I supposed to be grateful?"

"I don't care if you are or not."

"I thought," he exploded, "we were talking like two adults for a change!"

"I thought so, too," she said.

"You don't sound like any goddamn adult to me . . . I don't care if you are or not," he mimicked, as though she'd said it spitefully.

She waited. Thinking how strange it was, he'd been so calm when they were talking about her love life and now here he was, furious over . . . over what? Choice of words? Her very minor declaration of independence from his moods? She started to say that all she'd meant was . . . Stopped herself. They'd both understood what she meant and she wasn't going to help along a tantrum by trying to soothe it.

"You're faking it!" he said when she was silent. "You must think I'm some kind of an idiot. You're pretending to be some kind of fucking Buddha saint and I know damn well you're the same hysterical insecure Margaret if I can crack that fucking façade!" He picked up a water glass from the night table and dropped it on the floor. She glanced at Rosie, who was staring at her father in fascination. The glass shattered into hundreds of pieces. Margaret didn't move. Rosie made no sound. In rapid succession Roger dropped everything else from the top of the dresser —her brush and comb, a pile of clean diapers, some dirty underwear, her sunglasses. Then he turned and stalked out of the room.

🌿 HANNAH convinced Roger that he would be a marvelous art teacher. In one corner of the schoolroom in the barn they made a series of simple two-frame easels and a separate worktable for clay. They spent a whole day in town buying art supplies. Hannah and Roger and Daisy and Mario. Hannah taught Mira how to do cuisenaire rods and first thing in the morning Mira worked on them with the younger kids and Hannah with Lorna and her own. Then Carol had improvisations with the younger kids while Roger had art with Daisy and Mario and a couple of the others. At first Carol had done a separate improvisation class with the older kids but Daisy and Mario had dropped out of it for some reason no one would discuss, although Margaret sensed that Carol was upset by it. In the afternoon they had cooking and weaving and indoor gardening and various other activities which were part of the normal life of the farm. Margaret was doing chores in the house and caring for the twins most mornings so she didn't see the class itself, but marvelous art work began to come out of the class and get hung on various walls and placed on shelves.

Margaret and Roger seldom fought because they made few serious attempts at communication. Sometimes they made love simply because they were two warm bodies in the same bed. David continued to sleep in the barn and generally refused to converse with her. She felt closer than ever to De Witt, understood that part of her new strength derived from his presence, yet she couldn't easily communicate with him because she perceived her problems to be not susceptible to solutions from the outside, even masterful ones. Once or twice she almost began conversations with De Witt with some words like, "De Witt, about Roger being the way he is and me being the way I am," but such a conversation had to be dishonest because she knew it would turn out with De Witt reassuring her about the kind of person she was, denying her complicity in the cancers of their marriage.

If she explained how right it had seemed until recently for them to be the way they were, for Roger to need her terribly and pick on her terribly, he would point out that one didn't need to pay indefinitely for one's mistakes, and she wasn't certain that was so. Besides, that attitude involved overlooking all the good things in their marriage, the sometime excitement, the sometime pleasure, the deep involvement that could never be lessened, only totally buried as it had been when she left him. She had pleasant talks with Starr and Dolores but nothing in their conversation ever made her want to bare her soul; she wasn't even sure what her soul consisted of. When you married someone who was visibly difficult, a large number of people were automatically willing to think the best of you, and many people thought her an awfully "nice" person because she had accomplished the balancing feat of staying married to Roger for several years, yet she knew now, had always known, really, that Roger was less her opposite than her flip side. That he fought old battles for both of them. All of which told her very little about herself nor was she sure she was ready to know more than she did. As a matter of fact, when she thought back now to her life since she'd left her parents' home it sometimes seemed that she'd dedicated herself to a series of activities whose virtue was to keep her too busy to find out if she existed at all, that is to say if she existed uniquely, if there was any one thing that could be said about her that couldn't be said of thousands of other women. And the farm, if you cared to look at it that way, had helped her to escape self-definition by providing her with casual friendships to avoid serious loneliness and a role to play so that she was too busy and tired to try to find out what loneliness was and whether you could accomplish things with loneliness that you couldn't with company.

Roger spent more and more time with Hannah. After art class they would come in for lunch, and then after lunch they would take Hannah's kids for walks, to town, to buzz around finding local handicrafts places, libraries, art galleries. Roger would gladly take Hannah and the kids to observe free schools a hundred miles away, see films at colleges that required a two or three hour drive, or buy some organic produce that the nearby natural foods store didn't have—although he'd always been utterly sarcastic about Margaret's fondness for seeds and nuts—bird food, he'd called them. Hannah often invited Margaret to accompany them but even when their trips didn't conflict with the twins' naps or some scheduled chore, she didn't like to go. She felt very much the outsider when she was with them and she was convinced that the problem was not just in her own mind. If they talked to Daisy and Mario as though the children were adults, they talked to Margaret as though she were some sort of harmless idiot stepchild, never scolding her for not knowing what was on their minds but explaining matters in a calm condescending way which, if she hadn't had other adults around treating her as an equal, would probably have driven her straight out of her mind. Once or twice De Witt or Jordan made some joke about Hannah, usually about her incredibly intense—suffocatingly close, destructively overbearing, were some of the expressions they used—relation to her children, but that part of Margaret that had demanded and never found an intensity in her own mother, the part that had wanted to be held close to the point of suffocation and then released with instructions about what to do next, that part always kept her silent when the others were being critical.

❧ As the mud season dried into something you could reasonably call spring, their pattern altered somewhat. In the morning Roger would be doing farmwork with the other men while Margaret did indoor or outdoor chores, keeping the twins with her. In the afternoon, after the twins' nap, Margaret would take the twins to wherever Roger and Hannah were, perhaps in the trailer or still in the garden, and then she would take a walk. Very often as she struck out on the path David would materialize alongside her, and together they would continue walking, sometimes staying on the road, other times exploring the woods. Looking for new leaves and buds and mushrooms. Occasionally talking, more often not. He was quieter these days, less prone to ranting about phonies he had to put up with or the injustices she had committed against him. Hannah's name still evoked incredible tirades on evil and women who thought they knew it all. Roger's name brought no similar negative response and at first she wondered if he was being circumspect.

"You never say anything against Roger," she pointed out one day.

"Why should I?" he asked.

"No should. I was just wondering."

Silence.

"Do you like Roger?"

He shrugged.

"I thought you'd blow up at some of the things he says, like calling you kid." *What are you recruiting for, Margaret?*

"It's natural for him to not like me," David pointed out calmly. "He knows I was balling his wife, doesn't he? I knew you'd tell him."

"He asked me."

"Mm."

"Anyway," she said defensively, "you haven't been . . . we haven't been since he came."

"That doesn't matter," he said. "I could if I wanted to."

"Why do you say that?" She was, she decided, offended.

"Because it's true."

Should she point out to him that the only time he'd tried, the night of Roger's arrival, she'd refused? It sounded so goddamn *petty.*

"Because," he went on as though reading her thoughts, "all I'd have to do would be threaten to hit the road or slash my wrists or something and you'd be all over me."

She stopped short. She would never fly again because her insides had been removed and her wings in all their true colors pinned to a board. Helplessly she stared at him in the bright sunlight; he looked a little older than he had when they'd come eight months ago, maybe just because he was. He'd lost a little more hair; Hannah had told him baldness was caused by an inositol deficiency and he'd told her to fuck off. He seemed taller or bigger or something but that was doubtless because she was slender now and had ceased to feel that she dwarfed humans. He was still attractive to her but the nature of the attraction had changed; what was strange was that it had changed in the same way as her relation to Roger. She loved them both but had a greater distance from them than before. She hadn't lost all sense of responsibility toward them but could recognize now the self-serving quality of that sense. She wasn't sure which was more frightening, David's ability to pinpoint her weakness or the possible loss of that weakness that had bound her so snugly to others. In her daydreams now of running naked along a beach somewhere in the Caribbean she was invariably running alongside De Witt or some other grown-up type and sometimes they weren't even holding hands!

She took a deep breath. "David, there is some justice in what you say. On the other hand . . ." On the other hand, what? "Things happen. To people, I mean. People change."

He spat on the ground.

"You don't believe people change." *You're still the same goddamn hysterical insecure Margaret.*

"You think you're a big fucking hippie because you spent eight months in a commune?"

"No. I don't think that."

"Then what do you think?"

"I don't think anything, David. I just feel a little different than I did before."

"Maybe you should have a checkup."

"And maybe you're jealous." She'd said it without thinking and he turned on her in fury.

"You've got no fucking right to talk to me that way!"

"You talk to *me* that way, David."

"It's different."

"Why?"

"Because that's not the way you are!"

"Maybe I am," she said. "Maybe there's no law that says I always have to be Mother Earth and you're the Bad Seed."

In a rage he grabbed hold of her shoulders and began to shake her and shake her until she began struggling to get free, but then his hands only dug deeper into her arms. She kicked his shins but that made him dig deeper and

153

shake harder and finally she fell backward with him on top of her. When she tried to push him up he pressed into her with all his might and came down on her lips with his teeth, biting so cruelly that she could feel them swell before he'd even let go.

"Jesus Christ, David," she moaned, feeling blood trickle down from her lip, "we're right on the road." She was crying, which prevented her from getting up her full strength to struggle. He began groping at her jeans. She tried using her legs to push back off the road but all that happened was that her sweater rode up and she scratched her back on the dirt and rocks. She began banging at him with her fist but he was on top and he was stronger and she not only had an uphill fight against him but also against the part of her that was very excited and wanted him in her, wanted to salvage some pleasure out of this filthy, gruesome situation, wanted him to force her body to make love with him when her mind had refused to let her do it since Roger's arrival. And of course that part of her won because it had David helping, and so they made love mindlessly, passionately on the hard dirt road, tangled in their own and each other's unbuttoned clothes, stopping and resting without separating, then starting again, until they were spent. And then, as she lay exhausted on the ground, David got up, pulled up his pants, zipped his fly, pulled down his bright blue sweater, said, "So long," and headed for the highway.

DAZED, unable to believe that he'd meant it the way it sounded, that he was disappearing from her life, she lay on the road until the heat had died inside her and she began to feel cold. Then she wearily pulled herself up, straightened out her clothes, brushed her tangled hair back from her face, and walked back to the farm with slow, unwilling steps. Hannah was sitting on the steps of the trailer, reading. Amazingly Roger wasn't with her. She looked up as Margaret passed and registered horror.

"Margaret! What happened?"

Margaret stood lamely looking for an answer. Hannah told her to come into the trailer, saying she couldn't let the babies see her like that. Obediently Margaret followed her inside, let herself be made comfortable half-reclining on one of the bunk beds. Hannah put up some water for tea and then sat on the bunk bed facing Margaret's.

"Do you want to talk?" she asked softly. "Don't unless you want to." Her manner was extraordinarily—Margaret felt, *deeply*—sympathetic. Seductive to Margaret, in her depressed and helpless condition. There was none of that toughness and stridency that put one off sometimes in the group, there was only warmth and compassion in those limpid eyes. Margaret began to cry. Hannah moved over, put an arm around her, hugged her. Margaret kept crying. Hannah made tea and brought her a cup; gratefully she sipped at it. Hannah sat at the little table in the kitchen end, waiting.

"It's David," Margaret finally said. "We had . . . a bad fight. I think he's left for good."

155

"Didn't you expect him to go sooner or later? They always do."

"I don't know," Margaret said. "I guess I didn't think about it much. I have a thing about . . . I hate to see people disappear forever."

"You don't leave yourself any margin for error that way," Hannah said. "You have to be careful who you say hello to because anyone you say hello to you might have around your neck for the rest of your life. Everyone should turn in their friends for new ones a few times a year."

Margaret smiled.

"Why do people think I'm kidding when I'm being serious?" Hannah asked.

"I guess because there's something extreme . . . I can't believe half the time that you mean what you're saying."

"But I always do," Hannah said. "Even when I know it sounds crazy or it's only partly true."

Roger came in without knocking, told Hannah he'd left the girls sitting in the grass, saw Margaret, stopped. Grinned.

"How does the other guy look?"

"Jesus," Hannah said, "what a time for dirty jokes."

"My wife's appearance," Roger said, "is a dirty joke."

"There's a certain implication there that I don't like," Hannah said slowly. "As though Margaret did it to herself."

"What difference does it make," Roger demanded, "if she did it to herself or that psychopathic little bastard she screws around with did it to her?"

"I think it makes a big difference," Hannah said. Margaret leaned back in the bunk bed like some tiny UN protectorate at a Security Council debate. "You're reminding me of all those Freudian bullshit artists who convinced the public that a woman who was raped must have gone out of her way to get it. Not that I want to give this thing sexual undertones."

"Overtones."

"Whatever."

"And furthermore, you don't have to give it anything, it's there. It's always there."

"You don't really believe that."

A hostile note, previously absent, had crept into the conversation.

"Damn right I do. If there's a male and a female in a room there's sex in that room. It may be good and it may be bad and it may be perverted and it may be repressed or any other bloody thing, but it's there."

"Oh, wow," Hannah said, shaking her head, at once sad, hip and lofty, "I wish I'd known what was on your mind when we were having those long marvelous talks about art and education."

"Don't worry about it, Hannah Banana," Roger said, "you knew all right. Same thing as yours."

"One thing I will not stand for," Hannah said angrily, "is having someone tell me what's on my mind."

"Or theirs," Roger suggested.

Margaret was beginning to think the day would end better than it had begun.

Hannah was upset—and terribly wary, as though she were going through a scene she'd lived many times before.

"You seemed so straight to me, Roger. So open and honest."

"That's me," Roger said. "Open and honest."

"You never made a pass at me."

"I was saving it. A special treat. For your birthday or something."

"Very funny."

"I'm serious."

Hannah shook her head. "I didn't figure you for the kind of guy that's got to perpetually prove he has balls."

"You really think that's the only reason for having sex?" Roger asked sardonically. "To prove something?"

"No," Hannah said, undeterred by his manner. "There's having children."

Margaret searched the other woman's face for a hint of irony but there was none; Roger was openmouthed.

"I begin to perceive the problem," he said finally. "It's not that you hate men it's just that you hate sex."

"Why is that my problem?" Hannah asked. "If you wanna make me and I hate sex, that's *your* problem."

It gave Roger pause.

"You mean to say that you know you hate sex?"

Hannah nodded.

"What do you hate about it?" he asked curiously.

"The way it feels," Hannah said calmly. "When I'm getting fucked I feel as though I'm getting fucked."

Was this one of those times when she believed what she was saying even though it was only partly true? Of all the sexual confessions Margaret had seen, read or heard unsolicited from a variety of people over the years she could recall no simple declaration of distaste like this one. Her own experiences had run the gamut from extreme pleasure to moderate pain, the distinguishing difference, aside from the physical feeling, being that in the pleasure extreme her mind was disengaged while it dominated when sex was bad. Once when Roger was on acid which she'd refused to take he'd become extremely quietly loving to her. Smiling, never speaking, he'd led her outdoors to their shrub-enclosed back yard, where under the leafy umbrella of a beautiful dogwood tree he had undressed her, then himself, and they had lain looking at the stars through the foliage. The mosquitoes found them but when she complained to Roger that she was being eaten alive and wanted to go indoors he rolled over on top of her and in a manner at once graceful and deliberate covered every part of her body with his own, then made love to her in a tender all-encompassing way. And some strange, kinky, warped thing inside her had responded by feeling claustrophobic and resentful. He was trying to make her believe there was only one of them. He was all over her and now he wanted to be in her, too. And as he touched as far inside her as he could go she'd felt a sharp pain. She was suspicious of the idea that her pain had been physical, it seemed more likely that she was reacting to the violation of some metaphysical air space. A space she'd thought of herself as perpetually trying to fill.

"Are you sure it isn't just that you never had the right guy?"

"You don't really think it matters, do you?" Hannah replied. "I mean if you hate swimming what difference does it make if you're in a pool or a lake?"

There was something wrong with the metaphor but Margaret couldn't put her finger on it.

"How about stoned?" Roger asked.

"I don't like the way being stoned feels, either," Hannah said.

"Far out," Roger said softly.

"I know what she means," Margaret said. "I mean I don't always want to feel the way I feel when I'm stoned." Copping out on the larger question.

"That isn't what I really meant, though," Hannah said. "What I meant is that I don't feel the *need* to be stoned."

"Maybe you could enjoy sex if you got stoned," Roger said.

"But I don't *want* to enjoy sex," Hannah said calmly. "Sex is just another dependency thing."

Roger whistled. A long drawn-out whistle. Then he said, "Come on, Maggie, let's get out of here."

Did he know how it sounded? Hannah's expression didn't alter but her frame seemed to sag. Had there been any actual change or was Margaret touched by the other woman's fear of being in need? Half-willingly she got up, said to Hannah, "See you later," and followed Roger outside, only now feeling again the cuts and bruises David had inflicted on her. Her legs were Charley-horsed, as after a dance class. She couldn't keep up with Roger as he strode across the yard to where the twins were sitting happily in the grass, watching the birds and cats and playing with gravel.

"The little creep really worked you over, didn't he," Roger said when she reached him. It was hostile but it was also friendly.

"He's gone," she said. "I think for good."

"Too bad," Roger said. "If I knew then what I know now I'd have matched up the two of them, they're both out of their skulls."

So he was willing to be her friend now if they could step together blithely over the bodies of Creepy David and Crazy Hannah.

"I don't know about Hannah," she said, "but David isn't crazy."

"Right," Roger said. "He's just this sweet little kid who goes around beating up on people."

"He beat me up because he was furious with me." *For not loving him enough to make up for his inability to love me.*

"And you loved it."

"No. I don't think so."

"Maybe I could do it better."

She smiled, which made her lip hurt like hell. "That's practically the same thing you said to Hannah. Maybe I haven't had the right guy."

"Very funny."

"It is. And I guess I could give you the same answer. If I don't like how it feels what difference does it make who's doing it?"

"She really spooked me."

"She spooked De Witt at first. He figured out she scared him because she refused to need him."

"Oh, shit, what are you, shilling for the sisterhood?"

"What I'm trying to say is that part of me empathized with what she was saying."

"So?"

"So I thought I ought to say so."

"Why?"

"Because it would've been dishonest to pretend I had no idea of what she was talking about just for the sake of not arguing with you. You used to accuse me of being dishonest."

He grinned. "But I got accustomed to it."

"It doesn't matter," she said, "because I'm doing it . . . arguing with you, whatever I'm doing, being honest . . . out of my own needs, not yours."

"What makes you think I give a shit for your needs?"

"You're married to me."

"I married you to fill *my* needs, not yours."

"It must be possible to fill your own needs and not forget other people's entirely."

He laughed. "What if one of my needs is to forget about yours?"

"Then," she said, calmly and with no forethought, "maybe we shouldn't be married."

He blanched. Or so she fancied.

"At least," she said, "maybe we should think about it."

"I don't want to think about it," he said. "You think about it and let me know what you decide." He went into the house. She hobbled after him. He went upstairs and she followed him up, pushing into the room just before he could slam the door in her face.

"Roger," she said, "I don't want you to think this is something I've been thinking about because it isn't. It just came out when you said you didn't want to think about my needs."

161

"Okay. So it came out. I did say it and it did come out. So do you want to get a divorce and get it over with?"

"I don't think of it as something to get over with. I haven't even been thinking of it at all. I don't even feel the *need* for it. There are people here who care about me and my needs so it hasn't been so important."

"Right," Roger said. "You don't need me at all. If you want someone to kiss your ass and worry about how happy you are, stick with De Witt."

She stared at him, surprised and confused.

"De Witt doesn't kiss my ass, Roger."

"Sure he does," Roger said promptly. "He's just such a technician of other people's asses that you don't even notice."

She was about to tell him he was talking nonsense when she remembered, suddenly and vividly, her brief motel interlude with De Witt, when her body hadn't been able to be convinced by her mind that De Witt really lusted for her.

"Making love to somebody," she blurted out, then paused, disconcerted, ". . . being nice to somebody in different ways . . . isn't the same as kissing their ass."

"It is if there's nothing that's really moving you to do it, if you're doing it because *they* want it."

She couldn't answer that. "I'll have to think about it." She was getting a headache and all her cuts and bruises were asserting themselves. "I don't know if it's true . . . or if it applies here." She left him and went downstairs.

De Witt had just brought into the kitchen the large graph-paper chart on which he would plot the planting. The peas, beans, spinach and lettuce were already in the ground and beginning to sprout; in another week or so they would sow the seeds for some of the less hearty crops and then, by the second week in June when frost danger was past, they would transfer to the outdoors the tomatoes, cucumbers and eggplants that had been brought to the cold frame from the greenhouse to harden off. She sat down facing De Witt, who was spreading the charts but then looked up and saw her bruised face.

"Margaret!" He stood up and came around to her. "What's happened to you?"

"It's David," she said. "He had a fit."

"Wait a minute. That lip needs some ice." He got some cubes and wrapped them in a dishtowel then brought back the compress, sat down next to her on the bench, one arm around her, and with the other hand placed the compress on her lip and held it there. She felt a wave of sexual gratitude.

*This is not ass-kissing, goddammit! This is being a good person!*

She leaned her head on De Witt's shoulder. "I think he's gone for good."

"David? Was this his farewell present?"

"Something like that."

"I'm sorry." He kissed her forehead. She put down the compress and he took her cold hands between his warm ones.

"I know what I must look like," she said.

Very, very lightly he kissed the swollen middle of her lip. Very, very lightly she licked his lips. He smelled of rotted hay and cow manure, both of which smells struck her at the moment as being sensual in the extreme.

"De Witt," she said, "did I ever tell you that Mitchell was David's stepfather?"

"No," De Witt said. "I don't believe you did. I've wondered from time to time how he happened to find us."

"De Witt, do you think there was something about my relationship with David that made this practically inevitable? I mean, do you think in some way I may have been asking for it?"

"No, of course not," De Witt said. "Why should I think that?"

"I don't know. There's something that seems right about it, in some awful sort of way."

"It only seems right if you believe that people who do good things deserve to be kicked in the teeth."

Was he defending her or himself? Damn Roger for leaving his drops of poison in her mind.

"I was nasty to him today," she said. "I mean not exactly nasty but it was the first time I really talked to him the way he talked to me."

"Good," De Witt said, stroking her arm with his encircling arm, her hair with his other hand.

"He said I had no right to be that way. That he and I were—well, what he was saying essentially was that I was violating the nature of our relationship. That I'd always been giving and loving, however he'd been, and it wasn't fair for me to suddenly change."

"Do you believe that?"

"Well, I understand what he meant."

"Maybe he meant that he was jealous that you were capable of change and he wasn't."

She looked at him wonderingly. "That's exactly what I accused him of, being jealous. That's when he got so mad."

He smiled. "Okay, then. What's our next problem?"

"De Witt," she said, "don't ever leave me."

"I won't," he said tenderly. "I promise you that, Margaret. If I ever leave here, you can come with me."

Tears welled in her eyes. "I really love you, De Witt."

"I love you, too, Margaret."

There were footsteps on the stairs; she froze. Then there was Roger's voice.

"Get the fuck away from my wife, you fucking motherfucker."

De Witt released her gently, swung around on the bench to face Roger.

"It seems to me," he said mildly, "that you want all the

164

privileges of the extended family but you don't want Margaret to have them."

"You don't think I'm going to argue with you and your fucking idiot lingo, do you?"

"Now you sound just like David," De Witt said. "You can say whatever comes into your mind but nobody can talk back."

"Listen, you pimp—"

"Roger," Margaret interrupted, "he was comforting me because I was upset and you wouldn't!"

"Why the hell should I?" he shouted. "It was my wife getting fucked by that crazy little bastard, not his!"

"I wasn't fucking him!" she shouted back. "Not after you came! And what if I was? You've been fucking around yourself, you'd have had Hannah, if she could be had."

"She can be had, all right," De Witt muttered.

"And when I think back," she went on, too furious to pay attention to De Witt, "to the number of girls you've had since I knew you—"

"I never gave all those girls put together," Roger shouted at the top of his lungs, his face bright red with rage, "the love you gave that lousy kid in one day! ! ! !"

She was dumbstruck. By what? By the truth? By Roger's perception of it? By her own failure to perceive it before? De Witt was watching her. Roger, seeing her reaction, was calming down. Outside the kitchen window at least one of the twins was crying. How long had that been going on unnoticed? She couldn't relate to it.

De Witt said, "You're trying to penalize Margaret for being a more loving person than you are."

Roger said, "If I tried to give you an intelligent answer you'd think I was interested in talking to you."

De Witt said, "You should be, we live in the same house."

Roger was silent.

"We've been sort of walking around each other," De Witt said. "Not arguing but never being friends, either."

"So what?"

De Witt shrugged, "There must be more to be gained for both of us."

"What if I don't like you?"

De Witt's expression didn't change but it seemed to Margaret that he was hurt. "Then I think you should tell me why."

"Okay," Roger said, "Sure I'll tell you. You see, I disagree completely with Hannah's idea of you. Hannah thinks, you know, you're a fraud, some kind of dark, menacing power freak who's only being nice in exchange for control of the situation."

De Witt smiled, nodded.

"But I think you're just what you seem to be. Bland. Eager to please. Catering to other people's emotions. A fucking caterer to the emotions, never getting mad because people wouldn't like it."

"I don't think that's fair," De Witt said slowly. "Although it's true that I seldom get angry."

"But Roger has trouble getting anything *but* angry," Margaret said. Aching for De Witt.

De Witt smiled. "Then maybe it's an attraction of opposites."

"On *your* part, maybe," Roger said to him.

"All right," De Witt said. "On my part."

Silence. Outside the babies were still crying.

"What do the poor kids have to do?" Roger asked her. "Scream out their lungs before you go find out what's wrong?"

Reluctantly Margaret went out. Rue had apparently eaten some dirt and choked it up; she was practically purple with rage, and Rosie was crying along with her, in sympathy. Guilt stricken, Margaret picked up Rue, who continued sobbing uncontrollably, although Rosie, watching, stopped. Margaret paced around the yard with Rue until the crying had slowed down somewhat, then she sat down in the grass with Rue in her lap; Rosie nestled alongside. The yard was alive with activity. Paul and Jordan were repairing the chicken coop. Hannah was showing some people around the grounds; she seemed in good spirits. One of the alternatives bulletins had listed them as having a school and for several weeks they'd been having visitors at least all weekend. They turned away people who phoned first, requesting that they wait until planting time was over, but most of them found it difficult to be rude to any reasonably decent human being who showed up in person, however inconvenient his presence might be. Finally, by tacit consent of the group, Hannah, who was so ingratiating with strangers, had been given the job of greeting people and answering their questions. Most people asked questions about the nature of life at the farm and Hannah was the only one who could answer because she was the only one who was convinced that her answers wouldn't turn out to be irrelevant. How things worked had more to do with how you perceived them to work, how you made them work, than with anyone else's idea of the order of things. Only Hannah could assure people, straight-faced and utterly believable, that there were no emotional difficulties at the farm because they didn't have the time and energy to waste on fighting, and then point out that besides they didn't eat white bread and all that shit that poisoned people's minds. At the beginning, some types would do a double take on that one, but by the time she tripped off on the use of niacin to cure schizophrenia, no one seemed to think that she was kidding—or should be. The women in particular seemed to take to Hannah and often she would get letters saying it had proved impossible for someone to move up for economic or other reasons but the writer did hope that Hannah would visit sometime with her children.

What was going on inside? She'd been sitting outside for almost half an hour and no one had come in or out of the house. It was true that Roger got angry on the rare occasions when she let the twins cry, but it was also true that he'd seemed glad of the excuse to get rid of her. She decided the twins were probably thirsty, anyway, so she would bring them into the kitchen for some milk or juice. Rosie was drinking from a cup all the time now and Rue was doing it during the day. Rue could make it up the steps now, but Margaret carried Rosie. If there was an argument going on, she couldn't hear it from the outside, although she listened for a minute before cautiously opening the front door.

Sounds of quiet activity throughout the house reached her ears. From the crafts room came the hum of the sewing machine, from the kitchen the sound of the oven door being closed. It was late afternoon but the house was still full of daylight. The smell of freshly baked bread dominated but other good smells, soup or stew as well as something sweet, like baking fruit, were combining with it. She put down Rosie and went into the kitchen. Starr was muttering over the stewpot. And at the long table, sitting facing each other and chatting with an easy intimacy that suggested they'd been in telepathic communication for years, were Roger and De Witt.

So that was why he'd wanted her out of the way, he hadn't wanted her to see him capitulating to De Witt's friendliness! He waved her away when she tried to approach them. Resentfully she went into the other room. How like Roger, having decided he could tolerate De Witt after all, to eliminate her from the friendship.

"Roger," she asked later, "what did De Witt say that made you change your mind about him?"

"I didn't change my mind about him," Roger said. "I think the same thing as I thought before, I changed my mind about the way I *feel* about that."

"You mean you're compatible because you're so different."

Roger nodded.

"Why didn't you want me there?"

"We were talking business."

"So?"

"Women can't talk business without dragging a lot of other stuff into it."

"What kind of business?"

"Making the farm self-sustaining. De Witt has a feeling Mitchell wants to get out. Whenever they talk on the phone lately Mitchell bitches about money. He's having trouble with conservation groups over one of his paper company's forests, and so on. Higher taxes."

"You mean you want to buy the farm?"

"Yup."

"Does De Witt have any money?"

"Nope."

"How could you manage it? Your income might cover a mortgage but—"

"By selling the house in Hartsdale, to begin with."

"Wait a minute." It was an automatic reaction. Exactly the words she'd used when she got the phone call about her mother. *Stop and let's go back a few minutes to when it wasn't too late.*

"You see what I mean?" Roger said triumphantly. "You're in a panic already."

"This isn't just business you're talking, Roger," she pointed out. "This is my life!"

"*That* house?" Roger said sarcastically. "*That* town? You're kidding me."

She shook her head. She'd never liked the house or the town. But they were a bridge to the past and she didn't like to burn bridges behind her. If you burned too many bridges you became just like those neighbors who frightened you so, the bright-eyed corporation wives ready on a minute's notice to collapse the contents of their lives and transport them on to Texas, New Jersey, Detroit, San Juan. To the next Newcomers' Club, Brownies Troop, Cancer Drive, Book 'n' Bake Sale. If their husband's timing was right they could bake the same cake each year in a different village of the damned and then move on to the next one, knowing that the body of some other corporation engineer's wife would appear to inhabit their home, their spot, their life.

She began to cry.

"Oh, shit," Roger said. "How did I know this would happen?"

"I know it makes sense, Roger. I'm not saying it doesn't make sense to sell it."

*"You're* what doesn't make sense."

"I know, I know." Tearful. "Why couldn't we rent it furnished?"

"What would that solve? Where would we get a down payment? As it is we might have to take back the mortgage."

"I think I'm scared of the idea of committing ourselves to this place."

"Selling the house doesn't commit us to anything but getting out of Hartsdale."

"Well, that's just it, maybe," she said, feeling dishonest. "I need to feel committed *to* something, not just to getting out of something."

"I thought you were crazy about this place."

"I *am*, but . . ." But what? The tears stopped. *But what?* But she wasn't so sure, now that there was this change in their relations with De Witt? Now that she would no longer have De Witt's automatic support in her life battle with Roger? No, it was more than that. The truth was that while she'd had vague thoughts of De Witt in terms of the future, she'd never really thought of the farm as anything more than a refuge from her marriage. Just as De Witt had said—it existed for her in contrast, and she was no more ready to abandon her real life than Marie Antoinette had been about to abandon the court at Versailles for the aprons and milk buckets she was fond of playing with. The steady routine, the lack of mental stimulation, the absence of stores, neon lights and traffic, of all those city nuisances that somehow served to keep your blood pressure from getting sluggish and your brain from turning into uncrunchy Granola, if she was frightened by De Witt's vision of movement as salvation, she was no less frightened at the thought of giving up more or less permanently those urban qualities, positive and negative, that made life seem much more interesting than it really was. In New York apocalypse seemed little more than an extension of everyday reality while up here you could picture yourself in another few years waiting for *anything* that would break up the monotony. "I love it here, Roger. But saying that isn't saying that I could stand to live here forever. Stay on a farm and milk goats and grow vegetables and all that with no change."

"There's no law we'd have to do that," Roger pointed out. "Why would we be any more limited to this place than we were limited to Hartsdale?"

"A farm is a lot more work than a house."

"There's a lot more people to do it."

"We'd be able to go places?" Quaveringly. "Together? Maybe take a vacation and go to Europe?"

Roger laughed. "You never wanted to go to Europe." This was true. She was frightened of airplanes and convinced she would get seasick. "I used to talk about going back to Paris and you never wanted to get off your ass and do it."

"I know," she said. "But when I think about living here, Europe seems different."

Roger rumpled her hair fondly. "At the rate you're going in another five years of country you'll be a reasonably sophisticated human being."

❦ A letter from Roger's mother.

June 7th, 1970

Dearest Roger:

I have your little note of June 3rd. At least I imagine it was written on or about the 3rd. I do wish you would remember to date your notes, dear, it makes filing so much easier.

It was pleasant to learn that you and Margaret and the twins are in good health. We look forward to a time when you will visit with us as we are naturally anxious to see our grandchildren.

Now about the money, dear, I have something to say which I fear will come as a shock to you. I have instructed Mr. Leddington to withhold your allowance until such time as you choose to return to a decent home and a normal way of life, such as it is. I realize that this is a much more drastic step than we took when you made your disastrous first "match," when we only refused to pay the exorbitant bills we were frequently sent. The reason for this is that I have been seeing a psychiatrist, a kind

and brilliant man named Dr. Pfensig, who
has convinced me that your difficulties
stem from my failure to be firm with you,
to use the authority which he says is available to every parent. Dr. Pfensig says that
I am so in awe of your intelligence that I
have refused to influence you or to inculcate
you with our values as every parent should
do.

 Well, dear, better late than never. I am
withholding your allowance to express my
disapproval of the way those people live.
They are dirty, they are sex fiends and they
take drugs. Please let me know when you
have returned home so that I can instruct
Mr. Leddington to resume your allowance.

Your loving mother,
*Sarah Adams*

Roger's face was a playground for astonishment, hilari-
ty and rage. He would reread some line, like *they are
dirty, they are sex fiends and they take drugs,* and begin to
laugh and then stop abruptly and mutter furiously, "The
fucking idiot, goddammit, the fucking idiot." Or he would
read *I have instructed Mr. Leddington to withhold your
allowance* with fury but then begin to howl at her refusal
to refer to his first wife by name, or at the name of the
doctor, or *inculcate you with our values.* But then finally
he could only repeat over and over in a tone of ironic awe,
*Well, dear, better late than never.*

He stared at the letter. "Menopause. Or maybe she's
trying to kick Mr. Boston."

Roger's mother was a secret drinker who kept bottles of
Old Mr. Boston whiskey in her dresser drawers, shoe bags
and so on.

They were lying in the pasture, having spent most of the

morning tilling and removing the rocks from the land for the tender crops, which were ready to go in. De Witt had brought the mail from town. Paul had mown the pasture for the first time that spring and the smell of the damp, cut grass was sweet and powerful. Rosemary sat nearby, grabbing handfuls of the grass, stuffing them into her mouth then spitting them out. Tiring of the game she would watch Rue, who was gamboling fearlessly around the soft pasture land, once in a while stopping to pick some grass and dump it on Roger or Margaret. It was a clear bright day. A perfect jewel of a day. All the more precious because it couldn't last; tomorrow it would get warmer or moister or colder or something you didn't want it to do.

"On a day like this," she said, "it seems impossible to think of ever leaving here." Maybe it was that she'd been resigning herself to staying, anyway. There were really good things to be said for the idea. De Witt and Roger stayed up late into each night now, talking, and while she was jealous, she understood how good it was for Roger's mind to be working on something concrete. When he really got going on some job, whether it was a film or sculpture or whatever, he became quite a different person; the dissatisfaction, the intensity, the restlessness, the ironic fantasies got channeled into what he was doing and life became easy and pleasant.

"Don't worry," Roger said. "We're not leaving." He stared at the letter. "The fucking idiot."

Also, the letter from Roger's mother had given the farm the extra appeal of being difficult or impossible to achieve. Roger had arranged for brokers in Hartsdale to show the house but that could take ages. They had no idea of what Mitchell was going to ask for the farm. He'd picked it up for a pittance, something like eight thousand dollars, seventeen years before, but it was unlikely that this would be a factor; he was a businessman, after all, and the worth of

174

the farm and the adjoining acreage, which he also owned, had multiplied geometrically several times since.

"What are you going to do?" she asked.

"Obviously," Roger said, "we're going to have to go to Philadelphia and talk to the idiot."

"We?" Her heart sank. In Philadelphia she always felt as though she'd been embalmed a moment before dying.

He nodded. "All of us."

They looked at the twins. Rosie had fallen asleep near them; Rue had finally stopped reeling around and was pulling apart some daisies.

*Children, you are about to be manipulated for financial gain.*

She sighed. "It seems like such a . . . yicch thing to have to do."

"Mmm," Roger said. "Well, they'll never know the difference."

"Do we have to go right away?" she asked, her stomach already twisting with dread.

"No," Roger said, "we'll wait until we talk to Mitchell. He's coming up for the weekend of the Fourth."

Mitchell is coming in a few weeks. Mitchell and David's mother. *David's mother.* How was she supposed to talk to David's mother? Better not to think about it. Not to try to plan. *Oh, God, David's mother!*

HANNAH left under odd circumstances. She'd been depressed and withdrawn from the day of the incident with Roger. She'd attempted to maintain some sort of friendly contact with Margaret but the way she'd done it was by suggesting that together they'd been victimized by Roger and De Witt, a ploy which turned Margaret off because a) it was ridiculous and b) she felt that way herself. At the beginning of what was supposed to be the last week of school Hannah and Mira had a terrific row, or rather Hannah was terribly upset and railed furiously at Mira, who gritted her teeth and otherwise maintained a posture of benevolent condescension. As closely as anyone could tell—for Mira was charitably silent and Hannah immediately hitched up the trailer and took off—Hannah was upset because Lorna and Baba had been persecuting her children. Or rejecting them. Whichever was the greater. Hannah had a tendency to think that any child in an argument with her children's united front was persecuting them both but in this case, because of Daisy and Mario's greater age, size and sophistication, it seemed particularly ludicrous. Still, someone had seen Mario running to the trailer in tears with Daisy following languidly behind, and a moment later Hannah had burst out of the trailer, nearly crying herself, looking for Mira. Only Carol had mixed feelings about her departure; even Carol had grown weary of the heavy trip Hannah laid on her friends but she couldn't help regretting, she said sadly, the magnificent Hannah that could have been.

MITCHELL and Becky were coming Friday morning. Roger spent a couple of days checking out real estate in the area so they'd have some basis for negotiating with

Mitchell. There was a strange tense feeling in the house. Mira was going around cleaning and double cleaning after everyone else. Starr was saying they didn't have to put on any goddamn show for anyone; what she was doing instead was making it a point not to do her regular chores, which refusal De Witt accepted with a smile on the grounds of temporary insanity, which Mitchell's visits often brought on. Paul and Jordan, it turned out, both entertained an inordinate hatred for Mitchell, and they disappeared without saying when they'd be back. Friday morning passed into afternoon and the visitors hadn't come.

Margaret was upstairs when the wine-red Aston-Martin, the only one she'd ever seen outside of a James Bond movie, pulled into the yard. Nobody had told her in advance about the car although there'd been some veiled jokes, and now the effect of the thing, flipping into the farm like a clerical error from another time dimension, was mind-blowing. Everything around it looked ten times as dilapidated as it had before as the car slid into the space between their shabby pickup truck and the weathered old barn, like some radiant, placid, space-age animal waiting to be milked. A large man and a small girl got out. Or was it a woman? It was hard to tell from the bedroom window; the shape was womanly but the ambiance was very young. It couldn't be David's mother. It *couldn't* be. Carol and De Witt came across the yard and hugged the visitors. Margaret sat down numbly on the bed. She'd been feeling nervous and defensive about meeting David's mother but the doll-like figure in the courtyard wasn't the person she'd felt defensive toward. Now she didn't know *how* she felt except that her heart was beating rather rapidly and she felt a strong reluctance to go downstairs. The twins were both napping. Margaret stretched out on the bed and closed her eyes but she was fully awake and the tension of

177

trying to force her lids to stay shut began to hurt her eyes. She got up, combed her hair and wove it into one long neat braid, then went downstairs.

They were all in the common room, chatting pleasantly. De Witt got up and came over to her, put his arm around her.

"This is Margaret," he said. "Who I've been telling you about." His manner was just stiff enough to tell her that even he was not entirely at ease. "I was talking about David," he said to her. "Telling Becky how you took care of him while he was here."

She nodded but she couldn't talk. She felt as though she'd eaten a can of anchovies. She smiled feebly. Becky Kastle sat near Mira, drinking iced tea and eating strawberries and yoghurt. She was very pretty. She looked about twenty-five years old.

"We eat so much better here than we do in the city," Becky said. It was one of the standard *turista* lines; they'd all gotten accustomed to the implied condescension in it; the marvel was that the Kastles, with their close ties to the farm, should still seem such tourists on it.

"Mmmmm," Mitchell said, buttering a piece of bread. "We should send Pierre up here for some lessons."

Mitchell was a pleasantly surrealistic-looking man, about six feet tall, built or evolved in the form of a Koke-shi doll, with half a head of silky black hair and the face of a cherub salesman who was his own best customer.

Becky giggled. "Pierre's our chef. It's against his religion to cook anything with less than half a pound of butter."

"How my wife keeps her figure is another story," Mitchell said.

His manner was jovial but his eyes were strangely evasive—as though he had to keep moving them away from you because it would be inconvenient for you to perceive his intelligence.

178

"Can I talk to you about David?" Becky asked Margaret.

*No.*

She nodded.

"How long was he actually here?"

Margaret tried to answer but nothing came out.

"Quite a while, actually," De Witt said, rescuing her. "And he did very well, too. Participated in the group work, and so on. About half a year, I'd say. I'm not sure he could have done it without Margaret's support."

"Thank you, Margaret," Becky said with apparent sincerity. "He needs someone to take care of him, whether he knows it or not."

*He knows it all right.* She wanted to cry. She'd thought about David rather less than she'd expected to in the weeks since his departure but when she did think about him it was like rubbing an open wound. Sometimes the wound was that he'd quickly found someone else and sometimes it was guilt that he was terribly alone, but it hurt either way.

Roger came in and De Witt introduced him to the Kastles. He was civil. Not at all flirtatious with Becky. A sure barometer of his interest in the farm, for he never failed to flirt with any good-looking woman unless his mind was fully engaged in some project. They talked for a while in a roundabout way.

"Mitchell is finding the farm rather more of a burden than he can manage easily, with the new tax structures," De Witt said to Roger.

"That's his subtle way of saying I'm broke," Mitchell announced jovially.

Flash to the Aston-Martin in the yard. Once upon a time in Hartsdale she'd known a lot of people who could have a chef and a couple of cars and complain about being broke. They'd never made her terribly angry because she

179

was rich herself but she was sure that without money she would have been infuriated.

"So how much do you want?" Roger asked laconically.

Mitchell laughed. "You're taking my breath away." To De Witt he said, "I didn't really want to do it this way, De Witt, but it's getting to be too much for me. I've really *seriously* thought about coming up here permanently but even if I could swing it, this life isn't for Becky."

"Of course," De Witt said sympathetically. "I understand perfectly."

"You do? Jesus, I'm glad of that. I've been worried, one thing I didn't want was to—"

"So how much?" Roger repeated.

Mitchell whistled.

Silence.

"With or without the land?" he finally said.

"Both," Roger replied.

"I really didn't want to do it this way," Mitchell said to De Witt. "So cut and dried. I'm not forgetting the work you've put in here, or the rest of it. I don't want to screw you, De Witt . . . I'd give it to you for much less than I'd put it on the market for."

"How much is that?" Roger asked.

"Look here," Mitchell said irritably, "I have nothing against you but this is between De Witt and me."

De Witt smiled. "It's okay, Mitchell," he said. "I appreciate what you're doing but I don't have any money."

"I'm not asking that much."

"I mean I have none."

"None?" He seemed unbelieving.

"None." De Witt was still smiling. "That is to say, about four hundred dollars."

"What are you living on?" Incredulous.

"You, primarily."

"But I just pay for the farm."

"What other expenses do I have?"

"Jesus, I dunno!" Mitchell was flabbergasted. "Food, clothes, entertainment, medical expenses, taxes . . . EX-PENSES!"

"Well," De Witt said patiently, "as far as food goes, the farm provides most of it. Whatever little else we need we manage to get with the money other people bring in . . . unemployment checks, craft sales, etc . . . clothing . . . we had it when we came, there's hardly anything else we need." She'd seen him in two different pairs of pants since she came, a pair of jeans and a pair of corduroys. In the freezing weather long underwear peeked out from the bottoms when he took off his boots. "As far as entertainment goes, I guess you could say we provide our own. Our lives are our entertainment." He made it sound desirable yet it seemed to Margaret that this was the essence of her complaint about the farm, that their life style was both the subject and object of their lives, that Starr couldn't go out and fuck a fifteen-year-old boy without delivering a speech about the search for new life styles; that they didn't just eat and farm organically but worried over it so much of the time. Like the radicals of the thirties who had to think just the right thoughts for fear of being consigned to the dustbin of history, they were conscious of their haloes growing shinier with each whole-wheat loaf baked, every tidbit of garbage plowed back into the earth, each Kleenex not used. "We don't seem to have much in the way of medical expenses, maybe just because there aren't many doctors close by." Most sicknesses just went away with time and Vitamin C; had there been a time when anyone lived like that? "And then of course," De Witt said, "I naturally don't pay taxes."

"No taxes at all?"

De Witt shook his head.

"Then you really don't have any income." Now he believed it.

"Right."

"Jesus," Mitchell said, "that's pretty funny. I'm not sure I'd ever've trusted you with this whole spread if I knew you didn't have a dime."

"I think it shows you were really a good person," Mira said. "That you didn't even think of asking."

"I took it for granted," Mitchell said.

They were all embarrassed.

Becky laughed. "Gee, Mitch, how would you be sure you existed if it weren't for taxes?"

To Margaret it seemed an aggressive remark but Mitchell simply nodded. He seemed lost in thought.

"Jesus," he finally said, "I'd be a rich man if I didn't have to pay taxes."

"If you weren't a rich man already you wouldn't have to pay so much," Roger said.

Becky giggled. "He's got you there, Mitch."

"I never think of myself as being rich," Mitchell said.

"How other people think of you is a better gauge," Roger said. "Us rich kids are always raised to think poor but I foxed 'em. At a certain age I realized that the test of whether your parents are rich isn't whether *you* can have what *you* want but whether *they* can have what *they* want."

Mitchell nodded, Kokeshi-doll-like.

"So let's talk to each other," Roger said. "Two rich kids."

*Roger, you just had your allowance cut off, Roger.* Was he bluffing or was he choosing to forget?

Mitchell smiled. Something in his eyes focused so that he looked intelligent again.

"Aren't you undermining your position?" Becky asked Roger. Flirtatiously. "Letting us know you have money?"

"Uh uh." Not responding to her signal. "I'm letting you know I can go elsewhere. Only poor people have to take whatever terms they can get."

"Okay," Mitchell boomed out happily. "So make me an offer!"

"Ten thousand," Roger said, deadpan.

"You're kidding," Mitchell said.

Roger shrugged. "You told me to make an offer."

"Hadn't we better clarify what we're talking about?" De Witt asked. "The farm or the whole parcel of land of which the farm is a small part?"

Mitchell responded but to Roger. "The parcel the farm is originally part of is actually about eight acres. If I had to put it up through a broker I'd ask for forty thousand."

Roger whistled. "That's pretty steep."

"Not really. It's good usable land, the house is in good shape, the barn's superb, all the out buildings, the coops and so on are in good condition. Now I admit they wouldn't be in that condition if it weren't for De Witt's work, which is why I'd let you have it for a lot less if you were working with him."

"How much less?"

"Five grand."

"Plus $2,400 for the broker's fee you wouldn't have to pay . . ."

Mitchell laughed. "He's too sharp, De Witt, watch out for him."

"Makes $32,600."

"Okay," Mitchell nodded. "You talked me into it. If that's what De Witt wants."

"What about the rest of the land?" Roger asked.

"That's about three hundred acres," Mitchell said. "I'm in no hurry to part with that."

"I'm in no hurry to buy a farm with no land," Roger said belligerently.

"Wait a minute," De Witt said. "I feel a certain antagonism creeping in that has no place here."

"Sure it does," Roger said promptly. "Buyer-seller antagonism."

"Then please let me take part in this. As a neutral party. Friendly to both of you."

Did he really believe he was neutral? And if he did, was it true? Did the fact that only his life was involved make him neutral? She hoped he didn't believe it; she hoped he was conning Mitchell.

"First let me explain something, Mitchell," De Witt said. "The question of land isn't a matter of principle. Nor are we thinking in terms of investment. You see Roger and I have been talking for a while, even before we were sure you were going to try to sell the place . . . we've been talking about ways to make it truly self-sustaining. It being an artificial situation to be supported by you. What we finally settled on as a feasible source of income is raising beef cattle. Organically, of course. There's an incredible market right here in the East. You need plenty of pasture for cattle, though, and . . ."

He kept talking but Margaret had turned off. Beef cattle! They surely hadn't talked about beef cattle when she was around, at least not seriously enough for her to pick up on it. Beef cattle had a much more ominous sound than the generalities of making a farm self-sustaining. Screen memory: hard-working, hard-driving, leather-faced cowboys working hard on the range all day, then at night riding into town to wench and brawl at the frontier saloon. That would be Roger and De Witt, while her life would be just like in the suburbs! She and Mira—she glanced at Mira, who was smiling placidly. How nice for Mira, she'd have more time to meditate.

"Nobody said anything to me about beef cattle," she said to nobody in particular. "Doesn't anyone care how I feel about it?"

"When we do it," Roger said, "you can let us know how you feel. By staying or splitting."

*But Roger! This was my place!* Her eyes filled with tears of betrayal.

184

Becky giggled nervously. "Is he really the way he sounds?"

But she couldn't answer without crying so she swiftly got up and went upstairs to their room, closed the door, made sure the twins were still sleeping, then really let loose the tears, curling up in the bed, hugging herself, crying bitterly . . . wishing, *aching* for David to be there. Most definitely David, not Roger. David, whom she could curl herself around without being accused of trying to smother. Who if you gave him something thought it was his due, not your neurosis. Who never fazed you by having grand schemes . . . who never had schemes at all. Who was on the road someplace, looking for something. A little temporary something. What he'd come from didn't exist, a formica counter with nothing underneath, what was ahead was no good, and what was available was okay only as an alternative to the others. She drifted into a light, sad sleep full of images that disappeared before she could reject them by waking up. She and David painting a line down a long highway. She and David's mother sitting in rocking chairs in an otherwise empty house, not speaking to each other. Snow outside. More snow. Piles of snow. Snow-white towels in a hotel linen room. Two of David's mother, wheeling a laundry cart down a long corridor full of doors. There was a knock on the door. As much in her sleep as out of it, she called, "Come in."

It was Mitchell.

"I'm sorry," he said. "I didn't realize you were asleep."

"It's okay," she said, sitting up, rubbing her eyes.

"I'm upset," he said, sitting on the edge of the bed, nothing in his manner suggesting that he was telling the truth. "I'm terribly upset because I really dig you and I don't want you to be mad at me and I have a feeling you'll be angry with me if I let Roger have the farm."

"You don't seem upset."

He smiled. "How do I seem?"

"Horny." Unctuous-horny.

Mitchell roared as though she'd said something brilliant and adorable. So it was true. Downstairs Becky flirted with Roger while Mitchell came upstairs to dip his wick in the counter culture. He tried to kiss her but she pushed him back, full of uncomprehended hostility. There were footsteps and De Witt opened the door. Mitchell laughed guiltily.

"De Witt told me to stay away from you."

"Suppose you go downstairs and negotiate, Mitchell," De Witt said. "I have something to discuss with Margaret."

Mitchell went. Margaret waited sullenly. De Witt sat there where Mitchell had been. Her nose began to itch; she scratched it.

"Margaret, why are you angry?"

"Because you told him to leave me alone," she lied.

"They think it's exciting to be here," De Witt said. "I told him you weren't like the younger girls, Carol, Starr, and so on. Sex for them is a very casual thing."

"How do you know it isn't for me?" she teased, knowing he would be too kind to remind her how he knew.

"I don't think that's what you're angry about."

She leaned forward and kissed his lips lightly but he gently pushed her away. She laughed ruefully. Now to continue the chain he had to go to someone and get pushed away.

"That's why I'm angry," she said. "Because you don't want me any more."

"Nonsense."

"What's nonsense?"

"It's nonsense that I don't want you and it's nonsense that that's why you're angry. You got angry about the beef cattle."

"I don't think it's so much the cattle," she said slowly. "It's that it sounded very permanent, and very demanding.

186

But not of me. I mean I'd just be in the background some-place while you and Roger . . . the truth is, I feel left out. The truth is that I'm jealous of this friendship between you and Roger. I mean, part of me thinks it's a beautiful thing, enjoys it, knows it's important for men to have .. but part of me is jealous."

"But Margaret," De Witt said—softly, reproachfully—"you are the bond between us."

*Bullshit, De Witt. That is what David would call Pure Bullshit.*

"Oh, yes? How could I tell?"

"Now you're being sarcastic."

"What's in all this for me, is what I want to know. A concession maybe? A saloon or a whorehouse in Brattle-boro so I can get to see you two once in a while?" *You are not being reasonable, Margaret. You can't get mad at them about some old cowboy pictures!*

De Witt smiled. "I don't think that will be necessary."

"Already," she pointed out, "we've progressed from your wanting to make love to me to not even letting me kiss you."

"You know perfectly well you'd have stopped me, any-way. With Roger downstairs and the children two feet away in the crib. Rue's not even sleeping." In point of fact she was staring at him through the slats.

So. He'd called her bluff. It didn't diminish her anxiety; it only left her with one less excuse for it.

"All right, what if those things weren't true? Then would you have?"

"Of course I would have," De Witt said. "If we had an understanding with Roger."

"What if I wanted to desperately and the very thought freaked Roger out of his mind?"

"I think you know it isn't possible for us to live together that way."

She knew.

"Would you do me a favor and take Rue down? I don't feel like seeing everyone yet."

"You don't want to talk about the cattle thing?"

"What's the point?" she asked wearily. "Roger isn't going to change his mind, we might as well just play it out. Maybe he won't even be able to get the money."

A short while later Rosie woke up and Margaret changed her and took her downstairs. Becky Kastle was alone in the common room.

"The men are walking the grounds," Becky said. "They took the baby. And there's the other one. My goodness, isn't she pretty!" Margaret thanked her. Sat down. Her head felt as though it was in a vise.

"I'm sorry you're upset," Becky said. Suddenly everyone was concerned with her moods. "Is it because of the farm business, or is it because of David?"

"I don't know," Margaret said. "Maybe both."

Becky smiled. She was really very pretty.

"How old are you, anyhow?" Margaret asked.

"Thirty-seven," Becky said.

"I guess you know you don't look it."

"Nobody looks their age any more."

"Up here they do. The natives, especially. And some of us." From hard work, from no make-up, from clothes that were right for work but wrong for everything else. But mostly from hard work. From real life, you could say self-righteously if you were thoroughly convinced that work was life or vice versa.

"Maybe they just work too hard up here," said Becky. Untroubled by any such conviction.

Silence.

Becky took a pack of cigarettes from her pocketbook, extracted one sloppy-looking joint, offered Margaret a choice. She refused. Becky lit hers, dragged deeply on it.

"I'm nervous," she said, smiling in that direct, appealing way she had. "I'd like to talk with you about David but I'd understand if you didn't want to talk to me. If you're feeling hostile or anything."

"It's just hard for me to think of you as David's mother."

"David has the same problem," Becky said. Margaret found her an ashtray. "David was never difficult when he was little." She giggled. "Not that he was difficult later on . . . I mean it just became apparent later on that he had some problems, you know, relating to people . . . When he was little he'd want to stay home and play with stuff, gadgets, kitchen things, broken appliances and so on . . . but a lot of kids are like that and I didn't worry about it . . . I never worried about the kids anyway . . . I had a business at home . . . we were pretty broke when Davie was little, Monty my first husband was just switching over from being a union organizer to being a history teacher and he had to take all these courses and he couldn't earn much . . . we had these friends in Mt. Kisco, we were living in a cottage on their estate, they had a lot of money and he . . . it was Mitchell, actually, Mitchell and his first wife . . . anyway Mitchell set me up with an answering-service business right in the house . . . David could operate that board as well as I could when he was six years old, the only thing was, he didn't like to talk into it, he'd pick up a call and . . . is Davie a good lay?"

Margaret stared at her.

Becky giggled, mashed out the rest of her joint. "I'm

189

sorry. I took you aback. Or maybe afront. Did I affront you? I get very affrontal sometimes when I'm stoned. My true lousy nature coming out . . . or . . . no kidding, *is* Davie a good lay?"

"I can't talk to you about that."

"That's too bad," Becky said, without apparent ill feeling. "Is there something else you'd like to talk about?"

"No."

"Don't you ever think about sex?" Becky asked.

"Sure I do," Margaret said.

"That's a relief." Becky stood, stretched. "People who never think about it make me jittery. I think about it all the time." She walked over to the window, looked out toward the barn. "I've been married on and off for nineteen years and for nineteen years that's what I think about when I'm not busy. Before I had orgasms I used to think all the time how it would be to have orgasms and then when I started having them I wondered if they'd be better with someone else, and about bad orgasms and good orgasms and so on, and then I went through this period of being unfaithful to Monty and then I'd think about whoever I was doing it with, and what we were doing, and so on, and now I've been going through this pretty faithful stage but my mind still . . . David does have a beautiful body, doesn't he? I was so surprised when he went out for sports, Little League and all that shit, he didn't seem like that kind of kid at all . . . he always did have a beautiful body, though, even when he was little he had those shoulders . . . *Why* won't you talk to me about David? Do you have all kinds of hangups about sex?"

"Yes."

Becky laughed. "I can see why David loved you. You're really very lovable."

"David didn't love me." David didn't love anybody, but she wouldn't say that.

"David doesn't love anybody," Becky said.

190

Margaret stood up. "I think I'd better give Rosie some juice."

Becky nodded. "Sure. Listen, I hope I didn't . . . is there anyone in the big bedroom in front? I think I'm gonna take a nap. I'm soooo sleepy."

"I don't think so," Margaret said. "If there is, you can just use one of the other ones."

MITCHELL would sell the farm and land for a total of $125,000. When Roger asked where was the favor to De Witt in all this, Mitchell explained that it was only because of his love for De Witt that he was willing to sell the land at all. Roger asked what good his willingness would do if they couldn't raise that kind of money, it being nearly impossible to get mortgages on unimproved land. Mitchell allowed as how he would be willing to take back a mortgage of up to $50,000. He also agreed that if Roger and De Witt were unable to raise the cash to buy the entire parcel, he would sell them one half or one third of the land parcel for $50,000 or $35,000, respectively. He insisted upon shaking hands with Roger, claiming that he was convinced that someone with Roger's resources would have no problem raising the money. Then he and Becky went off for an overnight visit to friends in Newfane.

꿋ᵛ "I think we'd better have a meeting," De Witt said.

"What for?" Roger said.

"To discuss this idea with everyone."

"What if Roger can't get the money?" Margaret asked. "Roger, have you thought about how you'll get the money?"

"I don't see what there is to discuss," Roger said to De Witt. "If I can get the money I can get it, and if I can't, I can't."

"Sometimes with a group," De Witt said, "things aren't as simple as they seem."

"Give me an idea of what you're talking about," Roger said.

"I don't want to lay on something that may not be there," De Witt said. "But I really think we should all talk."

꿋ᵛ "I'M very confused and miserable," she said to Roger before the meeting. "I don't know if I'm more afraid you'll get the money or you won't. The whole thing of having to go to Philadelphia . . ." *What if David comes back looking for me and I'm not here? What if the farm catches fire? What if your parents don't like the twins?* She felt tearful again and turned away from Roger so he wouldn't see her crying. He would think the tears were directed at him. Men were slower than women to cry, correspondingly slow to perceive that you might be crying for some much vaguer reason than a desire to manipulate them. Maybe it was jealousy; they never told you to stop crying, they said don't be hysterical, a cunning bit of word play designed to suggest that the womb was a dishonestly acquired secret weapon for the manufacture of tears. She waited for him to say Oh Shit. To tell her to go someplace else if she felt like being hysterical. She looked at him; he was watching her. Waiting. If she got really impossible he'd just go off someplace with De Witt for a beer.

Instead he sat down on the side of the bed and beckoned to her to sit next to him, then put his arm around her.

"What's up, Maggie? What are you so jittery about?"

"I don't know," she admitted. "Everything seems so complicated. I hate the thought of going to Philadelphia."

"That's natural. We'll get it over with fast."

"And then, let's say you get the money and everything else happens the way it's supposed to, and then . . . well for instance it's one thing to think about living in a permanent situation with De Witt and something else to think about Mira."

Roger smiled. "I feel exactly the opposite."

"You do?"

"Sure. It's one thing to think about having this spooky do-gooder nobody relates to kind of floating around the house but it's something else to think about living with this guy your wife digs and you know he's always gonna be there ready to prop her up if you're being a louse, a perpetual alternative for her to flirt with."

"You could try not being a louse," she said.

"That's true," he said.

She watched him suspiciously. Was he putting on some

kind of brilliant act that would last just long enough for her to do what he wanted her to do? When he'd first arrived at the farm they'd had that one decent talk when Roger had been the way he was being now—however that was . . . *reasonable*—listening to what she said instead of just using it as something to bounce off of—and then what had happened? They'd been talking about David. Of course, that was it. He'd been upset about David and he couldn't admit it then for fear of being put in a time machine and sent back to the nineteenth century, so he'd just gotten nasty and sarcastic again. That was reasonable, actually. But he was being straight with her now about De Witt.

"De Witt might split anyway," she said.

"I wouldn't have any trouble finding a new partner, there're always people looking for a setup like this. Anyway, why would he do that?"

"If you have an argument. Or he might get bored. He told me once he hated the idea of staying anyplace forever."

"Who doesn't? I might get bored, too. You can't not do anything because anything you do you might get bored with. In theory, once you get something like this going you can rotate responsibilities and everyone can have some freedom."

She smiled. "And anyone who doesn't like it can split."

"You get so upset when I tell you that. But it's true. And not only that but I never said it until you'd really done it once."

"I was getting out of an unbearable situation," she said. "I hated you and myself and my whole life. I couldn't stand it any more but I never thought about leaving you forever. I thought about escaping for a while, or I'd think how nice it would be to have a husband I got along with, stuff like that, but I never thought about leaving you permanently."

"Is that true?"

"Yes." It was funny that it was true, but it was.

Long silence. He fondled her arm, kissed her cheek.

"You know," he said, "you never asked me what happened to me while you were away."

"I didn't think you'd want me to." In truth she hadn't wanted to know. What was she supposed to do, ask for a written list of his conquests?"

"Well," he said, "I'll tell you now. When you left, at first I felt pretty relieved to realize you were gone, you looked like such a freak, and you were so fucking spooked and jumpy after your mother died, it was like living in a haunted house. So when you went . . . I didn't think I was going to care. I figured now I could relax and enjoy myself . . . I stayed stoned a lot the first few months . . . screwed around some, constantly as a matter of fact. I think maybe in the back of my mind I sort of assumed you were coming back and things would just go back to the way they were before, except we'd have the kids. Then Christmas came and went and I guess that was when I began realizing you weren't coming back." He smiled ironically. "I got very nostalgic. I stayed stoned but the pictures changed, I kept seeing these very bucolic pastoral scenes, you and these beautiful little twin girls running through meadows, swimming bare-ass under waterfalls, stuff like that. I found I couldn't get interested in sex any more except when I was seeing those pictures. Then after a while the pictures didn't do it any more . . . I couldn't get it up . . . and that's when I panicked." He smiled. "That particular problem I'd never had before. I went through the next few weeks after that literally drunk, stoned and/or sleeping every minute of the time. I woke up scared. Then one night I was stoned as usual, and I had on some really good stuff, some ragas, I guess, and I started getting pictures of women. But I mean from way back. Like my mother and my aunts and every maid we ever had and every girlfriend

195

and every chick I ever lived with, and so on, and as the stuff wore off I started thinking, and I realized . . . this may sound dumb but I'd actually never thought of it before . . . I realized it was actually the first time in my whole life I'd lived without a woman in the same house for more than a few days at a time. Boarding school they took me home from after a week because I made such a stink. From the time I left home I always made sure there was some broad around. This was the first time in my life I'd been on my own. That really got to me. It set off a whole train of other things. I got very introspective. I thought and I thought and I thought and I thought and some of it was pretty painful . . . like I spent days thinking to myself, what would I have been thinking about all this time if I wasn't thinking about getting laid, bugging my wife, etc. But the interesting thing was that from that day on, the panic was over. If I got stoned once in a while it was because I felt like it, felt like seeing some new pictures, getting some new insights, whatever. Not because I was scared not to be stoned. I still had no sex feelings, though. Not until I got here and saw you again. That flirting business with Hannah and stuff . . . I don't think I would have bothered if you weren't around, and the David business . . ."

Silence.

"Roger," she said truthfully, "I love you much more now than I ever have."

They hugged each other.

EVERYONE was there for the meeting, including Starr's fifteen-year-old boyfriend, Jordan's No. 2 girlfriend, a freshman at the Putney School, Harry Kirschner, a wild-eyed, nouveau organic farmer who lived a few miles down the road, whom De Witt had met recently at an organic-food suppliers' conference, and Harry's five apprentices, a murmuring chorus of sweet-faced acidheads, as well as two men, Larry and Jim, who'd appeared that afternoon in dashikis and bell-bottom jeans, explaining that they were considering giving up their FBI jobs to farm organically.

"Oh, Jesus," Starr said, "do we have to let in every creep that comes to the door?"

"No," De Witt said, "we don't. But where to cut it off is the problem."

"Before *them*," Starr said.

"Can't we just ignore them?" Margaret asked. "It's not as if we're doing anything political."

"That's where you're wrong!" Harry boomed at them from the periphery of their little corner group. "Wrong wrong wrong wrong! Everything we do is political. This is where the politics is, now!"

"Thanks for telling me," Starr muttered. From their corner, Larry and Jim stared at Harry, wide-eyed.

"Whaddya mean, fella?" one of them finally asked.

"Where do you think the revolution's gonna be, man?" Harry asked. "In the Pentagon? You can't have a revolution in the Pentagon, they're all robots! And you can't have a revolution in the cities, nobody has any energy,

197

they're all half dead from eating plastic food and never letting their feet touch the earth. This is the place, man! It's the only place for the revolution to begin! It *has* begun! This is it!"

"Jesus," Jordan muttered. "Maybe *he's* FBI."

"This isn't a meeting," Roger said. "It's a fucking comic opera!"

"I'm not taking part in any meeting," Starr said, "with any fucking list-making tape-recording FBI pricks!"

"No kidding," Paul said, "do you think we're on their list?"

"Everyone's on their list," Roger said. "The Cancer Crusade's on their list because they discovered the Left has more of it."

"Will you settle for a vote?" De Witt asked Starr, who consented. By vote it was decided that Harry Kirschner and his apprentices could stay, as could Jordan's girlfriend and Starr's boyfriend and Dolores's girlfriend but that Larry and Jim would have to go. One of them was practically in tears as they left. The other one was telling him, audibly, not to be upset, that they were martyrs to left-wing racism.

"Okay," De Witt said, "Most of you probably know or have figured out that Mitchell's having a bad time of it financially right now . . . the recession, depression, whatever you want to call it . . . and he wants to pull back on some of his obligations. Aside from his general situation his taxes here have gone up enormously . . . anyway, he's decided to sell the farm, and possibly the land as well."

"Oh, no!" Carol wailed. "I was just beginning to think of this place as a real home, someplace I could go away from and come back to."

"Shit," Starr said, "I knew it was coming. Shit, shit, shit, shit!"

Dolores said nothing but looked more stricken than anyone.

198

"Don't let him do it, man!" Harry said. "Take possession of the land, it belongs to you."

Everyone ignored him and he subsided for the moment.

Jordan's face was impassive but Margaret couldn't tell if it was stoicism or indifference. Paul looked bemused. Carol was making it a point not to look at Jordan or Butterscotch or Jordan's No. 2 girlfriend; they had agreed in some way, open or tacit, Carol and Jordan as well as Paul and Starr, that they were to use the farm, instead of each other, as the center of their lives.

"It could take him a long time to sell it," Carol finally said.

"Oh, that's great," Starr said. "Sitting around waiting for the ax to fall."

De Witt said, "I think we may be spared that."

They waited.

"Roger is willing to try to buy it," De Witt said, "and go on with our plans as before."

There was a long silence. Then Starr, in a voice thick with suspicion and hostility, said to Roger, "What, are you rich?"

"My parents are," Roger said.

Margaret always enjoyed the admission; until him, the rich people she'd met in New York had been like the aunts and uncles; you had to see the summer house in East Hampton or the yacht to know that the toe-worn sneakers were a matter of style. The kids in ratty clothes who thought they were breaking with a tradition were merely pushing one into the realm of the ridiculous.

"I'm not sure they'll give me the money," Roger continued into the vacuum. "I own a house where we used to live though. Outright. It's worth maybe close to fifty grand, and I've called the brokers and put it on the market, and assuming I can sell it . . . I'll come down on the price if I have to, to do it fast . . . anyway, that would give me more than enough to buy the farm parcel but that only includes a few acres, and in terms of having a self-sustaining enterprise here I'm not sure it pays to buy it without the big piece of land. If it comes to that it might be a better idea to look up north of here and see if I can't do better."

Silence.

Starr: "I noticed you keep saying I and my instead of us and our."

Roger: "Does anybody else have any money?"

Starr: "That's not the point."

Roger: "All right. What is?"

Starr: "The point is, what you're offering is to replace our weekend-hippie-absentee landlord with one who's here all the time."

"Oh, wow," Paul said. "That's pretty heavy."

"Still," Jordan said, "I can see what she's talking about."

Margaret looked at De Witt; he'd foreseen something like this, which was why he'd suggested the meeting. His face was expressionless. Roger was looking annoyed but not half as angry, it seemed to her, as she would have imagined if she'd had to paint his face without seeing it.

"I know what's she's talking about, too," Roger said. "But I don't see any way of getting around it. First of all, I want to make it clear that nobody's sending me on any guilt trip over my money."

"Nobody has to send you, man," Jordan said. "You're there already if you know you've got something no one else has that you didn't earn."

"Or," Roger said, "to put it another way, that I didn't have to exploit anyone to get."

De Witt and Dolores smiled but the others were angry.

"You've managed to twist it around," Starr said.

"You have to realize," Margaret said, "that anyone who has money gets an awful lot of that . . . stuff."

"And *you* have to realize," Starr said, "that anyone who

200

hasn't got money would be happy to exchange that kind of stuff for the kind of shit you get when you're poor."

Margaret nodded reluctantly. She glanced at De Witt; he was still watching. He would wait for it to get worse before he made any attempt at mediation.

"Are you just getting it off your chest?" Roger asked Starr. "Or do you have an idea?"

Starr shrugged. "I have a lot of ideas. Like why don't you split up the money and let us all buy it?"

Someone whistled.

Roger said, "You're not kidding, are you?"

Starr shook her head.

Silence.

"You're HUNG UP, man!" Harry Kirschner burst out with sudden violence. "You're all hung up on your money! Don't you know that money is shit?"

"Fine," Roger said calmly. "Go squeeze some out."

"You know what I mean, man," Harry said. "How you gonna face the future if you can't get rid of your hangups from the past? Look at me! Look at my body!" He flexed his muscles, pulled up his chambray shirt to reveal a lean sun-tanned torso. "Look at the life I lead! Would you believe I used to be a two-hundred-sixty-four-pound chemical engineer?"

Roger said, "Yes."

"I'll tell you what's wrong with *you*," Harry said.

"Why don't you go fuck off?" Roger said. "What's this joker doing here anyway?"

"You see?" Starr said. "You're throwing your weight around already."

"My God!" Margaret exclaimed. "He's doing exactly what you were doing a few minutes ago with those other men."

"I've been here a lot longer than he has," Starr said defensively.

"You mean you'd like a dictatorship of time instead of money?"

"I wouldn't like a dictatorship of anything!" Starr said heatedly. "I'm saying it's bad enough to feel like someone controls your life who's a few hundred miles away, and now you're telling me some guy that walked in a couple of months ago is gonna be able to tell me to go fuck off."

"Oh, for crying out loud," Roger said, "nobody's telling *you* to fuck off."

"You could. Or you'll think you can."

Of course he would have even without the money but Starr probably didn't realize that. By the time of Roger's arrival Starr had been out of the winter madness and into her new boyfriend and a variety of other projects so that they'd never happened to cross. Roger was smacking his forehead in frustration.

"May I say something?" De Witt asked gently. They all turned to him. "As you know, I'm not against anger as a response to an immediate situation. A way of working out the knots that develop between people. But these issues we're getting into now, they're not like that . . . they're very large, complex, legitimate problems, that is to say they go beyond personalities. Questions like who has a voice, how you earn the voice, and so on, this isn't a question of clashing personalities, it goes to the heart of our culture and beyond it."

"Not *our* culture, man," boomed Harry to the smiling and nods of his chorus. "*Their* culture. Money has no place in our culture."

"Bullshit," several people said at once.

"How'd you buy your farm?" Starr demanded.

"I used up what I had in the bank. That was it, I'm finished with money now."

"Tell that to the tax collector," Jordan said.

"What if you hadn't had that?" Starr demanded. "You'd have had to find someone who did, right?"

"I'm sorry," Harry said, standing up and yawning. "I can't get into you people. You're too hung up for me." and he left, followed by his boys.

"Now it seems to me," De Witt went on as though he'd never been interrupted, "that there are several related issues involved. Maybe we can take them up one at a time, even if they overlap . . . Now the first question I think only you can answer, Roger, and that is whether the feelings of the group are crucial to you. That is, assuming that Mitchell really means to sell and you're able to raise the money to buy, would the feelings of the rest of the group matter to you to a point where they would cause you to go ahead or stop?"

Margaret held her breath; what admission was he asking of Roger, from whom she'd never heard the words I love you. How could Roger ever admit in public that other people's feelings were important to him?

Long pause. Then Roger said slowly, "*Your* feelings are important to me because we're talking about a partnership . . . Margaret's feelings are important to me because she's my wife . . ." *Mirabile dictu!* She exhaled. "The others . . . I care how the others feel but not as much."

*I love you, Roger. I really love you.*

"In other words," De Witt said, "you would prefer that we worked things out as a group."

Roger nodded. "The group thing seems to be working pretty well. I mean people've got all kinds of problems with themselves and each other . . . but they don't seem to keep the place from functioning."

"Now everyone knows Roger's feelings," Starr said belligerently. "And Roger's feelings are more important than anyone else's because Roger has money."

"Only from a procedural point of view," De Witt said. "Now I was going to suggest that we go around the room and give everyone a chance to express their feelings."

"I'll tell you my feelings," Jordan said, jumping up, scratching his head in an agitated way. "My feeling is, fuck the house and fuck the money and everything else! Who needs it? I don't want to own anything! I don't want to pay taxes! I want freedom, not ownership."

"Especially from your children," Carol said.

"What the fuck has that got to do with it?" Jordan demanded.

"Plenty," Carol said. "It's one thing to talk about keeping on the move when you don't have little kids and something else when you do."

"Bucky Fuller," Jordan announced grandly, "says that men are born with feet, not roots."

"Which is true of their bodies," Dolores said quietly from her corner. "But not of their minds." It was exactly what De Witt had said to her once. Which of them had thought of it first? They seemed to have perfect understanding, they never even crossed verbally but seemed to have identical reactions to people and events. If De Witt's attitude toward Mira bespoke tolerance and determination, there was nothing but love and respect for the wife who'd divorced him.

"Right on," Carol said.

Silence. Mira was deep in meditation. De Witt asked Dolores if there was anything else she wanted to say.

"I guess so," Dolores said. "I guess I want to say that I'm for anything that lets us hold onto this place. If Roger wants to buy it, fine, if there's some sort of share system where we share taxes or a mortgage, whatever, I'll try to pay my share, neither way freaks me out especially. But to me it's very important to have a home. Someplace to come back to, as Carol said. When I was on the move all the time, I came to dread the next time I'd have to pick up and go again. Once I had this place I could travel for fun again. Maybe it's just having been raised on a farm, having a strong sense of land, of place . . . but I think it's more than that."

"I think it's age," Jordan said, grinning. "You're over the hill, kid, how old are you, thirty-five or some fucking crazy number like that?"

Dolores laughed but Carol pointed out to him angrily that everyone grows older.

"Not me!" Jordan said, "I have this plan where every year when my birthday comes to get me I'm gonna be too busy fucking."

"I feel the same as Dolores," Butterscotch said timorously. "I don't know how I can contribute my share, but . . ."

"If you do just what you've always done," De Witt told her, "you'll be giving your share."

Silence.

"I think," Mira said in her Super Celibate Angel voice, "that it's a beautiful idea to have someone own the farm who's really deeply involved with it."

"Then it should be ten times as good having ten people own it who're really deeply involved," Starr said.

"What're you proposing?" Roger asked.

"Nothing," Starr said. "I'm just saying whatever comes into my head."

Her boyfriend stared at her adoringly.

"I'm not dividing up the money," Roger said. "It would be a phony trip, pretending to divide it up and then laying down a condition it has to go to the farm. I'm not even sure I can get what's needed, I'm going to have to sweat for it, kiss my old man's ass, I mean, and I'm not willing to have someone take a few grand of that sweat and spin out for San Francisco or something."

"One of the problems we've had in the past," De Witt said after a long silence, "is with this question of indebted-

ness. Of how one has to be with people to whom one is in-
debted."

"Or to put in English," Jordan said, "Mitchell acts like
a fucking asshole half the time he's here and no one ever
tells him so."

"Except me," Starr said.

"Except her," Jordan admitted. "And Mitchell's decided she's that way with everyone so it's cool. But if everyone decided the hell with him and his fucking hippie-capi-
talist ego trip and called him on his shit, we know damn
well what'd happen."

"It's happening anyway," Carol said sadly.

"Maybe it was inevitable," De Witt said. "He had to really grow and learn and become part of the farm, or get
tired of his plaything and give it up."

Silence.

"All right," Roger said abruptly. "How about dividing
it up after I buy it?"

Margaret stared at him. If in the past she'd felt strained
and exhausted by his high-wire articulation and callous in-
flexibility, she was beginning to feel threatened by this new
Roger, whose reactions she couldn't anticipate, whose actions she couldn't predict. She didn't mind his giving away
what they didn't have yet; it was a more basic feeling, as
though he were snatching out from under her a spot of
ledge where she was trying to gain a toehold. Not that he
hadn't given away money and possessions before; it was
the way he'd allowed himself to be questioned and moved
from his original intention!

"Not to do us a favor," Starr said, eyeing him cautiously.

"All right," Roger said. "Not to do you a favor. To
keep the group together."

"You mean it."

"Yeah. I mean it. I don't mean the big land parcel. If I
get that it's going to go into beef cattle or big-scale farm-

ing, and if someone wants to go in with De Witt and me, that'll be a different thing. And I'm not talking about splitting with any two-year-old that drops in for a meal and a quick lay."

"Don't be a shit," Starr said, "just because you're giving something away."

"Don't notice it for the first time just because you're being given something."

"I'm not used to that," Starr said seriously.

"We'll get it all over with quickly," Roger said, "so you can forget about it."

"If you're serious about this," De Witt said to Roger, "I think you'll have some details to work out on paper."

"Oh, shit," Jordan said, "I'm not into legal documents."

"That's all ownership is," De Witt pointed out.

"There's Margaret and me," Roger said. "De Witt and Mira, Carol and Jordan, Starr and Paul, Dolores, Butterscotch. Makes ten shares. We can make provision where if someone new comes in they can have a share if they want it after a certain amount of time."

"What about taxes and stuff?" Margaret asked.

"They shouldn't be too hard to handle," De Witt said. "Split ten ways. Especially if we can persuade Mitchell to let us give him a portion of the money in cash so that the records don't show too high a purchase price to the assessor."

"I'm not sure I'm into all this," Jordan said. "Can I sell my share?"

"No!" several people shouted at once.

"What're you trying to turn this into, man?" Roger asked. "Cherry Grove?"

"There're going to be so many things to work out," Margaret said apprehensively.

"Mmm," Roger said, "But first Philadelphia."

"Is that where your house is?" Carol asked.

"No," Roger said, "that's where my parents live. Ardmore, actually. If we can get enough money there we won't have to wait for the sale of our own house to buy here."

"We," Starr repeated, kissing Roger's cheek loudly. "He said *we*. Let's have a party!"

༄ MARGARET dreamed that her mother was walking along the edge of a fog-shrouded island not unlike the one in the Isle of the Dead, reaching out desperately over the water, calling in a pleading echo-heavy voice, "Don't go to Roger's side for the money, darling! Come to meeeeeee! Come to meeeeeeee!" When she awakened, puzzled and upset, Roger was already dressed. She felt a surge of resentment toward him. Because he was dragging her back to Philadelphia? Or was it a carryover from her dream? When Roger came near the bed she pretended she was still asleep.

The Adamses had never known her mother. This was somehow unbelievable to her. Roger's parents and her parents had never met. *Do you know, Mr. and Mrs. Crowley Adams, that she is dead? My mother? Whom you never expressed the remotest interest in meeting? Who when she was young, before her foothold was taken away, had so many little talents that the problem was thought to be which she might fully develop? She could sketch a little, sculpt a little, play the piano and dance but had insufficient drive to continue any of those activities when she could no longer have lessons in them.*

How many times had she seen Roger's family herself, outside of Christmases? Six Christmases, each more funereal than the last. The four of them, plus Roger's father's brother who'd never married, plus (sometimes) Roger's mother's kid brother who'd been married four times and was as likely to show up with a past or future wife as with his present one. The place was briefly alive while he was there but otherwise it was an unremittingly dismal formal occasion, more like a board meeting than a holiday, a polite stock-option-giving ceremony from which, as little as they seemed to have given emotionally, Roger's parents always had to recover by going to Nassau for three months. Not the least of the blessings of being at the farm this past winter had been escaping the Adams Christmas.

"Roger?" She sat up suddenly. "What did you tell your parents last Christmas?"

"I told them the babies were too young to travel so we wouldn't be down."

"They must have known that didn't make sense."

Roger laughed shortly. "You have to think about something to know whether it makes sense."

"Roger?"

"Mmm?"

*Do something to reassure me, Roger. Tell me that the more things change the more they remain the same or something like that.*

"I've been dreaming about my mother."

He groaned. "I thought you were past that."

*You've got to be kidding, Roger. The past isn't what's finished it's only what's invisible.*

"Everything's flooding back on me. I almost feel guilty I haven't thought of her more since I've been here."

"You can go to confession while you're in Philadelphia."

"Very funny." But it made sense for the trip to bother him as much as it did her. More, even, just as *he* was less upset by *her* father. Now he was building up his shell.

"Are you sure they'll be there?" They did spend most summers at home in Ardmore since they'd sold the camp on the Jersey shore when the area got built up. Why should they go anyplace, as Roger's mother had said, when the club had a marvelous pool and eight tennis courts? Roger's mother was a superb player, as unlikely as her squat frame and spindly legs made her seem for the role.

"Mmmm. We faked a call to Sillsy." Sillsy was Sarah Adams. They all had nicknames, that brave Wasp attempt at warmth roughly comparable to trying to heat a house with a can of Sterno. Crowley was Cowpey, Roger's baby pronunciation having stuck where nothing before had.

"Don't you think we should let them know we're coming?"

"Uh uh. I don't want to give them time to build up their defenses."

"Don't you think they'll resent it if we just drop in on them out of the blue?"

He shrugged. "If they're resentful then they'll feel guilty and we'll get the money twice as fast."

Roger the Master Manipulator.

"That sounds awful," she said.

"That's all right," Roger said. "We're talking about awful people."

꧁ DOWN 91, then ugly 95, then across Westchester to the Tappan Zee. She looked toward Hartsdale, waiting to feel a pang, but there was nothing. Roger had filled in the space between the front and back seats and put the crib mattress across the whole thing. In the hot breeze, naked except for their diapers, the twins slept on and off the whole time. Margaret did, too. Across New Jersey and into Pennsylvania.

"I'm so hungry," she said. She'd awakened with it, an absolutely ravenous feeling.

"You had three breakfasts, for Christ's sake."

It was true. She'd sat there at the kitchen table, not wanting to leave, thinking of one thing after another to delay departure, and as the others had come in for breakfast or fresh coffee she'd joined them. Coffee and bread and eggs, then coffee and cereal, then more coffee, and, when Starr and Carol brought them in, blueberries, the first of the season, with top milk. When Roger had finally scooped up both girls in exasperation and started out of the house, she'd buttered another piece of bread to take with her, in addition to the bread and fruit she'd packed for the twins so they wouldn't have to stop along the way. Roger always hated to stop along the way, no matter where they were going and how little he might actually want to get there.

"But we've been in the car more than six hours since then," she pointed out.

"Will you stop it?" Roger said irritably. "We're almost there and you've had enough to eat to last you a week."

"I'm fortifying myself," she said. "You should understand that."

◦⋙ AND then they were in Ardmore. Beautiful Ardmore. What people once thought suburbs were going to be like. If the houses were a bit close together, well Philadelphians were used to that sort of thing, and the stone was so thick as to constitute an adequate barrier between neighbors who didn't tend to spill over each other with noisy warmth, anyway. They were busy people, desirable neighbors. A gynecologist on one side, an ear-nose-throat man on the other and a heart surgeon across the street. Margaret's mother would have thought she was in heaven. The taste in the buildings and the landscaping was uniformly good and of course subdued. It had been a major coup of Roger's, the year he turned twenty-one and spent a summer at home while his parents were in Europe, to have ordered installed a kidney-shaped swimming pool that took up most of their back grounds. Taste was terribly important. It was their word for life style and it was mistaken for content just as often as the latter. The crucial aspect of bad taste was that it revealed something about you that it was inappropriate for others to know.

ICHABOD Moses, the family retainer, opened the door, greeted them calmly but warmly, ushered them in. Ichabod had once had an identity of his own. A wan, genteel, young soul, 4F during the Second World War by virtue of asthma and several other physical difficulties, he'd come to them in 1942 when they were still living in West Philadelphia. Roger was three and Roger's father had gone off to be a Colonel in the war effort and it was thought that Sillsy should not be alone in the house with only the maid and the cook, also female, for protection, but at first no one could think of a satisfactory method or excuse for having a workman actually living in the house; it wasn't like the camp, with its separate cottage a few hundred yards away. Then a friend of Crowley's had mentioned his nephew from Minnesota who was looking for a teaching position in Philadelphia, and Crowley had asked whether the young man might be interested in living with them as Roger's tutor. From the beginning Roger had adored and terrorized Ichabod; from the beginning Roger's mother had had to protect Ichabod from Roger's temper. But from the beginning Roger had truly learned from Ichabod, whom he had christened Itchy. He learned to read, he learned to write and he learned arithmetic well before entering school, a fact which, combined with his difficult temperament, created enormous trouble when he had to sit still in school and learn the same things all over again.

There were two strange facts, though, connected to the tale of Roger and Itchy. The first was that as Roger precociously acquired knowledge from Itchy, Itchy himself seemed to shed it. The second was that as Itchy in his years with the Adamses lost his education, so did he lose the second striking aspect of his persona, his physical ailments. The asthma that had plagued him since childhood; the nervous stomach that had prevented him from digesting well—all gradually disappeared, to be replaced by strong capabilities in fields like carpentry, plumbing and electric work. So that Margaret, meeting Ichabod years later, had assumed him to have become the family retainer by virtue of lowly birth and lack of education combined with strength and know-how.

Ichabod led them into the parlor. Outside it was still hot and sunny but the house was cool. She found herself wondering what time it was and realized that at the farm they never thought about time. There was the clock-timer on the stove for cooking and baking and a clock-radio in De Witt's room which was occasionally set for some special reason.

The parlor had been redone since their last visit, or

maybe just for the warm weather; everything was lovely and light and airy. A pale Chinese rug on the floor, pale yellow silk upholstery on the sofa and chairs, sheer white curtains at the windows. The clock on the white mantelpiece said it was five-thirty.

Where did you put the babies in a room like this? She held Rosie, who was still sleeping. Roger put down Rue on the rug.

"You're looking just fine, Margaret," Ichabod said. "And I see you've got yourself two beautiful girls."

She kissed his cheek. He blushed.

"How you been, Rodge?" he asked.

"Okay, okay, Itch," said Roger. "How's things?"

"Just about the same as ever," said Ichabod.

"Where's Sillsy?" asked Roger.

"Sarah's taking a shower, I believe."

You swam in the pool to wash off the sun and took a shower to wash off the chlorine.

"How about Cowpey?"

"Still at the Club, I believe."

This could mean that he was at the Club but was also a code phrase used to describe Crowley's whereabouts on days or nights when he disappeared without letting anyone know where he would be. If Sillsy and Cowpey went to the Club together they went in separate cars so Sillsy could come home earlier if she got tired—or if she'd been away from Mr. Boston too long, as Roger put it.

"Could someone make us something to eat?"

"Why surely, Maggie," Ichabod said, and headed toward the kitchen.

Her arm was beginning to ache from carrying Rosie, and the crook of her elbow, where the baby's heavy sleeping head lay, was hot and sweaty. You couldn't put down a baby on a lemon-silk sofa which would be stained irreparably by a bit of sweat or dribble; the carpet had no softness and would irritate her skin; the chairs had the same light covering as the sofa. In Brattleboro, with an anti-ecology guilt twinge, she'd bought a box of disposable diapers which was all the twins were wearing at the moment. What if they leaked? For the first time she had on the twins' behalf that sense she'd had on her own so often during her childhood, the sense of not having a fitting place to be. Of being rather larger and grimier than a proper human being had a right to be.

Damn it, she was going to sit on the sofa. Rosie would still be warm in her arms but not nearly as heavy. She tried to remember whether her smock was clean. She'd been wearing it since the day before. In previous times she'd carefully planned what she'd wear in Ardmore but at the farm she'd seldom given a thought to what she was wearing. Would she rise from the sofa to find that the seat of her dress had left on that lemon silk some remnants of flour dust, cooking stains, mucous wiped off her hands onto her ass because no dishrag was available? The hell with it! She would sit down! In her left hand she held the twins' sleeveless smocks that were cut from the same piece of red floral cotton as her own. At the farm you cut things from the same piece because it was the obvious thing to do; here they were mother-daughter outfits, too corny for words. Then, too, the cotton itself, purchased in Brattleboro for forty-nine cents a yard, had seemed bright and beautiful at the farm, while here she became aware of the coarse grain of the cotton and the gaudy nature of the print.

Rue was fully awake now and reconnoitering the territory. She stood up, reeled over to the cocktail table, pulled herself up, grabbed a marble cigarette box and was about to bring it crashing down on the shiny wooden surface of the table when Margaret reached forward and grabbed it from her.

215

"Oh, Jesus," she said. She put the box down next to her on the sofa. "Roger," she said nervously, "maybe you ought to clear away the ashtray and stuff."

"You're really throwing yourself into it, aren't you?" Roger said.

"I can't help it," she said. "I'm nervous."

Roger looked at her with distaste, an old expression of his she hadn't seen recently. She pushed the ashtray and bud vase to a point on the table where Rue couldn't reach them. Roger started to leave the room.

"Where're you going?" Margaret asked.

"To pee, for Christ's sake. Is that all right?"

She nodded miserably. Roger left. She tried to sink back into the sofa, which wasn't that kind of sofa. She closed her eyes. When she opened them Rue was standing at the *étagère* at the other end of the room, the *étagère*, full of blown glass and unborn china and gold-framed photos with oval mats—Sillsy and her brother as children on their horses; Crowley in uniform; Sillsy as a very young girl in her pony cart; Roger with his first deer; Crowley and Sillsy washing down the floor of the camp in New Jersey THE YEAR THE COUPLE AND THE MAID ALL QUIT JUST BEFORE SUMMER, proud as punch at their ability to do menial labor although they lacked the calling for it their servants had been born with; and as Margaret sat staring at her utterly paralyzed, Rue leaned against the shelf at her neck level and stretching out one arm in front of her swept off the second shelf every single piece of glass thereon. Rosie started in her sleep; Rue stood motionless, examining the pieces of glass on the floor.

"Ichabod," called a tremulous but calm voice at the doorway, "please tell Franchesca to get the broom, there's been a little accident in here."

Sillsy stood in the doorway, her short squat figure resplendent in gray chiffon lounging pajamas, her wispy brown hair piled on her head except for a lock that dangled down artfully on one side, her pleasant freckled complexion at a high sheen after her bath, her mouth smiling as it often did, her gray eyes watching coldly as they always did.

"The baby," Margaret said in a strangled voice, "could you please get her away from the glass?"

"Certainly." Sillsy walked quickly across the room, picked up Rue, came back to the sofa and sat down next to Margaret and Rosie. The air filled with a perfume so sweet that it would have been nauseating had it been any less expensive.

*My God! What do I smell like?* Frantically she tried to remember a shower or a dip in the pond.

"Sillsy, I'm so sorry about the glass."

"It doesn't matter," Sillsy said. "I'm so pleased to see you." She was looking back and forth from Rosie to Rue. "Look at our beautiful children. Which one is Rosemary?"

"This one," Margaret said. "You're holding Rue. Rosie's the sleeper, Rue's the one that gets into trouble." She laughed nervously. "I guess you know that already."

"She's not in any trouble with us, are you dear?" Sillsy said to Rue.

She should feel grateful for Sillsy's graciousness. Why didn't she feel grateful? Because she didn't believe it?

"What color are her eyes?" Sillsy asked.

"They change," Margaret said. They were gray.

"Mmm," Sillsy said. "They'll probably end up gray. She looks exactly like my mother."

"Now say Rosie looks like your father," Roger said from the doorway.

"Hello, dear," Sillsy said tranquilly. "No, nothing like my father. That's the Adams nose, not the Walton nose."

Roger laughed but Sillsy had learned long ago to ignore Roger's laughing. Franchesca came in with a teacart and a broom and dustpan.

"Rue knocked over some glass," Margaret explained. "On the *étagère*."

"Good," Roger said. "I hate that stuff."

Rosie stirred.

"You're staying for dinner, aren't you?" Sillsy said, eyeing the teacart.

"Mmm," Roger said. "But we were hungry."

"Fine," Sillsy said. "We'll have dinner when we get the children off to bed."

*But we just got here. You've never seen them before.* It struck her now that while Sillsy was holding her granddaughter in a perfectly acceptable way, she'd neither hugged nor kissed them. From Sillsy's lap Rue reached out for the food on the teacart. Rosie sat up and looked around.

"Such a good-natured baby," Sillsy said.

Margaret said, "Sillsy, try touching the back of Rue's neck, it's incredibly soft."

Sillsy smiled, still looking at Rosie. "Doesn't she cry when she wakes up?"

"Hardly ever," Margaret said.

Rue succeeded in getting hold of a sandwich.

"Maybe we should go into the kitchen," Margaret said. "There'll be a mess if we eat in here." Nervous dirty smelly anxious Margaret.

"Please don't worry about it, dear." Franchesca left with the swept-up glass and Sillsy put Rue down on the rug. Margaret put down Rosie and took some iced tea and a half sandwich.

"So what's new, Ma?" Roger asked.

"I do hope you were able to take my letter in the right spirit, Roger," his mother said, fairly reeking of serenity.

"What letter?" Roger asked.

Her brow furrowed slightly. "Didn't you get my letter? I sent it weeks ago."

"Mmm," Roger said. "The delivery isn't so good where we are. Some of my checks haven't been coming."

"Oh, dear," Sillsy said. Flustered.

"What'd it say?" Roger asked.

"Oh, well . . . it's hard to . . . just a minute, I'll get the carbon."

Roger began walking bouncily around the room, hands in his pockets, whistling because he was having a good time. Sillsy came back with the carbon and handed it to him. He read it quickly, gave it back to her.

"How long you been seeing this guy?"

"Almost half a year," she said. Not without pride. It had taken her only twenty or thirty years to find out that you didn't have to be Jewish to love psychoanalysis.

"Well," Roger said, "don't be impatient. It takes time for anything to happen."

"Things *are* happening," she said angrily. "Can't you see how much more serene I am?"

Roger stared at her thoughtfully. "No," he finally said. "But I'll try harder."

Rue wiped the sandwich filling off her fingers onto the sofa.

"I can see it," Margaret said quickly. "You really seem different to me, Sillsy."

Sillsy's mouth smiled and she relaxed back in the sofa.

"All this is beside the point," Roger said abruptly. "Where's Cowpey?"

"At the Club."

"Which club?"

She gestured helplessly. "Ichabod's trying to locate him."

"That could take days," Roger pointed out.

"Are you in a hurry about something, dear?" Sillsy asked, her calm restored by his urgency."

"I need some money." He always seemed to *want* them to know it was the reason they were seeing him.

"But I—" She waved the letter. "I tried to exp—"

Roger waved the letter away. "Irrelevant. I'm not talking about piddling amounts and that's a bunch of garbage, anyway. When will you stop trying to deal with things you don't know a goddamn thing about? There're all kinds of communes. There're religious communes where no one does anything but pray, they're like monasteries, practically, and there're revolutionary communes where they plan what they're going to do with houses like this when they liberate Philadelphia, and there're teeny-bopper communes where they don't do anything but fuck and fuck and take dope and fuck some more."

Sillsy flinched but was mesmerized.

"Now the thing we're at," Roger continued, "isn't so much a commune . . ."

"That's what you wrote me, Roger, you and Margaret were living at a farm commune with—"

"Let me finish. It's not so much a commune as a *model* commune."

Margaret gazed at him with uneasy awe; his manner left no room for doubt that there was a difference between the two. Rue was tearing up a magazine; Rosie was eating a plum and wiping her fingers on the rug. Sillsy said she didn't understand.

"Well I'm going to explain to you now," Roger said with relish. "You know what a think tank is?"

She nodded. "You mean the people who think for the government?"

"Exactly. Problem solvers. Well the farm we're at is like a think tank. Nobody's there to escape the world. Practically everyone's a sociologist or a scientist, that kind of person. Interested in solving problems like overpopulation and how it's going to affect the communities of the future. Are you beginning to understand what I'm talking about?"

"I think so," Sillsy said.

"We need to know things like whether it's possible to break up the cities into small self-sustaining units."

"Did you come through Philadelphia, Roger? It's worse than ever."

"We need to know how many people can have their basic needs supplied by how many acres of land, how much livestock, how detailed medical services, etc."

"What will you do when you find out?"

*Rosie, this funny lady is your grandma. You are related to her by BLOOD. By blood and gore, as Roger used to say.*

"We'll publish a book, naturally."

*Naturally.*

"Not just a book. A series of guides and references. Specific sensible information so that responsible people can be led into these communities instead of just a bunch of wild kids."

"That sounds very worthwhile," Sillsy said.

"Damn right it's worthwhile," Roger said self-righteously.

"Roger," Sillsy said in a tremulous—almost flirtatious —voice, "I feel that I may have done you an injustice."

"That's all right," Roger said. "You have a chance to undo it."

Silence.

"The fact is," Roger said, "that we're at a crisis point. The guy we've been renting the whole spread from has had an offer for it from a developer and he's going to sell unless we come up with the cash. Aside from Maggie and me there's no one there that has any real money, they're mostly salaried professionals." Rue tugged at his pants and he picked her up without interrupting himself. "I'm selling the house in Hartsdale to raise some of the money but I need more and I don't know how long that'll take." He was fondling the baby's head as he spoke.

Sillsy's mouth smiled. "I never pictured you that way, Roger," she said, inclining her head toward the baby's.

"The other possibility is a government grant," Roger said. "Which stinks for a variety of reasons."

"Some very fine people have government grants," his mother said. Thinking. Slowly, because the mechanism was rusty. "Adams Malties had a government grant to develop a new low-bulk nutritious cereal for the Armed Forces."

Crowley had been to Vietnam on cereal business two years before and come home with the clap.

"Just what Adams Malties needed," Roger muttered.

"What dear?"

"It is thought by people who know," Roger said loftily, "that government grants are to be avoided."

"But I don't see why," Sillsy persisted.

"There's something very funny about this," Roger boomed suddenly. "The communes are the last stronghold of laissez-faire capitalism and here you are trying to talk me into government control!"

"No, Roger," Sillsy protested. "Not control, just—"

"What do you think they give you the money for? If they pay you, they own you. And if they own you they can decide what they want to do with you. Maybe they'll decide to use you as a center to study controlled heroin addiction, there're government people involved in experiments like that right now, Project Head Start, it's called, I'm surprised you haven't heard about it."

"You always tell me such frightening stories, Roger."

"But I don't tell you lies, do I!" Blithely.

"I suppose not," Sillsy said slowly. "I remember when you told us you wanted the money for the house, to get out of New York because of the guerrilla warfare, and Crowley said it was pretty ridiculous and I said how can we be sure, and now when you read the paper . . . every day . . . bombings, people getting killed, department stores . . . you wonder how anyone can live there."

"In ten years," Roger said, "the suburbs won't be any better. You'll be begging us to let you live at the farm."

*And we'll be refusing.*

She was upset not by the way she was feeling about Sillsy but by the revulsion she was feeling toward Roger, whom she had recently loved so much. If it was true that his parents had created the foundation for his dishonesty, it was also true that he seemed not just to exercise it but to glory in it. And it was frightening to her that he shouldn't mind doing this in front of her, although for the life of her she didn't know why.

"I'd like to talk to Dr. Pfensig about this, Roger."

"Oh, for Pete's sake, what for?"

She paused. "He says that I tend to let you manipulate me."

"Bullshit," Roger said. "You're manipulating me right now. And I'm *letting* you do it."

"I wish he had a phone in Truro. He won't be back for a few weeks."

"That's great. If I don't have the money in two days I lose the farm."

"Oh, dear." Her voice was worried but her eyes were the same as ever. When had Sillsy come to inhabit that face? When she was two years old had her eyes not been upset when the rest of her was? When had she begun to so clearly act out the poles of what she was and what she was expected to be?

"Look, Mother," Roger said patiently. "I have a feeling this is a big fuss about nothing. After all, I'm really doing exactly what you want me to do. You don't want me to live like a hippie and now you know I'm not. I'm ready to become a responsible citizen, work on a model organic farm, maybe supply unpoisoned beef to you and people

223

like Pfensig right here in Philadelphia . . . he'd probably be furious with you if I lost out on this chance. What'll you tell him?"

Sillsy smiled shyly. "Did you hear what you called me, Roger?"

"Huh?"

"You called me Mother. You haven't called me Mother in years." Sounding as much like a little girl as she ever did.

"Mmmm." He was slightly disconcerted. "Well, that's because I'm trying to help Pfensig to get you to act like one."

"Roger," Sillsy said conspiratorially, "you can't imagine what that man has done for me! I think . . . I think I'm getting ready to give up alcohol!"

"Holy Moly."

Again that girlish smile. "He's giving me *his* strength."

Ichabod came in to say that he had located Cowpey, who was now on his way home. If Roger was impatient or upset he was concealing it fairly well at the moment.

"You don't have a beer in the fridge, do you?" Roger asked.

"Yes, of course, dear. Dark or light?"

"One of each."

Sillsy went to find Franchesca. A moment later Crowley and his brother Cooper walked in.

"Ah," Roger said. "Great white hunters."

They had supposedly looked very much alike when they were young. Both were tall and fair but Crowley had grown florid and rotund, balding only sightly by the age of fifty-eight, while Cooper was bald, slender and professorial in manner. Crowley ran Adams Malties while Cooper, a doctor by profession, spent six months of each year in Vietnam and the other six hanging around the Public Library and various favorite places of his brother's, like a black whorehouse in the city. It was Roger's theory that his mother had been in love with Cooper for years, a theory based on the rather complicated fact of Sillsy's confessing to him when he reached maturity that during the war years when both Crowley and Cooper had been overseas, she had been sleeping with Ichabod. Followed by Roger's realization that his mother often confused the two dissimilar names and had once asked Roger if he didn't think Cooper and Ichabod resembled each other.

"Margaret, my dear," Crowley said, ignoring Roger, "it's good to see you, you're looking ravishing!"

Margaret blushed for the part of herself that had wanted Crowley to see she was looking all right again. He had always been flirtatious with her until their one brief visit while she was pregnant, when he had disappeared after a glance. If Crowley had lost some of his looks, he still looked at you in a way that made you worry about what he saw. She thanked him demurely.

"Coop," Crowley said, "Look at this beautiful girl! Don't you think she's too good for my son?"

Cooper laughed gently. "I was looking at your beautiful grandchildren."

"Grandchildren?" Crowley was briefly, genuinely puzzled, then his eyes fell on the twins. Rue had climbed up onto the love seat at the far window and was looking through the window. Rosie sat on the rug nearby. Rue was making noises and Rosie was attentive, the effect being that Rue seemed to be relating to her sister what she was seeing through the window. Rosie was also watching what was going on in the room. Sucking her thumb and watching.

"Yes, of course," Crowley said. "They're lovely. They look exactly like you, Margaret. Thank heaven."

Franchesca came in with Roger's beer and Crowley asked her to get more. Roger and Cooper chatted pleasantly together, while Crowley, ignoring them and the

225

twins, led Margaret to the sofa, where they sat down, his arm around her.

"Now," he said solicitously, "I want you to tell me what kind of year you've had."

She laughed nervously. "Well, it's been a pretty crazy, I mean a mixed-up year."

He nodded sympathetically.

"Mostly what happened is that my mother died and my daughters were born."

"Margaret," he clasped her hands with his free one, which was warm and moist, Ichabod must have found him at some crucial moment and she was getting the spillover, "why didn't you let me know about your mother?"

She shrugged. "I don't know." *You never wanted to know she was alive, why would you care that she was dead?*

"Suppose you keep your hands off my wife," said Roger, who'd once told her that his father always made it a point to flirt with his girlfriends. Cowpey complied, but suavely, seeming to ignore Roger even as he was getting distance on the sofa.

"Tell me about this commune you've been at," he said to Margaret, who was afraid to speak because she was afraid of crossing tales with Roger.

"Well," she said finally, "we don't really think of it as a commune." She licked her dry lips. "It's really a working farm, with animals . . . goats, chickens, a few pigs that get slaughtered for meat in the fall. A couple of acres planted with everything from beans and potatoes to corn and green vegetables. We really work pretty hard."

"How many of you are there?"

"Mmm. Let's see. It's really, uh, four couples, married people, I mean . . . and then their kids, and then a couple of older kids, you know, teenagers."

"Aha, all very respectable," he said with a knowing wink.

"It really is," she said.

At that moment Rue chose to get down from the love seat by climbing on Rosie's head. Rosie let out a startled yelp and began crying. Roger quickly rescued her and she stopped crying. Roger's father was watching him.

"Do we have something for them to sleep in?"

Ichabod said that he had made a bed out of quilts on the floor of the guest room. Margaret thanked him.

"We're not staying overnight," Roger said.

"Oh," Crowley said. "How much do you need?"

"A hundred grand," Roger said casually.

Crowley laughed. He laughed because it was such a large amount of money and it was meaningless to him. He'd been a rich man long before he and Cooper became the joint beneficiaries of their separately rich parents' estates. "What for?"

"I'm going into business," Roger said.

"What kind of business?" Crowley asked.

"Organic beef cattle," Roger said. "I actually need more than that but I'm selling the house in Hartsdale." Roger would never pull the same kind of bullshit with his father as he did with his mother, doubtless because nothing in Crowley's background had ever taught him that it was seemly to believe everything he heard. He gave his father some details about the farm, the land, their cattle plans. All pretty straight. When he was finished, Crowley just looked at him in a remote, hostile way. Searching for flaws.

"Organic beef cattle," Cooper murmured. "That's interesting, I gather it's a growing market."

"It is," Roger said. "I don't expect to do this just for fun. I expect to make a going business out of it."

"I don't see why you shouldn't be able to do that," Cooper said. He had always been more sympathetic and encouraging to Roger than Crowley was.

"Even without the cattle business," Roger said gratefully, "the farm comes pretty close to being self-sustaining now."

"Since when did you worry about sustaining yourself?" Crowley asked.

"I don't," Roger said quickly. "I never worry about it, I just thought it would be interesting to try."

"Are you offering to relinquish any other claims on our money?" Crowley asked.

"I'm relinquishing nothing!" Roger shouted. "I came here to get some money, not to throw it away!"

Sillsy appeared in the doorway. "I told Roger," she said timorously, "that I'd like to talk to Dr. Pfensig before I—"

"Before you BREATHE, damn it!" Crowley snapped at her. "You want to talk to that idiot before you decide to wake up and breathe every morning!"

Sillsy shrank back into her chiffon pajamas, disappeared from the doorway. Tension hovered over all of them. It was touch and go for a moment whether Crowley might give them the money just because Sillsy had offered Dr. Pfensig as a delaying tactic. Cooper started to say in his gentle conciliatory way that he wondered if he and Crowley might not together take an interest in such a business but Crowley silenced his gentler brother with a glance.

"The market happens to be lousy my boy," Crowley finally said.

"Spare me the bull," Roger said. "I'm not one of your idiot employees standing on a line turning out Shredded Shitties."

Margaret felt tears coming. They weren't going to get the money. Maybe they wouldn't even be able to sell the house. Roger would be furious and frustrated and would surely take it out on her. In the past hour anyway he seemed to have traveled back a considerable distance in time and if he couldn't do what he wanted to do he might get stuck there, and she with him. She wouldn't ever again

228

let him use her as badly as he once had but to state that implied that she would always have the reserves of strength needed to propel herself elsewhere. She was scared. And exhausted.

She wandered out of the room as casually as she could, through the hallway and into the library. The library was a source of amazement to Margaret every time she saw it, not because of its large number of elegant, unread leather-bound books but because of the even larger number of less elegant thoroughly read ones, not to speak of vast collections of magazines—*National Geographic, Time, Life, Esquire, Sports Illustrated,* Crowley's other sporting and gun magazines, and so on (not to speak of Sillsy's secret collection of movie magazines, hidden away in cupboards beneath the open shelves). Idly she picked up a *National Geographic,* burrowed into a corner of the green-leather sofa and leafed through the pages without seeing them because she was crying.

"Margaret?" It was Crowley.

"Yes, Cowpey?"

"May I come in?"

"Okay." She sat up. He sat down next to her on the sofa, took her hands again.

"You've been crying, Margaret."

She nodded.

"Is it about the money?"

"I guess so. At least partly."

"You like this scheme of Roger's?"

"I have mixed feelings about it."

Crowley nodded. She found herself wondering how she would feel if her own father held her hands the way Crowley did. She thought of her last visit to Boston and found a heaviness in her chest that made breathing difficult. They hadn't come within three feet of each other. The last time he'd touched her had been after the funeral and then before that . . . who could remember? Tears, horrible embarrassing tears which Crowley would misunderstand, filled her eyes again.

"You're putting me in a very difficult position," Crowley said softly. "There's nothing harder to resist than a lovely young woman's tears . . . and yet there are some decisions that have to be made on a very hard-headed basis." He brought her hands to his mouth, kissed them.

"I know," she said, "I wasn't even thinking about that."

"What were you thinking about?" Looking deeply into her eyes.

"I was thinking about my mother." So effortless maybe it wasn't even a lie.

"Ah, Margaret, I wish you'd let me know! I would have wanted to be there."

"I was very confused."

"Was she ill for a long time?"

She shook her head. "She committed suicide."

He dropped her hands as though she'd just confessed to hereditary syphilis.

"Oh, my G-g-g-od!" Crowley said. "When was this?"

"Not so long ago." *Once a week for the rest of my life.* "I guess just before I—we went to the farm."

"There's no light in here!" Crowley said abruptly. He got up and turned on the overhead light.

"Didn't you ever know anyone who committed suicide?" she asked, because he was staring at her wildly.

"N-n-no," Crowley said. "It wasn't done." But he heard what he'd said and grimaced apologetically. "I mean except for economic reasons, like the Depression."

*How about noneconomic reasons, like depression?*

He asked, almost hopefully, "She wasn't bothered about money, was she?"

"She thought a lot about money," Margaret said. "Her family was wealthy once, I guess I never mentioned that. Until the Depression, as a matter of fact. But that wasn't

230

the whole thing. Mostly she just felt futile. She had no career . . . no real interests to pull her out of herself when she was low . . ." *No love* . . . "Money might've made it a little better, she could've gone on trips sometimes, things like that."

"God," Crowley said, "I wish I'd known. I wish you'd come to me for help, Margaret."

She smiled. "That's sweet of you. But in the long run it probably wouldn't have made any difference." *Rich people commit suicide, too. As a matter of fact, suicide may be enjoying a bit of a vogue. Ontogeny anticipates phylogeny.*

"Still," Crowley said. "You should have told me, Margaret."

"The truth is I didn't know myself." *The truth is that somewhere I did know, which was why I'd stayed away for longer than usual. I felt I couldn't go there pregnant, I felt guilty about it for some strange reason.* "I wasn't home for a while. I was pregnant and it was uncomfortable for me to travel . . . and I was so busy . . ." *Too busy to even write and tell her how busy I was.*

"It must have been agony for you," Crowley said, and that simple statement brought forth a quantity of tears unlike anything since the time immediately after her mother's death. Her whole body was racked with pain. Crowley held her while she cried and cried and cried and then eventually she was still.

"The farm has been an escape for you, hasn't it?" he said.

She nodded.

"I suppose it's the best kind of therapy, work. That's what I've always found."

"Mmmm," she said. "Kneading bread, milking goats, there's something soothing about that kind of thing." *On a short-term basis, anyway.*

231

Silence.

"Come with me, Margaret."

Hesitantly, ashamedly, suspecting what he was about to do, she followed him to the big leather-topped desk in the far corner of the room, where he made out a check in her name for $100,000 and handed it to her.

"I'll need three days to cover it," he said.

Reparations. But for which crime? She leaned over and kissed the top of his head. She was about to start crying all over again but then suddenly realized with disgust that crying had become her natural condition in the past week.

"I—thank you, Cowpey."

"Margaret! Where the hell are you?" Roger's voice boomed through the house.

"I'm coming!" She walked out of the study, through the hall. Roger was just coming out of the parlor.

"What the hell happened to you?" he asked, looking at her curiously.

"Nothing," she said. "I was crying."

"Where's Crowley? Did that old fuck—"

She shook her head.

"I wanna get out of here. He's not giving me the money. Sillsy'l come through from her own money if Dr. Schmucksig approves. I'm not holding my breath."

She handed him the check. He looked at it for a long time, then laughed ironically.

"I knew it was a good idea to bring you along."

She smiled wearily.

His expression changed to wariness. "What went on before you got this?"

"Come on, Roger," she said in a low voice.

"What made him give it to you?"

"He asked why I was crying and I told him it wasn't about the money, I was thinking about my mother. Then I told him about my mother. It really threw him."

"And that was it?"

"And that was it, he said he guessed the farm had been therapy, and then he made out the check."

"In other words," Roger said, grinning, "you did a little number on him."

"I guess you could call it that."

"I hope you don't expect me to be grateful."

She shrugged. "I have mixed feelings." *I always have mixed feelings. My ambition in life is to have an unmixed feeling.* "Part of me is disgusted with myself for doing that number."

He nodded.

"How about you?" she asked, beginning to feel hostile.

"You mean am I disgusted with you?"

"No, Roger," she said irritably, "with yourself. You did quite a number, too, it was just like the old days."

He paused to consider. "No," he finally said. "It's the only way to deal with them. They're not real people."

The dinner bell rang.

"Let's get out of here," he whispered.

"No," she said firmly. "We have to stay through dinner."

Crowley entered the hallway, walked past them without speaking and into the parlor.

"Cowpey," Sillsy's voice trilled through the archway, "did you know that Roger has given up smoking?"

"THE funny thing is," she said later in the car, "I wasn't even thinking about my mother. Crowley was holding my hands in that, you know, flirty-paternal way he has, and I was thinking about my own father. I went to Boston

233

just before I went to the farm. I guess I haven't mentioned it."

"No."

"It was right after I left home, you know, I was still pregnant. He didn't even recognize me." *I didn't know whether to laugh or kill myself; there didn't seem to be anything in between.* "When he did recognize me, he was miserable. Guilty. There was a young girl there. Taking care of him or something."

Roger laughed. "Where there's life there's hope. As a matter of fact, sometimes there's hope where there's no life."

Purely enraged by his own father, he was purely amused by hers.

"I was furious." *It was them I really wanted to kill, not myself.* "I didn't say anything, of course. I made some dumb joke."

"No point in anything else."

"Still, I wish . . . you're going to think I'm crazy." It had been coming over her ever since her session with Crowley. "I'd love to go see my father."

"You're right. I think you're crazy."

"It's not so much that I want to see him as I want him to see his grandchildren."

"You want him to say they're beautiful."

Silenced by the simple truth.

"Don't you know they're beautiful without hearing it from the old fart? Do I have to travel an extra five hundred miles just to watch you trying to wring blood from a stone?"

"It's not five hundred miles," she said, unable to quibble with his larger points.

"Damn close," he said, "by the time we come all the way back across Massachusetts."

"The thing is," she said slowly, "I really want to do it." *I long to make the connection between them, Roger. They're*

234

*my children and he's my father; their lives should touch.*
"I mean, I'm definitely going to take them to see him."

"All right," Roger said. "So you're going to take them to see him. Why now?"

"Why not? It isn't as if we really have to be back in such a hurry, that was just a story you made up for your mother."

"True," Roger said. "As a matter of fact there may be a tactical advantage in taking our time."

"I think so, too," she said, pleased.

"All right," he said suddenly. "We'll go to Boston and then we'll go to the Cape for a couple of days."

"Not to Aunt Margaret's," she said quickly. Without thinking of how it would sound, only reacting to the memory of the last time she'd been there. With David.

"When did going to the Cape mean anything else?" he asked curiously.

She smiled weakly. "Never, I guess."

"Then what was that about?"

"Nothing," she said. "It's probably full of people." She wasn't going to risk their good feelings by telling him.

"Twelve hours away from the farm and you're crapping out again."

It was true.

"At the farm," she said, "I feel as though I'll have someone else if you get mad and leave me."

"I don't leave when I'm mad," he said. "I leave when I'm bored." It was an echo of De Witt; only the qualifications differed. "Anyway, it's the bullshit that makes me mad, the truth never does."

"All right," she said reluctantly. "It's going to the house. I was there in the fall with David."

"You WHAT?" The car swerved off the road onto the grassy shoulder, where he braked so hard that her head nearly went through the windshield and both twins rolled across the mattress into the seat backs and woke up crying. "Are you telling me," he shouted, "that you brought that little fuck to the house at the Cape?"

"You said the truth wouldn't make you mad."

"Well, I was wrong, goddammit!" he bellowed, pushing back Rue, who was trying to climb over the seat into the front.

Margaret got out of the car and stumbled through the grass toward the trees. Roger came after her.

"Don't you run away!" he shouted after her. "Don't you fucking run away or I'll drive off and leave you here!"

She stopped and turned. He looked grim in the white light from the overhead highway lamps.

"It wasn't the way it sounds," she said tearfully.

"You're always telling me it's not the way it sounds."

"It wasn't a romantic idyll, Roger. It was when I just met him. On the way to the farm. We just needed a place to flop for the night."

"It's a fucking Bible story." Still at the top of his lungs.

"I was still pregnant, for Christ's sake. I weighed two hundred and fifty pounds."

"The little tit-sucker must've been crazy about you."

"You're still getting more mileage out of my one—"

"Whaddya mean, ONE?"

"All right, damn it, TWO! One and a half! Whatever! You're still getting more mileage out of my two piddling infidelities than I got out of the whole endless stream of girls you've been fucking me with practically since we got married!"

"I never took anyone to the house on the Cape!"

"What's so sacred about the house on the Cape?" she screamed. And then stopped. Dumbfounded at their reversal. Rue had climbed out of the car and onto the empty highway, then run onto the grass. Now she clutched Margaret's leg and screamed to be picked up. Margaret ignored her.

"You don't mean that," Roger said.

236

"It just came out."

"You were using anything to win an argument."

"*You* always said there was nothing special about the house." He'd always said it but she'd always known he loved it almost as much as she did. It was a happy place. The repository of much of the pleasure in a large, otherwise drab and unsensual family.

"But *you* did, Maggie. You thought it was special and you took that fucking kid there."

"I felt . . . it never occurred to me that I shouldn't. I really never thought you'd care. I didn't think you cared about me at all."

He regarded her thoughtfully. "Some of the best times we ever had were at that house."

"I know," she said. "That's why I felt awful about going there with you now. I felt guilty that I was last there with *him,* even if I didn't make love with him there."

Silence. She finally responded to the baby's wailing and picked her up. In the car, Rue's less mobile sister sobbed gently.

"You keep saying what amounts to that my infidelities are worse because I care more. But what it really is, obviously, is that mine hurt you more and yours hurt me more. That's all."

More silence.

Then Roger said, "I'll take you to your father's. But we're not sleeping there."

She smiled "I doubt we'll be invited."

"We'll drive right through."

"You're not too tired?"

He shook his head. "We'll get there in the morning, stay a couple of hours. Then we'll go to the Cape." He waited.

"All right."

"And we'll stay there for a couple of days. I'm in the

237

mood. We'll pick up bathing suits, anything else we need. I want to do it now more than I did before."

To exorcise young boys and other bad spirits.

"I hope there's room," she said. "At this time of year . . ."

"If there's no room indoors," he said, "we'll buy sleeping bags and sack out in back of the house."

◆◆ BOSTON. She bit off the long ragged nail of her right thumb.

"Well," she laughed nervously, "here we are."

It was just past seven in the morning and the street was still reasonably quiet. The twins had awakened at five; they'd stopped for breakfast at six. Now Rosie had dozed off again and Rue was playing with the box of diapers.

"He gets up early, doesn't he?"

"Sure. Six-thirty. Breakfast at seven-fifteen; lunch at twelve; dinner at six."

Roger laughed. "How could I forget?"

She looked at the brownstone, flashed back to the moment in her last visit when the girl had opened the front door, briefly now found her own body refusing to get out of the car.

"Well," Roger said, "here goes nothing."

He took Rosie and she took Rue. Up the front steps. He rang the bell. She felt nauseous; only a conscious effort held down her breakfast. The door opened almost immediately and there was her father, gaping at them in the sunshine.

"Hi, Dad," she said, "It's us. Your family. Together again." *Remember us?*

"Margaret, my dear!" he said, suddenly remembering his early Barry Fitzgerald. "And Rogerrr! How are ya, me boy? You're lookin' just fine. I haaaardly recognized ya, children!"

"We brought your granddaughters to see you, Father!" How fucking quaint she sounded. Elsie Dinsmore coming home to Daddy. He looked at the twins.

"Ah, yes," he said, "a fine pair of girls." Something in his manner reminding her of the classic Thanksgiving Magnificent Bird line. "Yes, of course, Margaret, ya wrote me about them."

*You never answered.*

Rosie watched him sleepily. Rue lunged toward him with a wooden spool in her fist; he stepped back hastily.

"Rosemary," she said, "Rue, this is your grandpa."

"Rosemary," he said. "A beautiful name."

"Do you want to kiss them, Daddy?" *Daddy?* Why was she having such trouble with what to call him?

"Yes, of course," he said, but made no move to do so. Impulsively Margaret leaned forward and kissed his cheek.

"Yes," he said, "we'd better go inside." As though until her loss of self-control he'd counted on holding court on the stoop.

They went into the house. The living room got about two hours of sun in the early morning and wasn't as dark as usual. Margaret and Roger sat on the sofa, the twins on their laps.

"Have you had breakfast?" her father asked.

"Yes," Margaret said.

"You'll excuse me then," her father said. "I feel The Headache coming on."

The Headache had as distinct a personality and cause as The Curse. It was what visited her father at 7:16, 12:01 and 6:01 if there was no food in front of him at those times.

"I'll have a cup of tea," Margaret said.

He left them. There was no sign of the colleen but there

were subtle changes in the room. Bright new fiberglass curtains at the windows; a ghastly red glass vase filled with plastic gladiolas on the sideboard; lace antimacassars on the sofa and easy chairs. Her father came in with his bowl of oatmeal, dish of toast and two cups of tea on a tray. He gave Margaret her tea and sat with the tray in the chair that swiveled toward the TV set. For the next few minutes he concentrated on his breakfast. She glanced at Roger; he grinned broadly. Rue was squirming so Margaret let her down on the rug. Rue promptly teetered over to her grandfather and grabbed a piece of toast from the tray; her grandfather, with a startled exclamation, grabbed it back. Roger laughed but Margaret nearly cried except that a second later Rue grabbed the other piece of toast from the plate and began jamming it into her mouth before he could take it again.

"The child's got to learn some manners, Margaret."

"The child's ten months old, Dad. Maybe you should've let her have the damn toast."

"Mind your language," he said abstractly, finishing his oatmeal and putting the empty bowl on the sideboard.

"Sorry, Dad." She sighed. "Do you mind if I make them some toast?"

Why? They weren't hungry, they'd eaten huge breakfasts.

"I suppose it's all right," he said. "I can always get more for lunch."

Why in all the great fucking world of places to go had she wanted to come here? The connection. Making the connection. But all they were connected by was a sick joke. Rue finished the toast and began investigating the room. She picked up a *Ladies Home Journal* from the coffee table and dropped it on the floor. Margaret picked it up and put it on the coffee table.

"Can't you put her in something?" her father asked.

"What'd you have in mind? A cage?"

"Come on, Rue," Roger said, putting Rosie next to Margaret on the couch, where she docilely remained. "I'll make you some toast." He stooped over to hold Rue's hand and guide her into the kitchen. Margaret bit off the nail of her right index finger.

"Are ya still bitin' yer nails, then, Margaret," her father said, shaking his head. He finished his tea, put the tray on the sideboard. Then he looked at Rosie for the first time since they'd come indoors.

"You're a pretty one, aren't ya."

"Actually," Margaret said, "they're identical. No one can tell them apart, not even me. For all I know this one may really be in the kitchen right now." She waited. Nothing. Hostile tones could be ignored indefinitely; he needed something concrete and important like a dirty word to latch on to before he could get mad. She chewed off the nail of her right pinky.

"Such a terrible habit for a young woman," he said.

"You didn't like it much when I was a kid, either." *Anyway, I only do it when I'm here.*

Silence. He was watching Rosie. He looked almost nostalgic.

"I'll tell ya, Margaret," he said after a while, "I'd love to see them baptized."

"WHAT?" Her mind was briefly blown into the various corners of the room.

"It would be a great comfort to me to see them baptized."

"You seem pretty comfortable already," she said, recovering quickly. *More comfortable than my mother is. More comfortable than I am.*

"It's the church, Margaret," he said, as though she'd paid him a compliment. "I've been going again, regular-like."

"What brought that on?" she asked. As if she couldn't

figure it out for herself. Guilt had driven people to stranger places than their own church.

"It came over me one day," he said solemnly, "that it was where I belonged. No reflection on anyone, Margaret, but I'd have been a happier man if I'd learned that lesson early in life."

*Of course you would never have existed, Margaret, but you were always such a troublesome girl, anyway. The first few years of your life your mother, the poooorrr creaturre, was laid up with a skin disease of the groin, no one knew what caused it but the fact of the matter was that she never had anything like that before you were born and so you see Margaret it seems only reasonable to say it would have been better for everyone if you'd never been born. Aaahhhhhhhh, the poor creaturrrrre.*

She had a tremendous urge to scream or cry or break something but of course she didn't do any of those things, she just sat there.

Roger came back with Rue.

"Roger," she said, "my father wants the girls to be baptized."

"Okay," Roger said. "Should we leave 'em here and pick 'em up in a few days?"

Her father looked so petrified she had to laugh. Roger took the toast from Rue, broke off a piece for Rosie, gave it back.

"Are you serious about not minding?" Margaret asked him.

"Sure," he said. "It'll roll off their backs like water."

"Not on the sofa, please," her father said.

She looked at him, bewildered.

"The toast. She's got the toast crumbling on the sofa."

Margaret stood Rosie on the rug where she could lean against the low coffee table as she ate. Once again her eyes fell on the *Ladies' Home Journal*. The *Ladies' Home Journal!* It hadn't registered before.

"Whose magazine is this, Dad?"

"It's a fine magazine, Margaret," her father said.

"Yes, but who gets it?"

"Thousands of people get it. Have you seen the beauuutiful article on the Kennedys?"

"Daddy," Margaret said, "did you go to the store yourself and buy this magazine?"

He stared at her blankly.

"And if you didn't, WHO DID?" The prosecution rests. Silence. Roger watched. Toast crumbled. Behind the triple-layer fiberglass curtains of her father's eyes, little things slipped and slid, searching for a way out, but they found none and so eventually he spoke.

"She did."

"She?" Triumphantly pained. She had found the scab on her heart and peeled it off. "Who's *she*?"

"Now, Margaret, you're acting foolish."

"Who is she?" Making up in aggression now what she'd lacked before. "Who? Rose Kennedy? The Virgin Mary? Your . . . your *concubine?*"

"Damn it, Margaret!" he exploded, and she should have been prepared then for she had never heard the mildest curse from his lips in her entire life, "you've got to stop using that language!"

"It's just a word," she said. "Why are you so scared of words? It's a word for someone who lives with you without being married."

"Father Dempsey wouldn't let her," her father said, lapsing into sullenness.

"Huh?" She was confused. As though she'd wandered into the wrong argument. Roger came over and sat down next to her and put his arm around her and that, too, should have told her something. "Father Dempsey wouldn't let her what?"

"Wouldn't let her live here without being married."

243

"Are you talking about the girl who was here?" Roger asked in a low voice.

"The girl who was here," Margaret said. "The young Irish girl who was here the last time I—" Finally it sunk in. She stared at him, wild-eyed. "Are you telling me that you were married to her the last time I was here?"

"I certainly was not," he said indignantly.

"Then *when?*" She demanded.

"October third," he said, as though naming a much later time, while in point of fact it was perhaps a week after she'd been there.

"There was no choice in the matter," he said.

"Where is this girl?" Roger asked.

"She sleeps late," her father said. "It's the pollution, her eyes smart if she wakes up early."

"Five months!" Margaret said, the nausea nearly overcoming her now. "Five fucking months after Mommy died!"

It jolted him to his feet. "Leave this house! You can't use language like that in this house!"

"She was dead five months when I was here!"

"I didn't want to do it but the girl had to be protected."

*What about me? Who protects me? Roger will protect me. Roger's arm is around me and he isn't laughing even though all this is very funny.*

"Doesn't everybody wait a year?"

"I'm not a man to live alone, Margaret."

*My mother wasn't a woman to live alone but she always did.*

"And Father Dempsey felt . . . well it's not as though the Church recognized my first marriage."

That snapped it. The thing, whatever it was, whatever it was made of, the thing that had bound her to him for all the years, in spite of the odds, in spite of her vision of him, in spite of *himself,* it snapped. She stood up and picked up Rosie. Roger took Rue.

244

"Fuck you," she shouted, looking down at her father with a full and righteous rage. "Fuck you, Dad, and fuck the little cunt in the bedroom and fuck your farts in the bathroom and fuck your lousy policeman's badge. Fuck you, that's all." And as he stood there frozen in a position of horror that was more satisfying than any fury could have been, his mouth open, the color gone from his face for the only time in her memory, his shoulders looking as though they'd been boned, his arms at once stiff and dangling at his sides, she marched past him and out of the house with Roger and the girls.

ROGER started the car.

Her nausea was gone but it had been replaced by exhaustion and a feeling of emptiness, as though she'd actually thrown up.

"I'm proud of you," Roger said.

"Really?" she asked dully. "You mean for telling him off?"

"Sure."

"Roger," she asked after a while, "aside from all the stuff you let out on your parents, the jokes and everything . . . have you ever really told them off in what you thought of as a final way?"

"Uh uh," Roger said. "I always left an opening."

"Consciously?"

"Consciously."

"Because of money?"

"Because of money."

She sighed. "It's so ironic."

"That point has been made much of," he said.

"I know, I know," she said. "Still, it's very ironic . . . Not that I ever want to see him again."

THEY parked in the house lot, next to a new Oldsmobile. It was nine in the morning. They walked through the gate back to the beach. There were three teenage boys stretched out in the sand, sunbathing. If they were her cousins or nephews they'd gone through enough growth or acculturation since she'd last seen them to be unrecognizable to her. She and Roger sat on the sea wall for a while, letting the girls play rapturously in the sand. They'd never seen sand before! After a few minutes Rue teetered over the sand to the edge of the water. They'd never seen the ocean before! The tide was fairly high and it lapped at Rue's feet as she stood there, looking down, swaying as the receding waves washed sand from under her feet. Rosie crawled to a spot a few feet in back of her sister where she could watch the water without being touched by it.

Aunt Diz came out of the house and greeted them warmly. Margaret's mother's younger sister by barely a year, she had the older-sister qualities Margaret's mother had lacked. She was direct and managerial, less tepid than the others, in that way the best of the lot. She was charmed by the twins. She said that she only wished Margaret's mother could have been alive to see her wonderful grandchildren and Margaret nodded, but what passed through her head was that if her mother had had any serious interest in seeing her wonderful grandchildren then she would not have killed herself while Margaret was pregnant with them. Then it occurred to her that it was funny for her to be having disloyal thoughts toward her mother when she had just split irrevocably from her father on grounds of disloyalty.

A short while later Uncle Chuck wheeled Great-Aunt Margaret onto the porch. Great-Aunt Margaret had had a stroke and was in a wheelchair and easier to deal with than she'd once been, although her eyes were as sharp as ever. Aunt Diz and Uncle Chuck, with occasional grunts or half-articulated words from Great-Aunt Margaret, discussed at length which of the twins' ancestors had provided them with which features, but the name McDonough did not enter the conversation.

"My father has twin uncles back in Ireland," Margaret pointed out during a lull in the conversation.

"How nice," Aunt Diz said. "Something from everyone."

Roger laughed.

"How *is* your father, Margaret?" asked Aunt Diz, the one who'd tried hardest to be pleasant to him.

"The same as ever," she said. "I'm afraid."

They laughed uncomfortably; they felt better ignoring him than having her be impolitic.

The conversation turned to Aunt Diz and Uncle Chuck's three teenagers, stretched out on the beach.

"I didn't recognize them," Margaret admitted. "It's been so long." A few years. None of that generation had come to the funeral, naturally. Like David they didn't believe in hassling themselves unnecessarily. Besides, funeral parlors were so Western; maybe if they'd arranged a pyre . . .

"I hardly recognize them myself," Aunt Diz said with a sigh. "I keep telling myself we have plenty to be grateful for. They're staying in school. They're boys." Aunt Diz and Uncle Chuck had been married a long time before they had their three boys; the oldest was twelve years younger than Margaret and Margaret could recall some lamentation, somewhere along the line, that Diz hadn't succeeded in providing herself with a girl. "They've all become vegetarians. It makes planning meals very difficult, especially up here where we have fish and seafood just about every day."

Did Aunt Diz know that where there was a vegetarian up front there was usually an acidhead not far behind?

"I must say they've kept their manners, though."

Was she terribly worried underneath her casual authoritative façade, or had the family reached some sort of Emperor's New Clothes agreement under which the kids could do any kind of dope they wanted as long as they washed their hands before they came to the table? Her own father had put up with anything he didn't have to know about.

They had a marvelous day on the beach, Margaret's major worry being to keep the twins from getting too burned. She oiled them frequently and by afternoon was making them wear long shirts and pants. She and Roger bought bathing suits and were bright red by the end of the day.

At five o'clock they had cocktails with distant cousins who had a house at the other end of town and had been invited over to see Roger and Margaret and the twins. Margaret, her system by now thoroughly unaccustomed to hard booze, got incredibly high on one martini and experienced enormously loving mellow feelings toward Great-Aunt Margaret, Aunt Diz, Uncle Chuck, the distant cousins, the house, the beach, the ocean and S. S. Pierce.

"God, I love it here!" she exclaimed happily. "I love this house! I love all of you! I don't ever want to leave here! Can we stay here forever?" She glanced uneasily at Roger but by a second later she couldn't remember what she'd had to be uneasy about.

For dinner they all had lobsters, even Rosie and Rue, who sat on Diz and Chuck's laps through the meal and grabbed at random from their plates, to the delight of the adults. At night, when they'd put the twins to sleep in one bed with chairs on either side, and the martini had finally cleared out of Margaret's head, she and Roger took a long walk on the beach. The tide was halfway in and they crisscrossed back and forth over the wet and dry sand, Margaret occasionally stopping to pick up a shell, a feather, a rock, throwing it away when Roger teased her about shit-collecting, but then almost immediately picking up something else. After the first few times she began stowing some of the prettier shells in the pockets of her jeans, but Roger saw.

"What're you trying to do?" he asked, but indulgently. "Bring the beach back to the farm?"

"Something like that, I suppose."

"What was that bit about staying here forever?"

"I was drunk." That wasn't entirely honest. "Not that it doesn't appeal to me, but that's how it slipped out."

"There's no law that says we couldn't do it."

She stared at him, dumbfounded.

"Not in this house, obviously, but we'll have enough to buy a place here if that's what we want to do."

"Oh, wow." It was more than she could handle. "Don't you think we have an obligation to use the m—"

"To ourselves," Roger said. "That's who we have an obligation to."

"Wouldn't your father be furious?"

Roger laughed. "With you? You can write him a letter. A composition. How I Spent My Mother's Suicide Money."

"My God!" She was flooded suddenly with images of De Witt and the farm. "How could we back out on the farm at this stage?"

"Easier now than later, actually." He paused as though challenging her to say they had to do it.

"I guess that's true," she said slowly.

"I'm fighting the idea there's anything we *have* to do unless we feel like doing it," Roger said. "I want to feel as if I can back out on the whole farm deal, or just the cattle business, or buy something down here. There're actually more possibilities for making money down here, if you're into that. Tourists are big business."

He would procure them and she would cook and clean for them. Just like the farm only the ocean would be right outside the window.

"I'll keep the books and you'll cook?" she asked.

"Oh, come on, Maggie, I'm just spinning off some possibilities."

"It sounds as if you were spinning them off before I started collecting shells."

"That's true," he admitted.

"How come?" she asked. "The magic of the Cape or something?"

"No," he said. "It started before we got here." The tide was getting higher; by tacit consent they perched side by side on the sea wall, looking out at the ocean. "It's this business of living with De Witt. I wasn't thinking about it all that seriously, it was like a casual thing when I mentioned it when you were talking about Mira, but then later . . . the truth is it was when my prick of a father was pawing you . . . anyhow, it hit me that I'm really not all that anxious to live so close with *anybody*. In the same house, I mean. I like De Witt, you know that, it's just a question of whether I want to live that close to this guy my wife has a running thing with. Even if it's only an almost. And it's always gonna be an almost. I mean, if it's people we're attracted to. And who wants to live with people we're not attracted to?"

"It's true," she said slowly. "I wouldn't want to live with any woman you liked as much as I like De Witt. I'd feel as if then you could turn me off any time you didn't dig me and you'd have someone all ready and waiting."

"Exactly."

"But I couldn't see living up in a place like that with nobody else. No other kids. The twins are so accustomed to having people around. I really think they don't know what loneliness is."

"They say twins never do."

"All right. Then I'm thinking about myself, not them."

"Even if I wanted to go back to Hartsdale or the city, you really wouldn't want to, would you?"

"No," she admitted. "No. They don't seem possible any more." *There's nothing there.* She thought of David with a guilty twinge. He'd tried to enter her mind a few times during the day but she'd pushed him away. *You're just another escape, David, really. I've got to grow up now, even if you can't.*

"On the other hand, we don't have to buy any place now. We could just travel around for a year or two, see what we like."

She sighed. "Shopping around for our lives."

"Don't get melodramatic."

"I'm sorry," she said. "Maybe it doesn't even matter. Maybe whatever we want to do we can do it practically anywhere."

"If we know what it is we want to do," he said. "And who we want to do it with."

"Maybe the farm is as good a place to start from as any," she said.

"I don't know," he said. "We'll have to think about it a lot. We'll have to talk to DeWitt, see how he reacts to the separate houses thing, assuming we're willing to go ahead. The others, too. The more I think about it the more I'm sure I don't want to live in the same house with anyone else. You can't be the way you want to be when there're always other people around. Like, we had to come out here to talk, and it's not just because they're who they are, it's because they're other people. Even living with one other

251

person you have to stretch yourself a little out of shape, the more people you've got the more you have to stretch. You end up using all your energy that way."

She smiled because she never thought of Roger as changing to accommodate other people; he was so much more honest and consistent than she was.

"The barn is practically a house already," she pointed out. "If we wanted to be, like, separate but equal."

"I was just thinking the same thing," he said. "And there's nothing to prevent us from putting up a third house. Nothing at all."

"Tell me again," she said, "that we'll always be able to come back here."

🙥 By the time they got back to the house all the adults had gone to bed. The boys sat stoned around the gas heater in the living room, ignoring Margaret and Roger as they walked through and up to their room. In silence they got undressed, feeling the sun-tanned warmth of their own bodies and then each other's. They made love. The twins slept.

"Soon," Margaret said, "they should go into a separate room."

"Mmmm," Roger murmured. "Then I can beat up on you."

She smiled, said, "Don't do that, you're the only man I've got." And realized that she wasn't talking about the loss of De Witt but of her father. Her hand flew to her mouth, ready to lose another nail.

Then she asked herself who she was kidding; it wasn't

that day she'd lost her father but many years ago. And it wasn't his disloyalty to her mother that had been the final blow but her ultimate inability to deceive herself that he had any loyalty to *her*. That he had even so much as a frame of reference that included her needs. He'd never let her be a part of his inner life. If the truth were to be told, she hadn't split from him at all, she had only made visible the split of his choosing. You heard stories about objects so closely connected to a dead spouse that the survivor couldn't bear to have them in the house. The only inanimate object that had been important in her father's marriage was the TV set, which was unevocative. But then there was Margaret, who had dropped into his life out of the blue and clowned around in that harsh way she had, trying to force him to believe that he'd once had another union whether or not it was recognized by the Church, and that union had indeed produced a mass of flesh and feeling named Margaret, whether she was recognized by the Church or not. Call the moving van! Get it out of the house, that large object over there which consumes its own fingernails!

She felt herself drifting off to sleep. Stopped herself. Had a funny thought. Giggled.

"Roger?"

"Mm?"

"I just had a funny thought."

"Mmm."

"I was just thinking what I should've said to my father."

"Oh, for Christ's sake!"

"No," she said. "Listen. I mean it. I should have pointed out to him—it only just occurred to me now . . . I was falling asleep . . . I should have told him that once upon a time, before scissors were invented, *everyone* must have bitten their nails."

# Fine Fiction By
# TOP WOMEN WRITERS

Novels that speak to women's needs,
desires, problems.
Novels about women who are sensitive,
talented, demanding and ready for anything.
Great new novels <u>by</u> women <u>for</u> women
who are not afraid to ask for what they want.

_____ 42183 ONCE A LOVER Diana Anthony $3.50

_____ 46968 DECEPTIONS Judith Michael $3.95

_____ 45048 DOUBLE STANDARDS Aviva Hellman $3.95

_____ 41270 OPTIONS Freda Bright $2.95

_____ 50189 WIFEY Judy Blume $3.95

_____ 49622 LOOKING FOR MR. GOODBAR
Judith Rossner $3.95

_____ 44100 ATTACHMENTS Judith Rossner $3.50

_____ 49589 BOOK OF COMMON PRAYER
Joan Didion $3.95

_____ 43780 LOVE Susan Schaeffer $3.50

_____ 52602 THE COLOR PURPLE Alice Walker $6.95

_____ 47256 MERIDIAN Alice Walker $3.95

# THE MOST FABULOUS WOMEN'S FICTION COMES FROM POCKET BOOKS

____ MORNING GLORY
Julia Cleaver Smith 42603/$3.95

____ PROMISE ME TOMORROW
Nora Roberts 47019/$3.50

____ JANE'S HOUSE
Robert Kimmel Smith 46083/$3.95

____ LACE Shirley Conran 46714/$3.95

____ DECEPTIONS Judith Michael
46968/$3.95

____ FOREVER Judy Blume 46942/$2.95

____ WIFEY Judy Blume 50189/$3.95

____ ANY MINUTE I CAN SPLIT Judith Rossner
50975 $3.95

____ ATTACHMENTS Judith Rossner 44100/$3.50

____ EMMELINE Judith Rossner 81681/$3.50

____ LOOKING FOR MR. GOODBAR Judith Rossner
49622/3.95

____ NINE MONTHS IN THE LIFE
OF AN OLD MAID Judith Rossner 42740/$2.95

____ ONCE A LOVER Diana Anthony 42183/$3.50

____ DOUBLE STANDARDS Aviva Hellman
45048/$3.95

____ OUT OF A DREAM Diana Anthony
46728/$2.95

____ OPTIONS Freda Bright 41270/$2.95

____ AS TIME GOES BY Elaine Bissell 42043/$3.95

____ THE FAVORITE L.R. Wright 45186/$3.50

____ A WOMAN OF HER TIMES G.J. Scrimgeour
44878/$3.95